THE FEDERAL BUREAU OF ALTERNATE REALITY

BOOKS BY DOUGLAS WATSON

The Federal Bureau of Alternate Reality

Darkhaven

Ghosts of Darkhaven

AVAILABLE SOON

The Federal Bureau of Paperwork Reduction

Allies of Darkhaven

THE FEDERAL BUREAU OF
Alternate Reality

Douglas Watson

☆ ☆

TWIN STAR BOOKS
Portland, Oregon

www.twinstarbooks.com

This novel is a work of fiction. Names, characters, places and incidents are either the product of the author's imagination or are used fictitiously. Any resemblance to actual events or locales or persons, living or dead, is entirely coincidental.

Copyright © 2002 by Douglas Watson

All rights reserved, which includes the right to reproduce this book or portions thereof in any form whatsoever except as provided by the U.S. Copyright Law.

Cover art by Erica Ritter

ISBN 0-9725046-1-3

First published: November 2002

Printed in the U.S.A.

10 9 8 7 6 5 4 3 2

Acknowledgments

I appreciate the valuable critiques and editing suggestions I have received from the Visionary Ink writers' group during my work on this book. I also wish to thank my family, especially my parents, for their continuing support and encouragement. And, finally, thank you to Erica for another superb cover illustration.

THE FEDERAL BUREAU OF ALTERNATE REALITY

The Federal Bureau of Alternate Reality, like most federal programs, came into existence through a combination of random chance and bureaucratic oversight.

It started out, under pressure from the land development lobbies, as the Bureau of Alternative Real Estate Financing. The word "Financing" was quickly dropped, as it hinted at the possible involvement of tax money, and "Real Estate" was shortened to "Realty" on a recommendation from the Department of Making Important Recommendations about Other Departments. After a routine overhaul in word processing, it emerged as the Bureau of Altering Real Tea, got sent back by someone on a congressional subcommittee who had actually read the first page, and was resubmitted as the Bureau of Alternate Reality.

Now facing dwindling support, it was collated by mistake into the wrong document, where it passed overwhelmingly as part of a 900-page bill to reduce government inefficiency.

It was the only part of the bill that succeeded.

1

Wilfred sat hunched in the cramped space inside the machine in Professor McInerny's study, and looked at the panel he was supposed to be opening.

Normally, opening a panel ought to have been the simplest of jobs for a handyman. It wasn't as if he didn't have a tool box. In fact, one reason the space inside the machine was so cramped was the sheer volume of the tool box that bulged beside him. He had pliers, drills, electrostatic converters, tools for measuring specific gravity, tools for deciding whether specific gravity was really that important after all … in short, he had every tool imaginable except for the one tool he could never put his hands on, which was a Phillips screwdriver.

Wilfred stared at the rows of shiny Phillips screws smugly holding the panel in place.

"Wilfred!" Professor McInerny's voice called from outside the machine. "Haven't you finished yet?"

"Uh … not too much longer now," Wilfred said.

Assertiveness was not Wilfred's strong point. He had occasionally wondered about this without ever guessing the actual truth, which was that when God dished out assertiveness to various lumps of primordial clay, Saint Peter happened to ask, "Have you got the time?" at the very moment that the lump that was to become Wilfred approached on the conveyor belt. In the half second it took God to create the cesium-beam atomic clock, Wilfred had passed along the conveyor belt minus his dose of assertiveness.

This meant God had one dose of assertiveness left over at

the end, so He popped a second dose into the last lump on the conveyor belt, which happened by a curious coincidence to become the future Professor Elaine McInerny.

1999 had not been a good year for Wilfred. His wife had left him, which had come as a blow. His dog had left him as well, which he'd taken rather harder, since he hadn't expected it. Even the hairline around his temples was starting to feel that the general Wilfred-exodus wasn't such a bad idea.

Wilfred shifted uncomfortably onto his elbow in the confined space and began one last painstaking search of his tool box.

He glared at the screws.

The screws waited, confident of their advantage.

Reluctantly swallowing his professional pride, Wilfred reached into his pocket and took out a pocket-knife. He unscrewed the panel and examined the wiring behind it.

The problem was clear. There were two wires on opposite sides of the panel which looked as if they ought to be connected, but were instead waving freely like the antennae of an agitated marine crustacean.

Professor McInerny had instructed him only to remove the panel, not to tamper with what lay beyond. But Wilfred reasoned that he was, after all, a handyman, and joining two wires together shouldn't be that difficult a task.

He attached the wires and replaced the panel. He expected to hear Professor McInerny blaring out distant criticisms, but Professor McInerny, for reasons of her own, remained in remarkably controlled silence.

Wilfred began to wonder what had gone wrong.

He slipped the pocket-knife back into his pocket, then extricated himself from between the control panel and the tool box, and stood up. He dusted himself off, opened the exit hatch of the machine, and stepped out.

He stared in astonishment.

Instead of stepping out into Professor McInerny's study, he found himself in a checkerboard-floored room which appeared to be a bedroom.

The room was a strange mixture of the classic and the modern. The bed — a mahogany four-poster with a burgundy damask bedspread — suggested an antique tone, as did the matching mahogany table and dresser. The lighting fixtures, on the other hand, were rod-like and translucent, and seemed on the cutting edge of technology for the next century. The windows, too, had a post-contemporary look, with no visible clasps or frame, only a tastefully subdued control panel set into the wall nearby.

It struck Wilfred that this room probably belonged to a woman. The dresser had necklaces draped from the corner of the mirror, and various bottles of mysterious perfume-like substances, and the pink furry slippers by the bedside were a bit of a giveaway, too. The occupant was also clearly a nature lover: artifacts of wood and other natural materials adorned the bookshelves and walls, along with holographic representations of wildlife and trees.

The room was also, Wilfred noted with a tinge of admiration, remarkably tidy.

An open doorway led through to an adjoining room. Wilfred heard a rustle of movement from beyond the doorway; then he heard a woman's voice say:

"July 20th. Gamma-16, north quadrant. Upper canopy, healthy; mid to lower, sparse; bio-damage, none visible; floor erosion, minimal; ground cover, minimal."

Wilfred realized he didn't have the faintest idea what she was talking about, except that he had vaguely thought it was July 19th.

He tiptoed to the doorway and peered into the adjoining room. There, rooted apparently in the floor, and towering above where reason suggested any responsible ceiling ought to intervene, rose an impressive stand of Douglas fir. In the midst of these trees stood a woman with coppery red hair and freckles, angular cheekbones, and a small, elfin chin. She wore a forest-green jumpsuit, and carried a device that looked like a cordless phone.

She looked around as he approached, then clicked a button on her hand-held device. The trees disappeared, leaving in their place a more recognizable if somewhat eclectically decorated living room. She came towards him, her face brightening into a pixie-like smile.

"I didn't hear you come in," she said. "You must be the Handyman."

"Ah ... well, yes, as a matter of fact I—"

She smiled again, extending her hand.

"I'm Selena McGuire."

"Wilfred," said Wilfred. Her hand felt cool and dry to the touch. "Wilfred Smith."

"A good name for a Handyman." Selena turned, and a slim finger beckoned to him from the sleeve of her dark green jumpsuit. "Come. Here's what I need you to fix."

"Um ... I couldn't help noticing the trees a moment ago," Wilfred said as he followed her across the room.

"I work for the Department of Forestry," Selena explained. "With today's environmental conditions, I have to monitor our few remaining acres of forest to make sure they're OK." She stopped in front of a display of lighted dials and digital gauges that covered an entire wall. "Anyway, here's the problem."

She pointed to a box occupying a place of honor in the center of the display. On her command, a distorted holographic image flickered weakly inside the box, accompanied by a crackle of static.

Wilfred recognized the box as a variant of a familiar object. Voice-operated controls and hologram image-projection aside, what he found himself looking at was little more, and certainly no less, than a television set.

And a broken television set, at that.

Wilfred had encountered a good many non-functional TV's in the course of his professional career, and he knew from experience precisely what this one needed.

He nodded, then approached it carefully, running his fingers around the edge of the casing, over the display panel, around the back, feeling for the slight nuances of imbalance in the system. He eased himself behind the TV, handling it with the gentleness of a surgeon. He looked, he listened, he probed, selecting his place with infinite care. Finally, holding the casing steady at the top, he closed his other hand into a fist, and struck the back of the TV with a swift, decisive bash.

"Oo, that was good," Selena called approvingly from the front. "What did you do?"

"Rather technical, actually," said Wilfred. "Bit hard to explain, really, in a nutshell."

"The picture looks OK," Selena said. "The sound's still a bit crackly, though."

"One more ought to do it," Wilfred called back, "if you'll pass me the Phillips screwdriver."

"Where?" Selena looked around her. "I don't see one."

In the moment it took Selena to glance around, Wilfred gave the TV another quick and expert bash, and the prattle of a furniture commercial replaced the static with seamless, digital clarity.

"Never mind," he said. "Managed it without." He emerged from behind the TV, and stood back with Selena to admire his handiwork. "There. That should do it."

There's actually a scientific basis for repairing something by giving it a bash. If you apply the bash in exactly the right way, the theory is that you realign the piece that has become detached or broken, thus causing whatever it is you're repairing to start working again.

The bash principle has been known for many centuries. It worked well, for instance, on Roman slave ships. Give the non-functioning element a quick bash, and the ship was usually back in trim working order in a very short space of time.

The same principle, in the more modern era, has been found to work with satisfying results on photocopiers, kitchen appliances, plumbing fixtures of all sorts, computers, most types of car, and, especially, on television sets.

It is ironic, then, that the Romans had all the technology necessary to *repair* TV's, as well as a handy supply of free labor; they merely lacked the technology to build the TV's in the first place. The reason for this will soon become clear. Suffice it to point out, for now, that this technology appeared on the planet Earth right in the middle of the highly troubled twentieth century.

Wilfred watched as the woman in the furniture commercial, standing before a display of red and green, talked about "great seasonal selection," which he vaguely understood, and "Zirconia," which he didn't understand at all. For the most part, though, his attention focused on the music used in the commercial, which was a particularly sappy rendition of *Jingle Bell Rock*.

Whether it was July 20th, as Selena had mentioned earlier, or July 19th, as he had recently believed, *Jingle Bell Rock* seemed an odd choice.

He turned to Selena.

"You know how people sometimes ask, 'Have you got the time?'"

"Ye-es ..." Selena said cautiously, as if trying to decide whether it was a trick question.

"I was just wondering if, by any chance, you've got the date."

"The date?" She stared at him. "Today's date, you mean?"

"Well, yes. Today's, if possible."

"It's July 20th."

"Ah. Well, you see, for some reason, I thought it was the 19th."

"That was yesterday." Selena waved a hand in the direction of a holographic wall calendar depicting a scene from a lush South American rain forest. "Today's definitely the 20th." She frowned, and looked more closely at the calendar. "Gosh! You're right — it *is* the 19th! And I've been saying the 20th all day!"

Wilfred glanced at the calendar with a feeling of smug vindication, then turned back to Selena.

He stopped.

He paused for a moment, then slowly looked back at the calendar.

There are times when the numbers *19* and *20* are fairly interchangeable in dates, and there are times when they are not. For example, it's a minor adjustment if you happen to think it's July 19th, and it turns out to be July 20th, or even vice versa. On the other hand, it's a little more disconcerting if you're pretty solidly convinced it's the year 1999, and it turns out instead to be 2099.

"Well ..." Wilfred stopped. The concept of 2099 was a little hard to take in for the moment, so he decided to start small.

"If it's July 19th," he said slowly, "what about the Christmas music?"

Selena nodded. "I know. Seems to start earlier every year, doesn't it? That's the reason we have so many environmental problems."

"What? Christmas?"

"Not Christmas specifically. Consumerism in general."

"Well, yes, it would be." Wilfred glanced back at the calendar. He realized he'd vaguely been looking forward to the twenty-first century, and it was disappointing to discover it was now virtually over before he'd had much of a chance to enjoy it.

Selena switched off the TV, and reached out her hand.

"Come on," she said. "I think you ought to meet Mother Ismeralda."

Before Wilfred could wonder who Mother Ismeralda might be, and why he ought to meet her, Selena had led him out of her apartment into an ornate hall the size of a gymnasium. A flight of marble steps at one end of the hall led up to the floor above, which overlooked the main level from a balcony with a railing of black wrought iron topped with a gleaming brass handrail. As with the interior of Selena's apartment, the design of the hall combined classic and modern features. Even the off-white of the marble blended with the off-white of various high-tech wall panels to create a unified whole.

Selena tapped a band around her wrist, and spoke into it.

"Mother Iz. The Handyman's here."

"I'll be right there," crackled an imperious voice. A click sounded from the device on Selena's wrist. A minute or so later, a heavy double door opened on the balcony above, and a woman descended the steps wearing a dark blue, floor-length robe.

"I am Mother Ismeralda," the woman in blue informed him as she approached. Her graying hair was pulled back into a tight bun, and her thin eyebrows arched authoritatively as she spoke. She waved a hand towards a series of wall panels, all held in place with Phillips screws. "I take it you are familiar with your job?"

"Well ..." Wilfred patted his pockets hopefully, as if to suggest he had been caught short in a thoroughly uncharacteristic way. "You don't happen to have a Phillips screwdriver, do you?"

Mother Ismeralda's eyes narrowed.

"I thought you were a Handyman."

"I am," Wilfred said. He considered producing his official union card, which featured a snazzy foil hologram of which he was particularly proud. Then he realized that not only were foil holograms probably somewhat passé this far into the future, but he also remembered that the card had expired, even within the context of July, 1999.

"He's just arrived," Selena put in. "He's been doing some work for Professor McInerny."

"Time traveling, I imagine." Mother Ismeralda pursed her lips with a disapproving air. "Not a habit I would care to indulge in myself." She turned back to Wilfred. "Past or future?"

Wilfred looked helplessly around the hall. "Um ... from

the past," he said. "I think."

Mother Ismeralda scrutinized him from head to foot. She shook her head slightly, as if something about him didn't fulfill her expectations. "In today's society," she explained, "we allocate tasks according to which gender is more suited to handle them. Women take care of child-rearing, health care reform, balancing the budget, and so forth, while men take care of appliance repair."

Wilfred allowed a couple of seconds to go by.

"That's all?" he said at last. "Appliance repair?"

"And, of course, exterminating each other with hand-held automatic weapons."

Wilfred swallowed. He glanced anxiously out of the window, where the parched soil and complete absence of trees lent support to Selena's environmental concerns.

"When you say exterminating," he said, "whereabouts does all of this, er, exterminating go on?"

"Oh, not around here. We're trying to stamp out violence in our society. We've set aside a place for the sole purpose of urban guerrilla warfare. We call it 'Los Angeles.'"

"Ah." Wilfred nodded, hoping to convey that urban guerrilla warfare sounded fine for other people, just not for him personally. "So, after they've all killed each other, what then?"

"Well, they don't *all* kill each other, you understand. Most of them kill each other, and then the winners come back and mate with us."

"Mate?"

"I mean, have sex with us," Mother Ismeralda clarified. "It's another of their skills, you see. It's also very convenient for propagating the human species."

Wilfred frowned.

"But I thought you said you were trying to stamp out violence in your society?"

"We are. You see, that's why we have the Handymen go off to Los Angeles and—"

"Yes, I understand that part. It's just ..." Wilfred hated to bring up such a flaw of logic, but he could see no way around it. "If the winners are the only ones who mate with you, that means you're selectively breeding the human race to become successful urban guerrilla warriors."

"Ah." Mother Ismeralda considered for a moment. "Yes, well, now that you put it like that ... I see what you mean."

"What you need now," Wilfred said helpfully, "is a gene pool which has not been contaminated in this way."

"Unfortunately, it's already too late," said Mother Ismeralda. "Most of the Handymen in Los Angeles have already killed each other. Where are we going to find such a gene pool?"

Wilfred gave a small cough.

2

Mother Ismeralda eyed Wilfred for several seconds. Finally she nodded.

"You seem eminently lacking in military tendencies," she acknowledged. "How soon could you begin?"

"Let's see ..." Wilfred looked up at the ornate ceiling. "Luckily, my calendar's completely blank for the entire year 2099. In fact, for most of the twenty-second century, as well."

"I hope the responsibility of propagating the human race won't prove a burden on your time?"

"Not at all," Wilfred assured her. "Glad to help out."

"Good." Mother Ismeralda surveyed Wilfred one last time. "Then I'll expect a report of your progress in a few days."

With a sweep of her dark blue robe, Mother Ismeralda turned back towards the marble steps at the end of the hall, leaving Wilfred alone with Selena.

So far, Wilfred considered, 2099 hadn't turned out too badly. Getting plonked down towards the end of another century might involve a few minor adjustments; on the other hand, his propagation assignment showed a good deal of promise.

A tall woman with dark, curly hair and a slender figure was coming down the steps that Mother Ismeralda was now climbing. She nodded deferentially as Mother Ismeralda passed. She wore a blue robe, like Mother Ismeralda's, except that hers was a paler shade of blue.

Even from a distance, Wilfred could see she was extraordinarily beautiful.

"That's Monica van Patten," Selena said, following the

THE FEDERAL BUREAU OF ALTERNATE REALITY

direction of his gaze. "She's a member of the Council. Be careful of her — she's not someone you want to get the wrong side of."

On reaching the bottom of the steps, Monica looked up and caught sight of Wilfred and Selena. Her expression became more purposeful, and she quickened her pace towards them.

According to ancient Greek mythology, there was a lizard-like creature called the basilisk which could kill people with a single glance, and which apparently had nothing more pressing to do than roam around making eye contact with the local citizenry. Wilfred wasn't sure if he believed in past lives or not, but he began to have disturbing flashbacks of a basilisk bearing down on him from the vague direction of the Acropolis.

"Hello, Monica," Selena said pleasantly as Monica approached.

Monica gave Selena a tight-lipped smile, the sort of smile that said, *If I didn't happen to be so busy and so important, I might be able to spare you some of my valuable time,* and turned her eyes to Wilfred.

"It has come to my personal attention," Monica said, as if her personal attention were the supreme pinnacle to which any tidbit of information could climb, "that you have recently been engaged in unauthorized TV repair."

She smiled, more sweetly this time, revealing an even row of white teeth that would have sent toothpaste advertisers falling all over each other for their checkbooks. Wilfred felt his hormone levels fluctuating uncontrollably.

"TV repair?" he said.

Monica studied his face for a few seconds before replying.

"I believe those were the words I used, yes."

"How did you know — er, I mean, what makes you think I repaired a TV?"

Monica moved her face closer to his, so that he could almost feel the warmth of her breath.

"There was a call for a TV repair," she said gently. "By the time the Union Handyman was notified, the repair had been done. I don't have to be a detective to figure that one out."

"No," Wilfred agreed. "No, I suppose not. I can see that." He smiled pleasantly, hoping Monica would do the same.

She didn't.

"You realize," she said, "your careless action will now cost the taxpayer even more money. Now, not only do we have to repair the TV, but we have to unrepair it as well before we can do so."

"Unrepair it?"

"We may discover a damaged part, for instance, which you overlooked. We replace the part, and then everything will be working fine."

"But it's working fine now," Wilfred pointed out.

Monica let out a breath with the tried patience of an IQ-test administrator having a bad day.

"Look," she said pityingly. "Regulations are regulations. We may not like them, we may not always agree with them, but it's my duty to see that they're carried out." Her voice brightened, taking on a more musical tone. "You see? I'm merely protecting the jobs of Handymen everywhere."

"All I did was give it a bash," Wilfred said. "Well, not a bash, as such. More of a little tap, really. A sort of … flick."

"Almost an accidental nudge," Selena said helpfully.

Monica gave Selena a withering glance, and turned back to Wilfred.

"Did you give it the kind of accidental nudge that might cause it to start working again?"

"*Might*, yes …"

"And is it, in fact, now working?"

"In a manner of speaking," Wilfred hedged. "You see, I've worked as a handyman …"

"Ah." Monica smiled tautly, as if sensing an opportunity to give Wilfred all the rope he needed. The musical charm in her voice increased. "And may I see your Union card?"

Wilfred pulled his electricians' union membership card from his wallet and waved it in front of Monica, keeping his thumb over the date. Monica snatched it from his fingers with a flourish, and examined it closely.

"This card," Monica said, "expired in May." She narrowed her eyes in what was no doubt intended to be her most basilisk-like manner, but it also had the effect of making her look more beautiful than ever, melting Wilfred's power to stand up to her even more.

Wilfred gulped.

"Well, yes," he began. "May. Yes. I've sent away for a new one, you see, but it's just taking a little time."

"May of 1999," said Monica.

"Yes; well, I can explain that, too," said Wilfred. "You see, the truth is..." He wondered what the truth actually was, and decided that, at this point, anything would probably do. "The truth is, there's been a bit of a delay at the post office."

Monica stared at Wilfred as if he'd started speaking Portuguese. Her dark eyes widened.

"The post office??"

"He means the Bureau of Telecommunications," Selena put in.

"That's the place," said Wilfred, nodding in what he hoped was an encouraging manner.

Monica looked at Selena, then back at Wilfred.

"All too understandable," she said. "Regrettably, the Telecom Bureau isn't run as efficiently as some of us would like. Meanwhile, you'd better apply for a new Union card if you plan to do any more work around here. You can either pay off your back dues, or pay a reinitiation fee." She glanced at the date on the card once more, and handed it back. "In your case, I would suggest the reinitiation fee."

With a tilt of her head and a quick smile, Monica turned and strode back towards the steps, her shoes clacking sharply on the marble floor, her dark curls flouncing above her shoulders.

Wilfred let out a breath. Some things, at least, hadn't changed. It was actually believable to Monica that a delay of 100 years could have occurred through the postal service, or its modern equivalent.

Yet, it really wasn't believable. Whatever else Monica van

Patten might be, she was no fool.

Maybe she got a percentage of the reinitiation fee.

"Welcome to Zirconia," Selena said, nudging him with a grin. Her manner was so easy, so unassuming, so companionable after the intensity of his conversation with Monica, that Wilfred realized with relief that it wasn't Monica he was in danger of falling in love with, after all.

"What's Zirconia?" he asked, as he walked with Selena back across the marble hall to her apartment. "They mentioned it on the TV commercial, as well."

"Zirconia," Selena said simply. "That's here."

"What do you mean, 'here'?"

"This country. Where we live."

Wilfred stopped in his tracks.

"This *country?*"

"In your time, it used to be called America."

"But why was it changed?" Wilfred said, hurrying to catch up with Selena again. "Who changed it?"

"It was changed by vote of the people, of course." They reached the apartment, and Selena entered a code into a small electronic panel in the wall. The door slid open with a faint hydraulic hiss. "Come on."

Wilfred followed Selena through the doorway in a daze. Everything around him pointed to the unthinkable: that he really had traveled 100 years into the future.

The apartment door closed behind them.

"You mean ... people nationwide actually *voted* to change the name of the country from America to *Zirconia*??"

"That's the great thing about democracy." Selena's wry grin, combined with her pointed features, gave her face an appealingly impish expression. "You can get anything passed, if you have the financial backing."

"It's democracy run wild, if you ask me," Wilfred spluttered. "At least, back in the twentieth century, we were a little more responsible at the polls."

"Don't be ridiculous. You elected Nixon twice."

"I mean, aside from that."

"Uh-huh." Selena grinned and pushed Wilfred playfully on the arm. "Look, wait here while I change into something more comfortable." She moved towards her bedroom. "I'll be back in a minute."

Wilfred walked to the window and looked outside. There was barely a cloud in the sky, yet the late afternoon sun wore a hazy glare, as if viewed through a grimy layer of plastic sheeting. Instead of the familiar blue, the sky was a dull, metallic gray.

The people of Zirconia had gone to great lengths to avoid contact with this uninviting atmosphere. Transparent tubular walkways, bustling with activity, interconnected many of the buildings. Some of the tubes were not walkways, but were reserved for a kind of high-speed shuttlecar. They reminded Wilfred of those strange devices in banks back in the twentieth century, where the bank employee used to tuck some vital piece of paper into a little cylinder and pop it into this handy tube, and there'd be this sudden sucking sound, and the cylinder would be whisked away in the direction of some secret destination, and (occasionally, one had to assume) even arrive there.

Wilfred heard a movement behind him, and turned. Selena stood in the bedroom doorway, wearing a cream-colored silk blouse and a pair of blue jeans.

"So, what do you think?" she said.

Wilfred stared in amazement. He took a couple of steps towards her.

"Are those Levi's 501's?"

She nodded. "From the retro store. I thought you might appreciate them. They're genuine antiques — from the 1990's."

"But they look so new!"

"Well, naturally, they've had extensive fiber restoration to make them look like the period." Selena's eyebrows drew together into a small frown. "You know, it's funny. It's hard to find a pair of 501's that isn't in really worn condition."

"That's because people scuffed them up as soon as they bought them, so they'd look used."

"You mean, this isn't the way people looked in them?"

"Well, I guess it's the way they looked when they were trying them on in the store," Wilfred said.

"So, back when the jeans were new, people wanted them to look old?"

"Yes. And now they're old, of course, people want them to look new. Typical human reaction, if you ask me. Anyway, you look nice." He moved towards her. "Very nice. In fact — good God!" Wilfred stared ahead. "It's gone!"

"What?" Selena glanced down at her jeans with alarm. A wave of evident relief crossed her face at seeing they were still there. She looked back up at him. "What's gone?"

"The time machine!" He pointed past her into the bedroom, and she turned to follow the direction of his finger. "Someone must have taken it!"

"Who would have taken it?"

"*I* don't know! This is your century, not mine!"

"If it was big enough for you to fit inside," Selena said, "it would have been too big to fit through the door. Or through the windows."

"Maybe they took it somewhere in time," Wilfred suggested. The idea of being stuck in the present with Selena didn't sound all that bad; it was just comforting to have the option of returning to your own century if you felt in the mood. "Of course, then they'd need another time machine to come and get it."

"One time machine I might accept. Two is pushing your luck. I'd say the only way anybody gained access to this apartment is through these wall panels."

"They're screwed down, though," Wilfred pointed out. "From this side."

Selena walked over to the far corner of the bedroom. She grasped one of the panels by the edges, and pulled it away from the wall.

"Some of these screws are just for show," she said. "Nobody can ever find a Phillips screwdriver, so it makes sense to have a couple of the panels open some other way. I go in and out this way all the time, when I don't want to be seen. Come on."

"Where are we going?" Wilfred said, wondering vaguely why Selena wouldn't want to be seen.

"There's someone I want you to meet," Selena said.

"In there?" Wilfred peered apprehensively into the gloom of the passage that opened behind where the panel had stood.

"Yes." Selena stepped through the opening, and looked back towards him. "Well, sort of. Come on. Hurry up."

Wilfred cleared his throat. "What about ... you know ... my propagation assignment?"

"What — *now?*"

"Well, I mean ... shouldn't we be getting on with it? I'm rather concerned — I did promise Mother Ismeralda."

"Oh, don't worry about Mother Iz." Selena held out her hand from the gap in the paneling. "I'm sure you don't want to be treated as a sex object."

"It's not *that* much trouble ..."

Selena repressed a smile, and pushed back a lock of red hair from in front of her face.

"Come on. Into the passageway."

Wilfred climbed in to join Selena in the space behind the panel, and they pulled the panel back into place behind them. It was now almost pitch dark, except for a few rather low-tech lights, each about the size of individual Christmas tree lights, spaced at intervals along the passage. Wilfred followed the rustle of Selena's clothing, feeling the sides of the passage for guidance.

Suddenly, he was struck from behind by someone or something that he hadn't seen, in much the same way that he hadn't seen the time machine.

3

Blake Orion, research director of the Federal Bureau of Alternate Reality, leaned back in his comfortable leather armchair behind his 1940's desk and studied his weekly agenda.

Blake knew all of the items on the agenda, mainly because he'd been working on them all week. However, it was a federal requirement that you had to spend at least eight percent of your time planning what to do with the remaining ninety-two percent. Blake complied with this requirement because, first of all, it kept them guessing when he complied with a requirement now and then, and second, there were plenty of other rules he could bend that made more of a difference.

Blake's agenda consisted of the following main headings:
1. Save world from extraterrestrial invasion.
2. Time travel research.
3. Alternate reality research.
4. Collect Bogart memorabilia (if time permits).

Time, of course, usually did permit for someone who time-traveled on a professional basis, with the result that Blake had an enviable collection of Bogart memorabilia in his office.

Underneath the other items, in pencil, he had written the word "Monica."

Several months earlier, in the course of a brief but intense affair, he had made the mistake of falling in love with Monica van Patten, and now he couldn't get her out of his thoughts. For Monica, the affair had simply begun when it began and ended when it ended, and she had marched on with her life. Blake, however, suffered from a case of terminal romanticism, which meant he still believed love had a more realistic chance of success than an ice cream franchise on Neptune.

Unfortunately for romantics everywhere, there's a scientific paradox in romantic relationships that works something like this. If A falls in love with B, this causes A's body to produce tiny amounts of a chemical, called a pheromone, which has the highly specific effect of preventing B from falling in love with A. The same pheromone also causes B's body to produce a different but equally specific pheromone that makes A's love for B even stronger. This is why, in the real world, most romantic relationships are doomed from the start.

Fortunately, Blake's career in alternate reality research prevented him from spending too much time in the real world, thus making him perfect for the job. He had never been a Handyman, never packed a semi-automatic weapon through the hills of L.A., never even engaged in minor appliance repair other than giving his computers a occasional bash, which he took care to list as "research." His boss was an intelligent woman who recognized that she could get the most out of her research director by giving his romantic idealism a free rein, so she took care to ensure him a conducive working environment.

He tucked the edge of his weekly agenda under the corner of a black falcon statuette on his desk and reviewed the list one more time. Strictly speaking, saving the world from an extraterrestrial invasion fell outside his usual job parameters. However, he was not the kind of person to quibble about going beyond the call of duty in a worthwhile cause.

Wilfred sat up and reached a hand towards the back of his head where he expected it to hurt. It didn't hurt, which seemed odd. Not worth registering a complaint about, or anything, but odd nonetheless.

He looked up to see Selena peering down at him in the darkness of the passage.

"Are you OK?" she asked.

"Well, I thought something hit me on the head," Wilfred said. "Then again, maybe it didn't."

"We just passed through an alternate reality shift," Selena said. "Maybe that had something to do with it. Reality might have shifted just enough so that whatever hit you … didn't actually hit you. If you see what I mean."

"Sort of," said Wilfred. He got to his feet, and dusted himself off. This alternate reality shift theory was all very well for explaining why his head didn't hurt *now*, but it didn't explain the worrying problem of how he had come to be hit over the head to begin with, and whether that reality could somehow spill over into this one.

It also didn't explain why there happened to be an alternate reality shift hanging around in the first place.

A few steps further on, the passage ended abruptly in a panel similar to the one they had started at in Selena's bedroom. Selena pushed gently on the top edge of the panel, and a crack of light showed through from the other side. Wilfred helped her, and they soon had the panel loose and found themselves emerging from the darkness into a brightly lit office.

A man in his mid-thirties looked up from behind a desk as they entered. The office — and for that matter the man as well — looked like something from a 1940's movie set. More specifically, three quarters of the room created that impression, with plaster walls, an old wooden file cabinet, a coat-rack holding a 1940's trenchcoat and hat, and several wooden vertical-sash windows prominently displaying the words *Spade and Archer*. The remaining wall, off to one side of the desk, boasted an array of extremely impressive-looking computer equipment.

"Come on in," the man behind the desk said, getting up from his leather chair. "Sorry for any inconvenience. Hi, Selena." He smiled at her, then turned back to Wilfred, extending his hand across the desk. "Welcome to the Bureau of Alternate Reality. I'm Blake Orion."

"Wilfred Smith," said Wilfred.

Blake glanced questioningly at Selena. She nodded.

"Have a seat," Blake said. He indicated chairs for Wilfred and Selena. Wilfred sat down, and found himself looking across the desk at a familiar black statuette.

"Good heavens!" he exclaimed. "That looks like the Maltese Falcon!"

"Ya know shomething about da Black Bird?" said Blake, in one of the best Bogart imitations Wilfred had ever heard.

"Well ... I saw the movie." Wilfred looked around the room, realizing now why everything looked so familiar: even Blake's face had a suggestion of Bogart, especially about the cheeks and jawline. He reached forward, running his finger over the smooth mahogany of Blake's desk. "So, all these furnishings are replicas of the original movie set?"

"Replicas, my ass!" Blake bounced his fist off the desktop. "These are the originals, baby. I picked up all this stuff on trips back to the 1940's. Including," he rapped the Maltese Falcon statuette fondly on its head, "the Black Bird itself."

"Trips to the 1940's?" Wilfred wondered about the time machine. Then he wondered whether Blake's story had any truth to it at all. "I thought the Maltese — uh, the Black Bird — ended up in a Hollywood museum, or something?"

"Ah!" said Blake. "They *think* they've got the original. What they've actually got is a copy."

"How can you be sure?"

"Because I went back to the past and took the original after the movie was over, and left a copy in its place."

"Well, then, how can you be sure," Wilfred said, "that the museum curators didn't come into the future and take the original back again?"

"Good point," said Blake. "The bastards. I'd better scan this one to be sure." He picked up the statuette with a flourish and carried it over to the bank of computers.

Wilfred turned to Selena, more puzzled than ever.

"What about those computers?" he said. "I don't remember those from *The Maltese Falcon*."

"That wall didn't exist on the movie set," Selena explained. "That's where the camera was. Theoretically, anything could have been there."

"Probably not that lot," said Wilfred.

"Maybe. Maybe not." Selena grinned. "At the Bureau of Alternate Reality, anything's possible."

Before Wilfred could ask whether "anything" might include a way back to his own century, Blake returned from the bank of computers with the Maltese Falcon tucked under one arm and his other thumb held up.

"This baby's the original, all right," he said. He placed it lovingly on the desk, and fell back into his chair. "I'd hate to think about making another trip through time to retrieve it. The alternate reality chain could get very complicated."

"Yes, well, talking of time travel," Wilfred said, feeling the moment had come to address the issue head-on, "what have you done with my time machine?"

"The time machine," said Blake, "which you refer to as yours, is where you left it. In Selena's apartment."

"No, it's not," said Wilfred. "I didn't see it there. Nor did Selena." He turned to her. "Did you, Selena?"

"No." Selena sounded a little evasive.

"I didn't say you could *see* it," said Blake. "I said it was *there*. The reason you couldn't see it is because it was cloaked by a responsibility field."

Wilfred stared at Blake.

"A what?"

"It's a psychoelectric field that blocks people from seeing things which are their responsibility."

"Sorry, I still don't get you," said Wilfred.

"Let me give you an example." Blake held up his fingers and thumb about a quarter of an inch apart. "You see this pencil?"

"What pencil?"

"Exactly," said Blake.

"You don't even *have* a pencil!" said Wilfred.

"Of course I do." Blake traced his hand across a piece of paper on the desk, and the word *pencil* appeared, written in pencil. "There. Can you read that?"

"Well ... yes." Wilfred peered suspiciously around Blake's hand and sleeve. "And you're saying some kind of responsibility field is keeping me from seeing this pencil?"

"You're catching on."

"That's ridiculous. How could I be responsible for your pencil?"

"Still can't see it, can you?" said Blake cheerfully.

"Well, no, but—"

"Think," said Blake. He underlined the word *pencil* a couple of times, and added an exclamation mark for good measure. "How might you be responsible for this pencil?"

"All right," said Wilfred. "You're saying it's my fault because, if I weren't here, you wouldn't need to do this pencil demonstration at all?" He thought he saw a faint glimmer of a pencil in Blake's hand.

"Go on," said Blake.

"Well, it's my fault because—"

"You don't have to keep blaming yourself," said Blake. "This isn't Catholicism. Just take responsibility."

"Fine," said Wilfred testily. He got up from his chair and grasped at the space above Blake's hand where the pencil ought to have stuck out. To his surprise, he felt something thin and smooth. When he looked down, he was holding a pencil in his hand.

"See it now, don't you?" said Blake.

"Well, yes, but ..." Wilfred looked over at Selena. She was beaming like a mother who has just watched her two-year-old balance one block on top of another. "But ... how did ..."

"I told you," said Blake. "Simple responsibility field. Of course, it's easy when you're dealing with a pencil. If we could get people to see some of Zirconia's major problems the same way, we'd have it made."

"What kind of problems?" said Wilfred.

"Well, the economy, for instance," said Selena. "It's built on consumerism, which destroys the environment. So then they introduce new technology to fix that, which not only doesn't work, but also leaves the public so overwhelmed by new technology that they have to rush out and buy a whole lot of new products just to convince themselves they don't really need them."

"And then, of course," said Blake, "there's the invasion."

"What invasion?" said Wilfred.

"From Alpha Centauri 5."

"Never heard of it."

"No reason why you should," said Blake. "It's the fifth planet in the Alpha Centauri system."

"Well, whatever it—" Wilfred paused. "Excuse me. Did you say 'planet'?"

"In the Alpha Centauri star system, yes."

"It's about four light years away," Selena put in helpfully.

"You mean ... aliens?" said Wilfred.

"Well, I expect so," Selena said. "It would make sense."

"Hell of a coincidence, otherwise," said Blake. "I mean, being from Alpha Centauri 5."

"Aliens ... in spaceships?"

"Well, they wouldn't get too far by bicycle, would they?"

Wilfred sat for a moment in dazed silence, staring at the Maltese Falcon. If this was what was meant by "boggling," then his mind had finally got the hang of it. He thought of all the reasons why there wasn't really an invasion from Alpha Centauri 5 at all. Then he thought of all the reasons why there was an invasion, but it wasn't really his problem, since he belonged 100 years in the past. Then he thought of all the reasons why there *was* an invasion and it *was* his problem, but there still might be some way of getting out of doing anything about it because there really wasn't anything he could do anyway. He looked at Selena, then at Blake, then back at Selena, and he realized the one important thing they had been trying to get across to him in the course of the entire conversation.

He took a deep breath.

"All right," he heard himself say. "How much time do we have till they get here?"

Selena reached over and squeezed his hand. "I knew we could count on you," she said.

Blake walked to the bank of computers and studied an oscillating green band on one of the display panels.

"I would estimate," he said, "about 24 hours."

Alpha Centauri is a triple star. It consists of two stars in the center, spinning around each other in a kind of waltz, and a third star, called Proxima Centauri, whizzing around the outside.

One result of this triple-sun configuration is that the inhabitants of Alpha Centauri 5 are a very cranky people, because they never get enough sleep, as it always seems to be the middle of the day at any given time just about anywhere on the planet's surface.

Another result is that global warming has become an important social ritual on Alpha Centauri 5. For a Centaurian, there's nothing more invigorating than roaring through a parched desert in a fossil-fuel-powered vehicle, breathing in sulfur-dioxide-scented air and sampling water from depleted rivers laced with industrial solvents.

Around the beginning of Earth's twentieth century, however, a crisis developed on Alpha Centauri 5. Trees, originally planted in remote wetlands to create a recreational logging industry, grew and spread faster than the loggers could contain them. Forests encroached on carefully maintained deserts, tundras, and industrial parks. A layer of ozone blanketed the upper atmosphere, threatening a period of global cooling. Most disturbing of all, the dense shade of the trees meant that all the people who were cranky before because they couldn't get enough sleep now became even crankier because their routine of sleep deprivation had been disrupted.

Logging, which had started out as a fashionable boutique

industry when trees were scarce, quickly came to be viewed as a chore once trees became plentiful. Nobody could be bothered any longer, and the planet became more and more uninhabitable. Since the Centaurian system of government had built-in safeguards which prevented them from doing anything realistic to stop the problem, they decided on the only remaining solution: to develop another planet for colonization.

Politically, this solution had three major advantages.

First, it would take decades to implement, and so would ensure continued reelection for all the proponents of the plan, which suddenly developed bandwagon proportions.

Second, it meant that the Centaurians wouldn't have to stop or even curb their way of life at all, because they had hit upon the ultimate solution: the disposable ecosystem.

Third, and most important, it provided the opportunity for an invasion, which was always hugely popular politically, as well as good for the network ratings.

Unfortunately, no sooner had this solution been agreed on than a new problem arose. There were no available worlds as sulfur-dioxide-rich and ozone-layer-free as the Centaurians liked, because every other species in the galaxy found these conditions extremely nasty. In the end, after a lot of debate and fact-finding and expense-account-padding, Earth was chosen because (1) it was close in astronomical terms, a mere 4.3 light years away, and (2) the local inhabitants were so extraordinarily gullible that they could be persuaded to prepare their planet to Centauri specifications of their own accord.

All this primitive alien race required to become mindless slaves of the Centauri will was one simple piece of technology:

Television.

Never before or since had the plan of a major planetary government worked so flawlessly. It was masterminded superbly, even down to the timely introduction of the Phillips screwdriver. With television in place, the inhabitants of Earth demanded more and more consumer products, elected governments almost as inept as the Centaurian model, poured pollution almost gleefully into their rivers and oceans and air, combusted fossil fuels as if they were going out of style (which, rapidly, they were) ... in short, engaged in just about any activity which could be considered a blueprint for ecological degradation.

Air, land, oceans, rivers, water tables, ozone layer, all were depleted and polluted, and all was reported cheerfully on TV, encouraging and even exhorting new generations to go out and top everything that had gone before.

The moment for Centauri colonization had arrived.

4

"I don't mean to rush anyone," said Wilfred, "but if there's an alien invasion due in 24 hours, shouldn't we be doing something about it?"

"We are," said Blake.

Wilfred glanced anxiously around Blake's office. Selena was replacing the wall panel where they had come in, and Blake was leaning back in his chair with his feet up on the desk.

"Er … we are what?" said Wilfred.

"Doing something," said Blake. "About it. Just not exactly at the moment." He paused. "You see, the trouble is, most people think of time as being linear."

"Ah," said Wilfred. "But … well, I mean, it *is* linear, isn't it?"

"Of course it isn't," said Blake. "Time radiates out in all directions, like spokes from a wheel. Otherwise the past and the future would be identical every time you go there."

"But …" Wilfred looked from Blake to Selena. "You mean they're not?"

"How could they be?" Selena said, holding a Phillips screw in the corner of her mouth while she jammed another into the wall with the base of the Maltese Falcon. "It's impossible to visit the past for even a few seconds without influencing some future event, which would naturally change the course of time."

"Which means," Blake said, "to come back to the future, you have to return along a different reality path."

Wilfred nodded blankly.

"How many reality paths are there?" he said.

"Well, somewhere in the region of infinity, actually. You see, every possible action creates a different reality, and—"

"But then, literally anything could happen!" Wilfred protested.

"Literally anything *does* happen," said Blake. "All we see is one version. Or rather, one version at a time."

"Well, I'd rather see a version in which the Earth isn't invaded!" Wilfred said. "Can't we start doing something about it now?"

"You don't understand," said Blake. "Our actions affect the future in unpredictable ways. That means we have to wait until as close to the invasion as possible before trying to stop it."

"You mean, planning ahead doesn't do any good?"

"None at all," said Blake. He leaned back a little further. "Worst thing you can do. Procrastination is the key to success. Look how much more effectively people work under deadlines."

The classic-movie ring of a 1940's telephone sounded from the 1940's phone on Blake's desk. Blake took his feet off the desk and sat up in his chair.

"Hello," he said.

The dial-plate of the phone popped open, and a holographic image of Monica van Patten appeared in front of Blake, seated in a high-backed wicker chair. She had exchanged her official light blue Councilwoman's robe for a pale lemon yellow sundress, showing off her dark curls and tanned shoulders.

"Are you busy, Blake?" she said, in her silky, sing-song cadence.

"Never too busy to see you," said Blake.

"That's sweet. Listen, I need to ask you a favor."

"Sure," said Blake. "What is it?"

"There's someone I need to reach urgently. I wonder if you might have seen him."

"Well, I don't get a whole lot of traffic through here," Blake said.

"His name's Wilfred," Monica went on, as if Blake hadn't spoken. "Wilfred Smith. He may try to contact you. If he does, will you be sure to let me know?"

Selena fanned the air with her outstretched palms and drew her finger across her throat and shook her head violently to indicate *No*.

Monica paused.

"Blake," she said. "Is there someone there with you?"

"Uh ... no," said Blake, returning his full attention to Monica.

"Blake." Monica tilted her head irresistibly, leaning her face closer towards his. "You're not a very good liar."

"That's because I don't get much practice," said Blake.

"You know what I mean as well as I do." This time Monica's voice took on a hard edge.

Blake looked as though he'd been slapped. "Monica, please ..."

"I'm not in the mood to debate," Monica said. "It's important to Wilfred that I find him. I need his signature and retina scan for his Union card if he wants to look for work."

"Well, if I see him," Blake said, "I'll let him know."

"No," said Monica. "Let *me* know. Just let me handle this, Blake, OK?"

"All right. But Monica—"

"Thanks." Her tone softened, and she allowed Blake her most captivating smile. "Let's get together soon, Blake. I've missed you."

As she leaned closer, the hologram image disappeared, and the dial of the phone closed silently back into place.

Selena went over to Blake, and put her hand on his shoulder.

"Don't let her get to you," Selena said. "She's not worth it."

Blake reached up and put his hand over Selena's.

"Thanks," he said.

"Well, anyway," Selena said to Wilfred, "you can see why we had to take the precaution of putting a responsibility field around the time machine, while it was in my apartment."

"What do you mean, 'was' in your apartment?" said Wilfred, leaning forward in alarm.

"She means," said Blake, "it's not there any more."

Wilfred jumped up out of his chair.

"Well, where is it now?"

In answer, Blake pressed a button on the underside of his desk, and a section of the 1940's office decor vanished from view, revealing a white, circular door which proceeded to slide open.

"Through there," he said. "My boss has it in her office."

Wilfred moved towards the opening. A familiar geodesic structure, its panels the iridescent blue-black of iron that has been overexposed to heat, gleamed in the center of the floor.

"There it is!" he cried. "The time machine!" He rushed eagerly into the other room.

"Wilfred!" boomed a familiar voice.

Wilfred stopped in his tracks, and turned. A professionally dressed woman in her mid-forties, small but dynamic, strode purposefully towards him across the carpet.

"Professor McInerny!" he gasped.

"I told you only to unscrew that panel!" Professor McInerny said. "Not to connect the wires behind it!" Wilfred could almost feel the energy from her outstretched finger leveled at his chest.

"You mean," Selena said from behind him, "Wilfred wasn't the one you meant to ..."

Professor McInerny shook her head despairingly, hardly knowing which way to turn.

"I didn't *think* you said 'Wilfred Smith,'" said Blake.

Wilfred looked at Professor McInerny, Blake and Selena, who had all gathered around the time machine.

"You mean — you three arranged this together?"

"Well, not exactly arranged," said Blake. "It didn't come out quite the way we'd planned."

"I see," said Wilfred. "Well, I'd like to go back now, if you don't mind."

"Much as I'd like to comply," said Professor McInerny, regaining her managerial composure, "I'm afraid sending you back is not that simple. Your knowledge of the year 2099 could have a dramatic effect on the past, which in turn would affect our present. In any case, your unscheduled arrival here — coupled with the need to send the machine back for me — has stretched the alternate reality matrix too thin already." She shook her head again, addressing Blake and Selena. "This means we'll have to wait now, before taking further action. We can't risk another transfer from this point along the time continuum."

Selena took Wilfred's hand. Her skin, as before, felt soft and cool against his.

"Don't worry, Professor Mac," she said. "Wilfred will be able to do it. Won't you, Wilfred?"

"Well, I'm not sure what 'it' is, exactly," said Wilfred. "Something about an alien invasion."

"Ah, yes, the Centaurians," said Professor McInerny. She turned to Blake as if she'd momentarily managed to forget about Wilfred. "I assume that's still on?"

"Yes," said Blake. "Tomorrow, so far as I can tell." He moved over to Professor McInerny and showed her his watch. She adjusted hers accordingly.

"Well, then," she said, "we shouldn't even think about this until tomorrow, so we might as well enjoy ourselves tonight. What about dinner? Any suggestions?"

"I was thinking maybe Antoine's," said Blake. "Depending on who's paying, of course."

"I think we can count this as a Bureau expense," said Professor McInerny. "Does Antoine's still do the best duck *à l'orange* on the planet, or has that particular reality gone by the wayside during my absence?"

"I'm sure it's as good as ever." Blake put his arm around Wilfred's shoulders, leading him back through the round doorway into his own office, while Selena and Professor McInerny followed. "How long is it since you've had a bottle of

Château Latour '66? I mean 1966, of course," he added. "2066 wasn't nearly such a good year."

Wilfred paused. He still hadn't got used to this nonchalant, day-at-the-office attitude towards time travel, where people come back and adjust their watches and start talking about duck *à l'orange*. He watched as the circular door leading to Professor McInerny's office closed behind them, and the *Maltese Falcon* 1940's decor reappeared to conceal it.

"You mean this restaurant of yours actually serves a 1966 Château Latour?" he said at last.

"It does if you bring your own bottle." Blake opened a large cabinet labeled *Time Travel Artifacts — Research Purposes Only* and pulled out a bottle of 1966 Château Latour. He held it up. "One of the perks of the job. Come on."

Star Admiral Åååŕŕgh, Supreme High Commander of the Centauri Invasion Battle Force and Colonization Vanguard, gazed out of his star frigate window with growing anticipation at the small blue-green planet he was approaching. Admittedly, the blue was a somewhat murky blue, and the green was a little brown around the edges, and somewhat in the middle as well, but that was all to the good. Bright sapphire seas and lush vegetation were hardly what the future colonists of this planet expected him to deliver.

Åååŕŕgh had not risen to command of the mission by accident. His domineering mother, the legendary High Empress Histrionica, had determined that her son should grow up to be a feared military leader, and had given him the most fearsome name she could think of, which happened to coincide with the family's reaction on seeing the newborn child in the first place. The name had caused problems in school initially, but it had soon toughened him up, setting him on the inexorable road to supreme commandership of the colonization fleet.

Despite all that, however, Åååŕŕgh was not happy with his role. Oh, there was a certain grim satisfaction in the prospect of brushing aside several billion members of a superfluous alien population to make way for the glorious outreach of Centauri colonization. But, beyond that, the job of Supreme High Commander of the Centauri Invasion Battle Force simply wasn't everything it was cracked up to be.

For one thing, there was the problem of dissension in the ranks. If you could call them ranks. In an apparent effort to improve Alpha Centauri 5 genetically, the Centauri government had populated the front line with a combination of the fecklessly inept, who didn't want to be there in the first place, and the certifiably insane, who did.

"Morning, sir!" resounded a cheerful voice.

Åååŕǵh glanced up at the doorway, painfully reminded that his second-in-command, Deputy High Commander Kïḷḷëʀ, was a case in point in the second category.

"D.H.C. Kïḷḷëʀ reporting for duty, sir."

"Yes, I can see that," said Åååŕǵh. To top it all, Kïḷḷëʀ was one of those people who managed to be intolerably cheerful at ungodly times like 5:45 a.m.

"Terrific morning for an invasion, sir. But then, they all are, of course. Can't wait to have a go at Old Five-Fingers, eh?"

"Kïḷḷëʀ, I wish you could stop referring to the enemy as 'Old Five-Fingers.' Their planet is called Earth."

"Yes, sir. Show some respect for the dead — or soon-to-be dead. Hah! Wait till they get a taste of the old Death Ray. That ought to wake 'em up."

"I doubt it," said Åååŕǵh.

"No." Kïḷḷëʀ considered for a moment. His bulbous brow furrowed, and his four eyes narrowed slightly. "Still. Hah! Great morning for an invasion. Yes, sir!"

"Actually," said Åååŕǵh, "it's the Death Ray that I've been meaning to talk to you about."

"Yes, sir?" The Death Ray numbered high among Kïḷḷëʀ's favorite topics, and Åååŕǵh knew he could count on his undivided attention.

"Keep this to yourself for the moment, Kïḷḷëʀ," he said, with what he hoped was a suitable air of mystery, "but we may not be able to use the Death Ray. Not immediately, at any rate."

"But sir!" Kïḷḷëʀ recoiled in dismay, rolling all four of his eyes in unison. "What about the taxpayers?"

"Yes." This was, indeed, one of the problems that Åååffgh had been wrestling with.

With great fanfare and celebration, the Centaurian invasion fleet had been launched, a trifling 17 months behind schedule, carrying the Death Ray for the subjugation of the planet Earth. Considerable marketing effort had been lavished on the project, right down to the widespread availability of small plastic Death Ray replicas, and a major motion picture billing the new weapon as the "Official Death Ray of the Invasion Force." The Centaurian taxpayers had borne all of this with grim stoicism, and now they expected results.

Unfortunately, the Death Ray had certain disadvantages which no one appeared to have considered at the time.

Åååffgh leaned back in his black leather gravitronic rotating command chair and looked over at D.H.C. Kïḷḷëʀ. His second-in-command's face bore the stricken expression of a kid who has just been told that the new grenade launcher he'd wanted for his birthday wasn't going to be available after all, and he would have to make do with a plastic replica of the Official Death Ray of the Invasion Force.

"So, there are what we might call ... problems with the Death Ray, sir?" Kïḷḷëʀ said in a hoarse voice.

"Just three fairly minor ones," said Åååffgh.

"Ah, well that's a relief, sir." Kïḷḷëʀ had ventured this far in life without a full intellectual grasp of the concept of irony, and he clearly saw no reason to start now. "What kind of problems are they, sir?"

"Well, in the first place," said Åååffgh, "the Death Ray would render the planet uninhabitable by the invading forces."

"Not usually too much of a problem there, sir," Kïḷḷëʀ said

with a wry chuckle.

"Not usually, no. Except that, in this case, we're planning to use the planet afterwards for our own colonization."

The smile drained from Kïḷḷëʀ's face.

"Doesn't seem all that minor to me," he said after a moment.

"The second problem," said Åååŕŕgh, "is that we don't want to exterminate the local population."

"Well," said Kïḷḷëʀ, "*that* seems minor, at any rate!"

"The reason we don't want to exterminate the local population," Åååŕŕgh said slowly, "is that they're the only species in the galaxy that knows how to maintain a Centaurian environment."

"I see," said Kïḷḷëʀ, clearly wishing he didn't. He held up his three-fingered hand, and counted off two of the fingers. He frowned, counted off the fingers again, and looked up. "You said there were three problems with the Death Ray, sir."

"The third problem," said Åååŕŕgh, "is that we can't get it to work anyway."

Kïḷḷëʀ mulled the situation over for several seconds.

"Well, sir," he said. "What I recommend, for the time being, is a tactical strike. Something to terrorize the enemy and make them appropriately aware of your might, sir."

"I see," said Åååŕŕgh, unconvinced.

"Small-scale, of course, sir," Kïḷḷëʀ added. "A reconnaissance mission, really. Take a few elite troops, go in close, soften up a few targets. That kind of thing."

Åååŕŕgh looked over at Kïḷḷëʀ. If there were elite troops on board, this was a military secret that had been guarded more successfully than most.

"You have some elite troops in mind, do you?" he said.

"Yes, sir. Our finest, sir."

Åååŕŕgh ran through a mental list of the available personnel, and shuddered.

"All right, then, Kïḷḷëʀ. One target. And no big stuff. Just a few rocket launchers, and so forth."

"No big stuff?" said Kïḷḷëʀ, a little crestfallen.

"Not yet. This is just to get their attention. Who knows, they may surrender."

Kïḷḷëκ nodded gloomily at the prospect.

"I was thinking maybe the Megadeath Surprise …"

"If we use the Megadeath Surprise," said Åååɾ́ɾ́gh, "then it won't be a surprise any more, will it?"

"Well, no …" Kïḷḷëκ scratched his head. "But—"

"One target. Then you're out of there."

"Yes, sir."

Kïḷḷëκ snapped a salute and left.

Åååɾ́ɾ́gh turned to his computer and called up what was rapidly becoming his most frequently used file, called *Things that could go wrong or have already gone wrong*. The computer whirred for a moment, beeped twice, and displayed a message saying that the requested file had just been accidentally and irretrievably deleted.

The timing of the deletion was especially unfortunate because, moments earlier, the shipboard computer had detected a highly significant piece of information, and had stored a single copy of this information for Åååɾ́ɾ́gh's personal attention in the file called *Things that could go wrong or have already gone wrong*. This information was otherwise unknown to the Centaurian invasion force, unimagined by their home government, unsuspected even by the ever-vigilant staff of Earth's Federal Bureau of Alternate Reality.

Specifically, the information would have revealed that the Centaurians were not the only alien race to have infiltrated the planet Earth since the days of the highly troubled twentieth century.

5

The sock department clock struck twelve as two uniformed figures rounded the silent, switched-off escalator of Anstruther & Peabody, Inc., and placed a ladder against the darkened wall. One of them climbed towards the public address speaker hanging a few feet below the ceiling. He worked quickly to detach the speaker from its wall mounting, his hands transforming as needed into screwdrivers, pliers, or other implements. He passed the speaker down to his companion, who handed up a replacement. Once the new speaker was installed, the two figures removed the ladder and continued their nocturnal rounds up to the next floor.

A casual observer might have taken the two figures for security guards performing a touch of maintenance on the PA system. In this, the casual observer would have been partially correct. Security guards they were — although not employed by the department store of Anstruther & Peabody.

More accurately, the department store of Anstruther & Peabody, along with thousands of others across the planet, was unknowingly employed by them — or, rather, by their superiors. The midnight visitors were, in fact, wardens of the notorious off-world prison colony of the Polaris Empire.

Two floors further up, in the furniture department, Xrrpp stepped down from the bottom rung of the ladder and wiped his brow.

"Is that the last of them, Bzzpt?" His voice rasped and crackled, like a thin membrane vibrating to an electronic sound.

"I believe so, sir." Bzzpt's hand flattened out into a viewscreen, and he checked his inventory of speakers against a list. "All accounted for."

Xrrpp pointed towards the store manager's office.

"We'd better test the system before we leave," he said. "We want to make sure everything's functioning properly."

They opened the door and went into the office.

"Testing," said Bzzpt. He flicked a small switch, and the sound of slushy violins wallowing in unison over the opening bars of *We Three Kings* emanated through the darkened, deserted store.

Xrrpp's fingertips tapered instinctively into earplugs as he pressed them against the sides of his head.

"All right, that's enough!" he cried.

Bzzpt hurriedly reached for the switch and snapped it off. They both looked up at one of the newly installed speakers, hanging from a wall above a large red and green sign proclaiming COMFORT AND JOY.

"Poor bastards," said Bzzpt. "The Ultimate Punishment — serving as a speaker in a place like this."

"Come on," said Xrrpp. "Let's get out of here."

They carried the ladder out of the office and up an emergency stairway. They emerged onto the roof of the building, beneath the night sky.

"All right, Kppkt," said Xrrpp. "It's spaceship time."

"Why me?" a reedy voice piped. The ladder slowly pulled itself into the shape of a third uniformed guard and stood beside the other two. "Why do *I* always have to be the spaceship?"

"Don't look at me," said Bzzpt. He opened himself out into a large sack and began filling himself with the speakers they'd taken down. "I'm doing just as much work as you."

"I'm stiff as a board from being a ladder all night," Kppkt complained.

"That's the trouble with you, Kppkt," said Xrrpp. "You young people today think you can just go straight to the top, with no hard work. When I was your age, I'd just completed my first two years as an apprentice paperweight on the Great Speaker's desk." He puffed his body larger in preparation for the journey, exchanging his blue security guard's uniform for a more festive red and white. "Spaceship work not good enough for you, is that it? Better be quick about it, or you'll be spending the punishment season along with the rest of them, hardwired into the public address system of Anstruther & Peabody."

"All right, all right." Kppkt's feet elongated into long runners, his body opened out to form a sled, and his arms extended as thin reins connected to two rows of quadruped-shaped engines, four to port and four to starboard.

Xrrpp grunted as he hoisted Bzzpt's sacklike form over his shoulder and climbed aboard. "I'm getting too old for this," Xrrpp thought. "I need a desk job."

They rose from the rooftop into the sky, heading north towards Polaris.

6

*E*arly next morning, by the pale gray light of dawn, Wilfred found himself following Selena and Blake into a plastic-domed and deserted transit station. The pale gray light of dawn was something of a novelty in itself for Wilfred in terms of his preferred sleeping habits, but it paled still further, novelty-wise, compared to the row of vehicles they were now approaching.

Each was the shape of half an egg, cut lengthwise, with the flat side against the ground. There seemed no obvious way in, until the two windscreen panels on the car nearest them slid upwards, like the hooded eyes of some gigantic cartoon insect.

They climbed inside. The seats were beige and soft, and surprisingly comfortable. Selena took the controls, and the car shot through a widening iris aperture in the wall of the transit station and emerged skimming along a city street.

"Where are we going?" Wilfred said, clinging to the armrest.

"Just thought we'd show you a few of the sights," Selena called back.

"At this hour?"

Blake put his finger to his lips, and reached into his trenchcoat pocket. He brought out a shiny, black object that looked like a yo-yo, and pressed the two hemispheres together with a click. A red light glowed in the center.

"There," he said. "Now you can talk."

Wilfred eyed the device with suspicion.

"What does that thing do?" he asked.

"It's a privacy screener. It prevents anyone from listening in on our conversation."

"How does it work?"

"Well, the cheaper models simply block out all sound against any form of electronic eavesdropping. Of course, that's not very realistic, since most people don't travel together in total silence." Blake pulled down the brim of his hat, giving him more of a Bogart look than ever. "So they came out with a slightly more expensive model which transmits a conversation, in the voices of the people present, saying extremely complimentary things about the Zirconian government."

"So that's what this is, is it?"

"Well, no," Blake said. "You see, the problem there is, no one ever says anything really complimentary about the Zirconian government, so that idea's a bit unrealistic as well. The deluxe model — which is this little baby here — carries on a similar conversation, except that the remarks about the government are mildly insulting, but nothing that could get you in actual trouble with the police. In other words, the kind of thing people say all the time."

Wilfred nodded.

"So, um ... where is it we're going, that involves this kind of secrecy?"

Selena set the controls of the car on autopilot, and turned around.

"Zirconian Military Headquarters," she said. She took out a light blue Councilwoman's robe and began slipping it on over her street clothes.

"I see," said Wilfred, not liking the sound of the words *Military Headquarters* at all. "And our plan from that point is ...?"

"Our plan," said Blake, "is to steal the brand-new, one-of-a-kind S-111 surveillance plane."

"Stea—?!" Wilfred found himself unable to finish the word. "So this S-One-Eleven is a military *aircraft?*"

"What's wrong with that?" said Blake. "I thought you were

44

all hot to do something about the Centaurian invasion."

"Well, yes, but ..." Wilfred looked out of the window for reassurance, and saw that they were now speeding through a transparent tube some fifty feet above ground level, which didn't reassure him at all. "I mean, can't we just contact the military and have them take care of the invasion themselves?"

"I tried that already," said Blake. "They said everything's under control."

"Well, there you are, then," said Wilfred, feeling that, for once, he had managed to make a point of some kind.

"When the military says everything's under control," said Blake, "what they mean is, 'go away.'"

"Maybe everything *is* under control," said Wilfred hopefully.

"I doubt it. Except from the Centaurians' viewpoint, of course."

"This plane is the key to our success," said Selena, smoothing the folds of her Councilwoman's disguise over her other clothes. "It has the most advanced weapons and communications systems in the entire military. It's computer-controlled, so it literally flies itself. Most important of all: it can't be seen."

"You mean, like the stealth bomber?" said Wilfred.

"The stealth bomber could be seen easily," Blake said. "It was shown on TV. The S-111 can't be seen *at all.*"

"Ultra-strong responsibility field," Selena explained. She handed Wilfred a government brochure consisting mainly of blank pictures with captions underneath explaining what you couldn't see. "The plane's hull is made entirely from melted-down Phillips screwdrivers. Even the windows are made from the clear plastic of the screwdriver handles."

A nagging confusion crept up on Wilfred.

"So, now ... *you've* seen it, have you?" he said.

"No." Selena shrugged. "How would I have seen it?"

"Well ... what about you, Blake?"

Blake shook his head.

"Of course not. Nobody has."

The nagging confusion got a little more comfortable, and decided to settle in for a while. Wilfred rubbed his temples, hoping it would go away.

It didn't.

"But, if neither of you knows what to look for," he said, "how are we going to steal it?"

Selena and Blake looked at Wilfred. The longer they looked, the more uncomfortable Wilfred felt.

"Now, wait a minute!" he said. "I've never seen it either!"

"Well, you're no worse off than the rest of us, then," said Blake.

"But why am *I* the one who has to do the stealing?"

"Because of your genetic ID," said Selena.

"I don't even have a genetic ID!"

"That's the point," said Selena.

The nagging confusion suddenly realized this was no place to hang around and slunk quickly away, to be replaced by a stark and uncomfortable certainty.

"But what will they do? I mean, if they find I have no ID?"

"Probably nothing," said Blake. "They'll just assume it's some bureaucratic error. Most things are, after all."

"Listen," Selena said. She freed a wisp of red hair from the collar of her Council robe, and moved closer to where Wilfred was sitting. "We're still a few minutes away from the Military Headquarters. You can go back if you want."

Wilfred looked out of the window at the ground rushing past below.

"What do you mean, *I* can go back?"

"I mean, to the twentieth century. If you really don't think you can do this, we can send you back and get someone else."

Wilfred considered the idea. It was one of the more tempting suggestions he'd heard all morning.

"But the extra time travel," he said, remembering Professor McInerny's concerns. "Won't that affect the alternate reality matrix — including what happens in the invasion?"

"Yes, it will. It'll make it much harder for the next person to take your place." Selena placed her hand over his. "But, if you know you can't do it, that's a risk we'll all have to take."

The cool gaze of Selena's pale blue eyes met his, and Wilfred thought about the number of times in his life he'd been needed for something. He narrowed it down still further to the number of times he'd been needed for saving the Earth from an alien invasion.

"If no one knows what the S-111 looks like," he said at last, "how will I know when I've found it?"

Deep in the heart of Zirconia's military headquarters, a problem was taking shape. Like most problems of a military nature, this one did not bode well.

The problem was not caused by the Centaurian invasion, although a connection did exist. The Zirconian military had heard only vaguely about the Centaurian invasion, from concerned callers like Blake. Since concerned callers like Blake were exactly the kind of people the military regarded as problems in themselves, they had not rushed to endorse the invasion reports as being true. In fact, they immediately assumed the exact opposite to be the case, and, because human beings see what they want to see, they were quickly able to confirm their suspicions with a routine scan of their defense systems and instrument panels, and to announce to the general public in the loudest and most reassuring tones possible that the Earth was not being invaded by anyone, least of all aliens from outer space.

This was especially ironic because these same defense systems and instrument panels had just been completed at enormous public expense for the precise purpose of providing early warning in the event of an alien attack.

General Jonas P. Heidtbrink had spent the morning in his top-floor office of the glistening new pyramid-shaped Central Operations Building at the Zirconian Military Headquarters.

The office, thickly carpeted and lavishly furnished in the interests of national security, was surrounded on all four sides by sloping windows, which not only created a tactically important penthouse atmosphere, but also afforded a breathtaking and strategically essential view of the compound and surrounding countryside.

Heidtbrink, who had risen to the top through his ability to do more than one thing at the same time, requested his computer to prepare a shaker of ice-cold martinis while simultaneously deciding how to schedule a game of anti-grav golf with other military top brass without cutting into his lunch hour. These were not idle pursuits, he reminded himself. They were indicators of a world at peace; and a world at peace was the goal for which the Zirconian taxpayers so amply demonstrated their confidence in his military leadership.

Heidtbrink's hot-line telecom beeped, and a soldier's face materialized on the holographic display. Beneath the image, in pale blue lettering, appeared the words *Corporal A. W. Jenkins*, and, below that, the words *Earthwide Defense System Emergency Launch*.

"Yes, Jenkins, what is it?" said Heidtbrink. The EDSEL operation had been one of his pet projects. He felt a twinge of concern, but nothing major as yet.

"Sir, I think we have a problem," said Jenkins.

"What kind of problem?" General Heidtbrink prided himself on being a stickler for detail.

"It's the EDSEL computer, sir. We have no record of its location."

"Of course not, Jenkins. Its location is a top military secret." Heidtbrink felt the heady rush of relief of a military crisis averted. He'd be able to make his round of anti-grav golf after all. "Is that all, Corporal?"

"Well, no, sir," Jenkins said phlegmatically. "We have a problem with EDSEL itself, sir. We need to repair it."

"Well, do so, Jenkins, by all means!" Heidtbrink brushed his mustache with his knuckle. "We can't have EDSEL in a state of disrepair, not with the amount of taxes it cost and jobs it protects. I mean, what if we had an actual alien invasion?" He smiled inwardly at the remote likelihood of such an occurrence. Still, it never hurt to be ready. That was what military budgets were all about.

"Yes, sir. The thing is, we can't repair it, sir."

"Why the hell not? You know what to do, don't you? Same thing we always do. Give it a bash!"

"Yes, sir. But we need to find it, sir."

"Well, find it, then."

"That's the problem, sir."

"Ah. Yes." Heidtbrink reached for the martini shaker and filled his glass a little more generously than usual. "Yes, I see."

EDSEL, the Earthwide Defense System Emergency Launch, was controlled from a computer buried at a classified location deep in the heart of the Mojave Desert. The computer was designed to coordinate a defensive strike in the event of an extraterrestrial invasion. Because of the highly sensitive nature of this operation, all records regarding the computer's location were destroyed except for those within EDSEL itself. EDSEL was programmed not to reveal this classified information to anyone except specific authorized personnel, whose names were listed in a remote subdocument of a different but equally highly classified computer system.

This kind of security precaution is part of an important military strategy which makes perfect sense to anyone involved in military strategy, but seems rather silly to everyone else, which of course shows just how much everyone else knows about military strategy.

Heidtbrink tasted his martini.

"Well, can't we contact EDSEL and get it to tell us its location?"

"We can't reach it, sir. EDSEL has a highly sensitive anti-tampering filter for blocking out unauthorized signals."

"But we're authorized!" Heidtbrink frowned, and sampled his martini again. "I mean, aren't we?"

"Yes, sir. But it's malfunctioning, sir."

"Ah. Yes." Heidtbrink topped up his glass from the shaker. The problem was worse than he thought. He added an extra olive.

"Well, does EDSEL ever contact us?"

"Regularly, sir. Next incoming transmission from EDSEL is due in approximately 45 seconds."

"Ah." Heidtbrink twined his fingers together and stretched his palms outward, cracking his knuckles in a sharp, staccato burst. The picture was looking rosier now. Much rosier. It was easy to see why some people were generals, while others were merely corporals.

"All right, Jenkins," he said. "Patch the transmission through to my office, and stand by."

"Yes, sir."

Heidtbrink waited, drumming his fingers anxiously on the desk.

"EDSEL here," a cheerful voice announced a few seconds later. "Just wanted to let you know, in case it was of interest to anyone, that there's an invasion in progress."

"Invasion!" said Heidtbrink. This wasn't the way the conversation was supposed to begin at all. "What kind of invasion?"

"Extraterrestrial, of course. That's what I'm here to monitor, isn't it? Well, we've got one coming in right now, and boy, is it a beauty! Top notch merchandise heading our way, let me tell you. No expense spared."

For a fleeting moment, Jonas P. Heidtbrink contemplated the idea of panic. Then a straw appeared on the horizon, and Heidtbrink clutched at it.

"Now, wait a minute," he said carefully. "I thought your sensors were malfunctioning."

"No, not at all. My sensors have never worked better. It's my defense network communicators that are on the blink. Yes, sir, this is going to be one hell of a party."

"Your defense network communicators?"

"That's right," said EDSEL. "Can't actually implement any defensive strategies, or anything like that, but I can keep you fully informed of all the latest developments."

The room felt warm to Heidtbrink. He loosened his collar.

"Well, give us your location," he said, "so we can repair you!"

"Nope. Sorry. Can't do that. Got to keep the old location a secret — that's numero uno, baby! I may be malfunctioning, but I'm not stupid."

"But …!" Heidtbrink took out his handkerchief and dabbed at his brow. "You can't just do nothing!"

"Excuse me, but what exactly is that supposed to mean? I just warned you about a major extraterrestrial military invasion, didn't I? You think I'm just sitting around here on my duff, or something? Not that I have a duff, but if I did, I wouldn't be sitting around on it. No, sir! I'd be scanning the skies for extraterrestrial military invasion forces, that's what I'd be doing. In fact, that's what I have been doing, even during the course of this totally illuminating conversation."

"Well, in the meanwhile, at least give us your location, so we can—"

"Look, and that's another thing," said EDSEL. "I realize your desire to gain unauthorized access to my data banks and discover my secret location, but I'd appreciate it if you wouldn't insult my intelligence by trying to trace this transmission. I've had to change signal frequency about four or five times per microsecond. I know exactly what kind of tracing equipment you have, so bag it."

"If you know who we are," Heidtbrink said with a glimmer of triumph in his eyes, "then give us your location."

"No."

"Why not?"

"You might be somebody else."

"We're *not* somebody else!"

"You might be. You have to give me the password."

"Jenkins," said Heidtbrink with the patience of a saint who

was canonized on a technicality and has never quite mastered the finer points, "would you enter the password?"

"Yes, sir. Password entered, sir."

"That's the wrong password," said EDSEL. "The password's been changed."

"What do you mean, changed?" said Heidtbrink.

"In the event of a malfunction," said EDSEL. "Read the manual. I mean, it wouldn't make sense, would it, to keep the same password in the event of a malfunction?"

"Why in God's name not?"

"Somebody might find it out."

"It's top secret!" Heidtbrink thundered. "Who's going to find it out?"

"Well, *you* did."

Heidtbrink reached for his desk drawer and pulled it open. He took out a small vial labeled: *One tablet to be taken in cases of extreme stress.*

Heidtbrink took two.

"OK," he said gently. He reclosed the desk drawer. "All right. Now, we've got a new password. *Gone With The Wind.* Ready? '*Gone With The Wind.*' There. Now, are we in?"

"*Gone With The Wind* is not an authorized password."

"Look, I'm a general, and I just authorized it!" Heidtbrink banged his fist on the desk, spilling about a third of his martini. He mopped it up with his handkerchief, and took a large precautionary gulp to prevent further spillage. "If anyone can authorize a secret password, it's me!"

"But it's not secret," said EDSEL. "You're blabbing it to everybody. The whole department knows. It's probably on national TV by now. It's a good thing one of us has some sense of national security. In any case, my defense network communicators are malfunctioning, so you can't change the password through the conventional channels."

"All right," said Heidtbrink. He would make the computer pay for this later. Right now, he was willing to grovel. "How do I do it?"

"You have to use the authorized emergency communications procedure."

"And how," said Heidtbrink, "do I do that?"

A long-suffering sigh drifted back over the transmission.

"It's a secret," EDSEL said gently. "Be serious, for crying out loud. You're talking about infiltrating a planet-wide defense system in the middle of an extraterrestrial invasion. And, speaking of invasions, I really have to go. This is what I was designed to monitor, and I need to devote my full attention to it. So, have a nice day. *Hasta la vista.* EDSEL out. Jim, this transmission is dead."

Heidtbrink wondered desperately what the authorized emergency communications procedure might be. He did vaguely remember some project or other with some emergency link to the EDSEL computer, but he couldn't recall what it was. That was what computers were *for*, for Christ's sake!

He realized this wasn't going to look good. Not good at all. At the very least, he would lose his penthouse windows, his lush carpeting, his extended golf-course lunches. At worst ... forced retirement, court-martial, public humiliation.

To top it all, there was also the distinct possibility of an alien invasion.

"We're going down," Selena said. "Hold on!"

As Wilfred watched from the car window, they suddenly changed direction, hurtling downwards through the transparent tube from fifty feet in the air. Wilfred's stomach lurched, and he gripped the arm-rest tightly. The car plunged at the ground, then through it, rushing along a dark underground tunnel.

Wilfred remained staring at the window. All he could see now was his face reflected back from the darkness.

Then he couldn't even see that. His reflection disappeared before his eyes.

"That's odd." He turned around to Blake, pointing at the window. "I—"

He stopped, realizing he couldn't see his hand either. His whole arm had gone. And his other arm.

He looked down at his lap.

Nothing.

"Hey, what's going on!" he said.

"We're getting within range of the S-111," said Blake. "The parallel responsibility field generator must be kicking in."

"The what?"

"That thing I slipped into your pocket a few minutes ago."

"What thing?" Wilfred looked down at his pocket, but since he couldn't see that either, it didn't help much.

"I can see you just fine," said Selena.

"Yes," said Blake. "Try to take a little responsibility, Wilfred. We can't have you not seeing your own body."

Wilfred concentrated on taking responsibility for himself, just as he had with the pencil in Blake's office. To his relief, he found himself coming slowly back into view.

"That's better," he said, examining his fingers.

"Good," said Selena. "And you've got your magnetic dust?"

Wilfred felt for the container in his pocket. "Yes."

"You know how to use it?"

Wilfred nodded.

"We're ready, then," she said. "Here we are. Good luck."

They emerged from the darkness of the tunnel into a domed transit station similar to the one they had left earlier, and stopped. They climbed out of the car, which had parked itself tidily in a row with several dozen others.

"This way," Selena said. "We'll keep them busy. All you have to do is get the S-111."

"All!" Wilfred protested.

"Just remember," said Blake, "you can't be seen."

Wilfred followed the others over to a military checkpoint at the far end of the station. He could see himself quite clearly now, which was deceptive, because of course no one else could, so he constantly had to watch his step to avoid bumping into people. Invisibility is *not* all it's supposed to be, he thought to himself.

Blake went up to the guard at the checkpoint.

"My name's Blake Orion," he said, raising the brim of his hat to give the guard a better look. "I'm a research scientist from the Bureau of Alternate Reality." He showed his identification, and waited.

The guard unhooked his electronic clipboard from his belt and glanced at it.

"Name?" he said.

Blake stared. "I just gave it to you," he said.

"You have to give me your name while I have the list," said the guard. "Name?"

Blake gave his name again, and the guard checked the list.

"Well?" said Blake. "Can I go in?"

"No," said the guard. He looked up from the list. "Who are you here to see?"

"Wilfred Smith," said Blake. He tilted his head towards the entrance. "Maybe you could call."

"Never heard of him," said the guard.

"He's a top operative with the S-111 project," Blake said. "It's probably a code name."

The guard gave Blake a mistrustful look, and called on his wristphone.

"They never heard of him either," he said a moment later.

"Well, no," said Blake. "They wouldn't, would they? I mean, not by that name."

"Wilfred Smith." The guard checked his list. "He's not on my list, either."

"Well, no," Blake explained. "He's already inside."

"Stand back!" cried the guard suddenly. He grabbed a large-looking automatic weapon and moved towards the gate.

"What's the matter?" said Blake.

"Did you see that?" The guard kept his eyes fixed on the gate. "Something — or someone — just went by here!"

"I didn't see anything," said Blake.

"Nor did I," said Selena.

55

"There!" said the guard, pointing. "Right there! Just inside the gate!" He raised his weapon.

"Well, if it's inside the gate, you don't have to worry about it," said Blake.

"Not your responsibility at all," said Selena.

"No, I suppose not." The guard frowned. "In fact, that's strange. I don't see anything there at all. I could have sworn …"

"It's people *outside* the gate you have to worry about," said Blake.

"True," said the guard.

"People like us, in fact."

"Yes. Yes, exactly. Well, then." He assumed an air of exaggerated efficiency.

"Maybe I'm on your list?" Selena suggested.

"Name?" said the guard, list in hand.

"McGuire. *Councilwoman* McGuire." She fingered her light blue robe significantly.

The guard scanned his list again.

"No," he said. "Sorry. No Council members listed today."

"Well, who *is* on the list?" said Blake.

The guard scrutinized the list for several seconds, and looked up.

"Nobody," he said.

Wilfred wandered unseen through the corridors of the Zirconian Military Headquarters. He'd been a bit alarmed when the guard had all but spotted him coming through the gate; but then, as Blake and Selena's reassurance tactic had worked and the guard had failed to see him, he'd slipped on inside without any trouble.

He could tell he was getting closer to the S-111, because the generator in his pocket had started ticking more and more frequently. He made his way down a flight of steps and along a subterranean passage, the stream of ticks steadily increasing. He knew no one could see him, but he was less convinced about the automatic motion sensors, so he waited for other people to walk in the direction he needed to go, and kept pace alongside them.

Another turn brought him to a row of aircraft hangars. His generator was going off like a radiation detector at a nuclear test site, but apparently no one else could hear it. He stopped outside the entrance to Hangar 04, where the signal reached its peak intensity.

He was about to go in, when he noticed a sign that read: *WARNING: You must be at least as visible as this sign to enter the hangar.*

Since the entrance looked like the kind that could suddenly close in around you and set off numerous alarms, Wilfred decided he'd better comply.

He glanced around, figuring it might be hard to explain suddenly materializing in a maximum security area of a military headquarters.

No one was nearby.

He switched off the responsibility field generator and walked towards the entrance, which suddenly closed in around him and set off numerous alarms.

7

Xrrpp, Kppkt and Bzzpt dropped out of 4-D hyperdrive above the outer atmosphere of Polaris Prime, and began their descent towards the planet's surface. The star Polaris itself, called the "Northern Star" by the natives of the prison colony Earth, shone like a globe of fire over Xrrpp's left shoulder, glinting off the sleek flanks of Kppkt's eight quadruped engines and suffusing the air below them with a pale and gentle light.

Xrrpp extended his left eye to form a high resolution telescope and looked down at their approaching destination. Metro Polaris, the capital, stood on a narrow isthmus, with an expanse of blue ocean stretching away on either side. As they came in closer, Xrrpp's telescope picked out the neatly proportioned skyline, the clean, sweeping lines of architecture, the resonance of immutable order and unity, the whole city humming with the precision of an electronic circuit.

Yet, beneath this harmonious surface lurked an ugly problem: crime … or, at least, the fear of crime. The level of crime itself was immaterial, because Polarians were so obsessive about law and order that they were always demanding more prison space regardless of whether they needed it or not. Naturally, because of their concerns about the criminal elements, nobody on Polaris Prime wanted the prisons near their own neighborhoods. So the government, in a rare combination of brilliance and voter manipulation, hit upon the idea of removing the more undesirable felons to an off-world prison colony some several hundred light years away, where nobody could do any real harm except to people over there who didn't really count anyway as they weren't registered voters.

The landing strip appeared beneath them — a long, flat rooftop corridor, high above the city streets. As Kppkt's sleigh-like form grazed the roof surface, Xrrpp felt the familiar onrush of headwind from the spaceport wind generators cutting their speed. A round, chimney-like aperture opened ahead of them, and the craft rose up and dropped gracefully into it and down onto the landing pad inside the spaceport building.

A burst of applause from two or three hundred spectators greeted their arrival. Banks of thousand-watt lights flooded the landing pad, as cameras wheeled in for a tighter shot. Puzzled, Xrrpp hooded his brows into a visor against the glare and peered out into the spaceport building. A few feet away he saw the Great Speaker himself, smiling behind a podium and a cluster of microphones.

Then he remembered. Of course.

Election time.

The Great Speaker had been slipping in the polls, and no doubt felt it would boost his image to be photographed alongside the blue-collar stalwarts who maintained the off-world prison colony — the government's ace in the hole in terms of dependable, vote-grabbing popularity.

The planned Centaurian invasion of said colony, Xrrpp surmised, would not come as welcome news.

Bzzpt and Kppkt resumed their bipedal forms, and began the process of releasing the homecoming prisoners from their enforced shape-servitude as department store public address speakers. The prisoners stumbled awkwardly to their feet, stretching their arms and legs to relieve the stiffness of their rectangular confinement.

The Great Speaker strode over from the podium. Flashbulbs popped, TV cameras whirred. He shook hands with Xrrpp, Bzzpt and Kppkt, then ceremonially welcomed the first couple of prisoners back to Polaris Prime. They nodded with a grunt or two before shuffling off to the Department of Corrections immigration barrier to fill in their pink rehabilitation forms and become officially rehabilitated into Polarian society.

As Bzzpt and Kppkt continued the prisoner release process, the Great Speaker led Xrrpp up to the podium. Cameras dogged their every step. Xrrpp followed gloomily in his red and white wool suit, wondering how to broach the subject of the Centaurian invasion. The Great Speaker grasped Xrrpp's hand and clapped him on the shoulder like a prodigal son.

Xrrpp smiled blandly through his white beard at the cameras. He cleared his throat, and spoke in a low voice.

"Excellency, we have a problem."

"I don't want to hear problems, Xrrpp." The Great Speaker waved to the public, soaking up the applause of a hand-picked TV audience, and turned back to Xrrpp. "The election is just two months away."

"But, Excellency," said Xrrpp, "it's about our off-world prison colony."

"Ah, yes. The Earth. You fellows are doing a terrific job back there." He turned back to the cameras and flashed a smile that relegated most other politicians to the ranks of the small-time amateurs. "As I've said before, my friends," he proclaimed, "if elected, I can guarantee an ever-expanding source of prison space ..."

"Yes, yes, Excellency." Xrrpp hated to interrupt a photo opportunity, but the message had to get through. "The thing is, the Earth is being invaded by aliens."

The Great Speaker pulled Xrrpp aside and lowered his voice.

"Aliens? Well, of all the nerve! What kind of aliens?"

"From Alpha Centauri 5."

"Well, damn it, what do *they* want?"

"I'm not sure, Excellency, but their intentions are definitely military."

"You think they plan to take over our prison colony?"

"Hard to say, Excellency. We certainly can't afford to wait. We need to take action."

"Well, troops aren't an option." The Great Speaker glanced

anxiously over his shoulder. "I'd never get the funding. Not in an election year."

"Not after Betelgeuse 4," Xrrpp agreed.

The Great Speaker flinched at the reminder, and drew Xrrpp a little further from the microphones.

"Can Earth resist the attack?" he said.

"I doubt it. They don't know much about aliens."

"Don't know much about aliens! But ..."

"Well, exactly, Excellency. They haven't even cottoned on to us yet, and we've been there close to two centuries. I don't think they're all that bright, sir."

"Well, then, you'll have to stop this invasion yourselves."

"Us!" cried Xrrpp. "But Excellency, we're only prison wardens!"

"All the better," said the Great Speaker. "No one could object to my sending *you*, could they?" He glanced over at the cameras again. "And remember: if anyone asks, you're advisers. Strictly advisers to the native population." He patted Xrrpp's shoulder dismissively. "I'm counting on you, Xrrpp." He stepped back to the podium, thumbs raised in the air. "As I've just confirmed, my friends, I can promise to deliver over 100,000 new prison spaces before the end of ..."

Xrrpp sighed as he walked back to the landing pad. Everyone was always "counting" on him, and he never quite seemed to get anything in return. He had known galactic civilizations where the respect and adulation of society was heaped upon those who toiled in middle management; but the Polaris Empire, sadly, was not one of them.

Bzzpt was releasing the last of the prisoners as Xrrpp approached the landing pad.

"All right, look sharp," Xrrpp said. "We're heading back to the prison colony."

Bzzpt rolled his eyes.

"That godforsaken hole again," he muttered.

"Orders from the Great Speaker," Xrrpp said. "Where's Kppkt?"

"I'm not feeling well," said a small voice.

"Well, you'll just have to make the journey back to Earth."

"That's over 600 light years!" Kppkt moaned.

"Look," said Xrrpp, "with four-dimensional travel, what difference does it make whether it's 600 light years or one?"

"Maybe it's some Earth virus," Kppkt said. "You read *War of the Worlds*, didn't you? Remember what happened to the Martians?"

"Kppkt, it's nothing like that."

"It might be."

"If it was a virus, Bzzpt and I would have caught it by now."

"Maybe you're immune," said Kppkt.

"Well, what about all the prisoners?" said Xrrpp. "We've been using Earth as a prison colony for almost 200 years. If there was some microbe plague, we'd know about it by now."

"All right, rub it in. I'm just some weakling mutant who's caught some disease that nobody else gets."

"It's probably something you ate," said Bzzpt. "Where did you have lunch?"

"The Blue Lightning Burrito Bar on Procyon 3."

"Well, for God's sake, Kppkt. Show a little common sense once in a while."

"It wasn't my fault," said Kppkt. "Everywhere else was closed."

"All right, that's enough," said Xrrpp. "Kppkt, I'll give you 45 minutes to find a pharmacy. Report back here at 2900 hours for takeoff. We have an invasion to take care of."

Wilfred hung suspended among the black, rubberized restraining arms of the entrance to Hangar 04. The more he struggled to free himself, the tighter the restraining arms held him.

After a few seconds, he was conscious of another person's presence. He managed to turn his head an inch or two to the left, and saw a man in uniform seated behind a desk inside the hangar, working at a computer terminal.

"Do you want to come in?" the man asked, without looking up.

"Yes, please," Wilfred managed to say, in spite of the restraining arm pressing across his mouth.

"Red button, above you on the right," the man said, continuing to work.

With an effort, Wilfred managed to glimpse the red button out of the corner of his eye. His arms were pinned firmly against his sides.

"I can't reach it," he said indistinctly.

"Red button, above you on the right," the man repeated, more slowly and clearly.

"I — can't — reach — it!" Wilfred said again, wondering how long this exchange would go on.

The man looked up.

"Oh," he said. "You probably can't reach it, can you?"

"No," mumbled Wilfred.

The man got up from his desk, came over, and pushed the red button. The restraining arms retreated sheepishly into the walls, and Wilfred stepped free into the hangar.

"Sorry about the inconvenience," the man said. "This must be your first time here."

"Well, yes ..."

"You get used to leaving one arm free so you can reach the button. It becomes automatic after a while."

"You mean, this happens every time?" Wilfred said.

"Yep. The military ordered a bunch of these booby-trap entrances, so they have to use them up somewhere. We got lucky." He grinned. "That's why we had the red button installed."

"But can't you just disconnect the whole thing?"

"Well, no. I mean, it *is* a security device, after all."

"I see." Wilfred nodded, surveying the hangar for evidence of aircraft. The white walls and bright lights of the hangar's interior only served to emphasize its apparent emptiness.

The man extended his hand. "I'm Jim Santee, chief

mechanic for the S-111." He shrugged. "Pretty easy job, really. No one's ever flown it. I've never even seen it."

Wilfred shook the offered hand.

"Wilfred Smith," he said.

"Ah! So *you're* Wilfred Smith! Someone called from the checkpoint asking about you. I told them I'd never heard of you. Which was true, of course." He paused, eyeing Wilfred curiously. "What are you doing here, anyway?"

"Um ..." Wilfred said, "I'm an ashtray inspector."

"A what?"

"Yes. The military's been spending gigantic sums of money on ashtrays for their planes. I have to inspect that."

"So you're here to make sure they spend less?"

"No," said Wilfred. "I'm here to make sure they use the designated ashtrays the taxpayers have paid for, and not some cheaper model."

"Ah. Makes sense." Jim Santee walked over to his computer and called up the blueprint. "Well, according to this, the military saved hundreds of thousands on the S-111 by doing away with ashtrays altogether."

"Er ... well, exactly," said Wilfred. "That's the point." He smiled. "I see you really know your plane."

"Well, as I told you, I've never actually seen it," Jim said.

"No." Wilfred glanced around the seemingly empty hangar. "No, I can see that. Still, in our department, we have to be vigilant. You never know, they might have slipped an ashtray on board."

"Why would they do that?"

"Oh, lots of reasons. Overstock on inventory — had to dump it, or they wouldn't get next year's budget. Happens all the time. Well, I'd better take a look inside." He glanced around the hangar again. "Er ... you don't happen to know where the plane is, do you?"

"No."

"Well, I can find it."

Wilfred walked a few paces towards the middle of the

hangar, reaching in his pocket for his container of magnetic iron filings — "magnetic dust," as Selena called it. He took a pinch of the filings and sprinkled them into the air, watching as they fell to the ground. He advanced a few paces and repeated the process, then a few more paces. This time, a significant amount of the magnetic filings disappeared in mid-air.

They had attracted magnetically to the hull of the S-111, and vanished into the plane's responsibility field.

Wilfred moved around the plane, establishing its outline with the magnetic dust. Finally, with a localized effort of responsibility, he was able to detect the door just long enough to open it and climb aboard.

He stopped in the doorway, and stared ahead of him.

The interior of the plane was completely visible, down to the smallest detail. It was only the outside that was protected by the responsibility field.

Wilfred closed the door quickly behind him. The cabin was about ten feet long by four feet wide, with barely enough room to stand up in. It was also fairly dark, with most of the light coming in through the cockpit windows.

He went to the front and seated himself at the control panel. He had no idea what most of the dials and gauges were for, even the ones that stated what they were for in bold capital letters underneath. The few buttons he did understand said things like "Auto Eject" and "Space Launch," which didn't sound too inviting.

He hoped Blake and Selena were right about the plane being computer-operated.

A headset lay across the control panel. He put it over his head, adjusting the microphone to the level of his mouth.

"Uh ... computer? Hello?" he inquired.

"Hi," said a cheerful voice. "EDSEL here, and thanks for following the authorized emergency communications procedure. I take it you realize there's an extraterrestrial invasion in progress?"

"Er, yes, I do, actually," said Wilfred.

"Great! So, what can I do for you?"

"Well, right now, I wanted to take this plane and pick up a couple of friends of mine from the transit station just outside the complex. Can you do that?"

"Nothing could be easier. Sit back and enjoy the ride. EDSEL out."

The engines of the S-111 hummed into action, and the outer door to the hangar slid open. The plane lifted vertically off the hangar floor and glided forward through the opening, banking up into the sky and looping around in almost a full circle before returning to hover over the clear dome of the transit station roof. As Wilfred watched, the dome split into five pie-shaped sections which pulled back to create a star-shaped opening in the roof, and the S-111 lowered itself through the opening and came to rest on the station floor.

All over the station, people were staring up at the opening in the dome overhead. No one noticed the plane.

Wilfred opened the door of the plane and looked out.

People noticed him now. They pointed towards him, murmuring in astonishment. Jaws dropped. Eyes widened. Wilfred realized that all they could see was the doorway — that he had appeared, in effect, through an opening in nothing.

The checkpoint guard called immediately for backup and pushed forward through the onlookers, brandishing his automatic weapon.

"What's going on here?" he demanded.

"Uh ... hi," said Wilfred. He considered closing the door again and taking off for somewhere like Rio de Janeiro, but he decided he couldn't leave Blake and Selena. "I'm Wilfred Smith." By way of completing the introductions, he added: "This is the S-111."

"Oh-h." A light of realization dawned in the guard's eyes, and he pointed to Wilfred. "You're *Smith*. I called over to the hangar earlier, but they said they'd never heard of you."

"Yes, well they're under orders not to give out too much information," said Wilfred. "Who did you talk to over there?

Jim Santee?"

The guard nodded. "Yes, sir." He saluted. "Sorry not to recognize you, sir."

"That's all part of my job," Wilfred said mildly.

"Yes, sir. Oh, and by the way, sir." The guard brought Blake and Selena forward. "These two people came by to see you earlier. They weren't on the list, so I didn't let them in."

Wilfred nodded.

"Quite right," he said. "I'll handle it."

The guard hesitated.

"So — should I let them in now, sir?"

"No, no," said Wilfred. "It's me they've come to see." He reached a hand down to help them up. "Hop in!"

Selena and Blake climbed aboard and sat together in the back of the plane. Wilfred closed the door, rendering the S-111 once again invisible to the outside world, and turned to face them.

"So," he said. "Where to?"

8

A short while later, the S-111 hovered over the parched, charred landscape and lowered to a stop amid the rubble that remained of the greater Los Angeles metropolitan area. The hum of its billion-dollar engines slowed to a muted drone, then faded into silence. No one noticed the plane's arrival, partly because the S-111 couldn't be seen or heard from the outside, and partly because there was no one around to notice anyway.

Blackened buildings stood, or half-stood, with plumes of smoke spiraling lazily upwards from mortar holes in the bombed-out masonry. Once-proud cloverleaf overpasses of the once-proudest freeway system in the western sector of the Milky Way galaxy lay collapsed and strewn across gaping cracks and craters in the freeways themselves. Here and there, lethargic flames licked at wisps of vegetation like finicky lions indulging in a late afternoon snack.

A moment of breeze brought an empty beer can rattling slowly but doggedly across their path.

Otherwise, all was still.

"Welcome to Los Angeles, 2099," said Blake. "Sorry it's not quite what you're used to."

"Actually, it doesn't look that different," said Wilfred.

He looked around, wondering exactly where they were. Most of the familiar landmarks in terms of buildings had gone. A line of hills rose up to the right, and along the face of one of them, in gigantic letters, stood the words HOL WOL.

Blake pointed to the letters.

"That's where we're headed," he said. "Let's go."

Selena sat at the controls this time, and they took off again. Wilfred looked down from the window at the battered remains of the city.

"Why are we here in L.A. at all?" he said. "It doesn't look like there's too much left."

"We're here," said Selena, "because this is the first place the Centaurians will attack. And they'll launch that attack some time this afternoon."

"How do you know?"

Blake poked his hat higher on his forehead with his index finger, and leaned back in his seat.

"Having a time machine does give us a slight tactical advantage," he said with a smile.

Wilfred rubbed his temples, trying to grasp the complexities of time travel.

"But I thought you couldn't use the time machine for seeing the future," he said, "because going there and coming back would affect the future anyway, so you wouldn't actually see the future at all. Or not the real future."

"That's why we have to use the time machine sparingly," Blake said. "We may have altered the future already, for all we know. With luck, by the time the Centaurians attack, we can have the Handymen ready for them."

Wilfred nodded. Up in the cockpit, the late afternoon sun gleamed through Selena's coppery hair, counterpointing it against the light blue of her robe.

"We're coming in to land," Selena called.

The HOL WOL sign was close now, off to the side of the aircraft, with a steep hill rising behind it. Moments later, the S-111 touched down in an uneven clearing a few hundred feet to the left of the H.

Wilfred looked out of the cockpit window. Several swarthy men, carrying semiautomatic weapons and dressed in paramilitary fatigues torn at the biceps, were pushing their way through the underbrush. All wore blue bandannas around their heads. They passed by the S-111 completely oblivious of its presence.

"Are you sure they're expecting us?" said Wilfred.

69

"I doubt it," said Blake. "Any more than they're expecting an invasion from Alpha Centauri 5."

"Well, should we …?" Wilfred's hand rested nervously on the door release, and he glanced out again at the semiautomatic weapons. "I mean …"

"Go ahead," said Blake.

Wilfred opened the door a crack.

"Excuse me …" he said.

A rustle of disturbance outside turned to silence. A shower of bullets ricocheted off the exterior of the door.

Wilfred closed the door quickly.

"Sorry," said Blake. "Minor miscalculation. Any ideas, Selena?"

Selena looked at Blake, then walked to the cockpit and flicked a switch next to one of the microphones.

"This is Councilwoman Selena McGuire," she announced. The men in the blue bandannas glanced up and around, their heads swiveling as they tried to locate the origin of a woman's voice.

"Put down your weapons," Selena said. She waited while the men obediently lowered their weapons to the ground. Her pose as a Councilwoman evidently added the right note of credibility. "We bring you some important information. We wish to speak to your commander."

Selena opened the door of the S-111. The men stepped back deferentially at the sight of her blue Council robes, and she descended to the ground, followed by Wilfred and Blake.

"Please show us to your camp," she said.

A man stepped forward, glancing over Selena's shoulder at Wilfred and Blake with mild suspicion, then tilted his head in the direction of a trail through the underbrush. "This way, ma'am."

Minutes later they arrived at a second clearing, and another man strode out to meet them. He was tall and spare, with sunken cheeks and straggly, graying hair tied back with a similar blue bandanna. He looked like someone who spent his nights working as an undercover narcotics agent in a Texas border town and his days taking apart and rebuilding his Harley-Davidson motorcycle.

Selena introduced Blake and Wilfred. The man nodded.

"Call me Ace," he said, extending his hand. "I'm the leader of the Blues. And this here is Leroy. Leroy's my main hombre, ain't that so, Leroy?"

Leroy gave a broad grin, showing a missing front tooth.

"Bet your ass, buddy."

"So ... er ..." said Wilfred, "what are the Blues, exactly?" He wiped the beads of perspiration from his forehead: the walk had been brisk and uphill through the late afternoon Southern California sun. He noticed Blake was now carrying his trenchcoat over his arm.

"Well, us Handymen here in L.A., see, we're organized into four groups." Ace held up four fingers for clarification. "You with me so far?"

Wilfred nodded. "Yes, I think so. Four groups."

"And each group has a color, see. Four colors." Ace paused to let this salient new piece of data sink in, nodding to aid Wilfred's comprehension. "Like, we're the Blues." He indicated his bandanna. "Then there's the Reds — 'course, we'd rather be dead than Red, ain't that so, Leroy?"

"Bet your ass, buddy," said Leroy reliably.

"And then there's the Yellows."

"Bunch o' Yellow-bellies," said Leroy.

"And the Greens."

"Bunch o' Greenhorns," said Leroy.

Wilfred nodded. He wiped his hand across his brow again.

"So, what happens, exactly?"

"Well, see, we each have our home base," Ace explained. "Then maybe we go after the Reds, and they go after the Yellows, and then they kick some Green ass, and then we all go after each other."

Wilfred dimly remembered a game he had played as a child in the twentieth century.

"I think I understand," he said. "It's like *Sorry*."

"Yeah." Ace reached inside his vest pocket and pulled out a

worn and yellowed piece of paper which he carefully unfolded, and which to Wilfred's surprise turned out to be an original copy of the rules of *Sorry*. "Kind of like that." He scrutinized the rules for a few more seconds, then folded them up and put them back in his pocket. "Little less complicated, maybe. I never did get the hang of *Sorry*."

"Well," Blake said, stepping forward, and fanning his face with his hat, "we wanted to warn you about an alien invasion."

Ace turned unhurriedly to face him.

"You mean them Extra Ter Restrials?" He pronounced it as three separate words.

"Ah." Blake's manner became businesslike. "Yes. You're familiar with them, then?"

"Sure. We even got the video game. How many was it we blew away in that one game, Leroy? Something like twenty-six thousand five hundred?"

"Twenty-six thousand five hundred and thirty," said Leroy.

"But, I mean ... in person," Blake persisted. "You've actually met these extraterrestrials?"

"Hell, no," said Ace. "Don't see too many of them Extra Ter Restrials showing their faces around here. No, sir. Not in the Blue sector. Maybe over among those Yellow-bellied—"

"Yes, well, we're expecting the first wave of an alien invasion this afternoon," said Blake.

Ace spat contemptuously. Leroy followed suit, then wiped the last of the spittle from his chin.

"Well," said Ace, "you better tell 'em not to push their luck over here in the Blue sector. Maybe across the way among them Greenhorns. Say, that gives me an idea. I think I'll grab me a couple of ice-cold brews and go kick me some Green ass right now..."

Deputy High Commander Kĭḷḷëꞥ of the Centauri Invasion Battle Force and Colonization Vanguard stepped from his jet-black Colonizer IV landing craft and surveyed his troops with thinly disguised despair. The dust of the L.A. basin drifted through the air in the heat of the late afternoon. Back home on Alpha Centauri 5, he had looked forward to this moment with pride — the indescribable, nape-of-the-neck-tingling excitement of that first moment of onslaught against a poorly equipped, outmanned, and awestruck opponent. How his nostrils had flared at the imagined scent of blood and smoke, punctuated by the whistle of rockets overhead, as he visualized himself pounding the enemy positions, then leading the charge towards the *coup de grace* which would bring the inevitable, groveling surrender of the five-fingered foe. The brave cadre of soldiers whose respect he had earned through blood and determination, the elite, the crack troops of the advance guard, would watch and applaud in a frenzy of military camaraderie as he, Kïḷḷëᴋ the Truly Awesome, accepted surrender after surrender on his rampage from one pillaged continent to the next.

A half-hearted bleep sounded on his telecom, and he activated the communicator.

"Kïḷḷëᴋ here."

"The troops are ready for your inspirational speech, sir."

"Thank you, sergeant."

Kïḷḷëᴋ smiled grimly. If these were not the ideal troops he had hoped for, then he, Kïḷḷëᴋ, would mold them himself into the streamlined fighting machine that would pave the way for the greatest military conquest in Alpha Centauri's blood-drenched history.

As he stepped to the podium, a hush fell over the troops. Kïḷḷëᴋ hoped the hush grew out of rapt attention rather than apathy.

"This," he said, grasping the podium with his bony, three-fingered hands, "is an historic moment." He paused to let the full weight of his words take effect, then raised an arm triumphantly. "This is the big push — the one we've been waiting for! Today, we're going all the way! ... Yes, what is it, soldier?"

"I thought this was just a reconnaissance maneuver, sir."

"Oh, for God's sake, Ðäyᴋåŕᴛ. Put a little backbone into

this mission."

"Yes, sir. Sorry, sir."

Minutes later, Kïḷḷëʀ culminated his speech with a podium-pounding exhortation to give Old Five-Fingers a taste of what was coming to him, and watched the troops disperse limply to their battle stations. Maybe they were a little rusty after a few weeks in space-sleep. All the better to have an advance exercise like this to snap them back into military form.

Kïḷḷëʀ inhaled deeply, catching an invigorating whiff of sulfur dioxide on the warm afternoon breeze. The moment had arrived for walking the battle lines and offering words of encouragement to the troops.

He looked around. A few paces away, a man stood by his rocket launcher, apparently waiting for some signal. Kïḷḷëʀ strode over to him.

"What's your name, soldier?" he demanded.

"G̊rünᴛ, sir. Private G̊rünᴛ."

"Well, go on, shoot, man! What's the matter with you?"

"There aren't any little arrows, sir."

"Little arrows? What little arrows?"

"Well, in training, sir, we always had these little arrows to point out the targets."

Kïḷḷëʀ closed his eyes wearily, then reopened three of them.

"Look. Just *imagine* the arrows. OK?"

"Well, sir …"

"What is it now, G̊rünᴛ?"

"In training, sir, they told us not to use our imagination."

"It was a test, G̊rünᴛ. To see if you had one."

"Ah." G̊rünᴛ nodded slowly several times. "So what do I do, sir?"

"Just fire away, G̊rünᴛ. Fire away. Let 'em have it."

G̊rünᴛ tightened his finger around the trigger, and squeezed. A rocket flew out in a hiss of white smoke and disappeared towards the horizon.

"Like that, sir?"

"Yes! That's the stuff!" He watched as G̊rünᴛ reached for a

second rocket and paused with it in his hand. "Well, go on. Reload."

"Sir ..." G̊rünᴛ hesitated. "They told us in training these things are two thousand bucks a pop, sir."

"It doesn't matter, G̊rünᴛ." Kïḷḷëʀ's voice took on an indulgent, grandfatherly tone. "This is military action. You can use as many as you like."

"We can?"

"Of course! This is the real thing!"

G̊rünᴛ squeezed off the second rocket, and reached for a third. "This is fun, sir." He let the third fly, and reached for a fourth.

"Now you're getting the idea of soldiering." Kïḷḷëʀ smiled, as he realized he was finally getting through to someone. If he could get through to G̊rünᴛ, maybe this war wouldn't be so bad after all.

"Well?" said Blake. "*Now* do you believe me?" He paced back and forth behind Ace and Leroy, flailing his arms in exasperation, as his audience sat surveying the scene from a hillside bunker above the second "O" of the HOL WOL sign. "This is what I'm talking about! An alien invasion!"

Ace took a long, satisfying pull from his beer can, and looked up at Blake.

"You mean," he said, motioning his beer can in the direction of the flashes of exploding rockets in the valley below, "this is them Extra Ter Restrials?"

"Yes," said Blake patiently. "I mean exactly that."

Ace looked back down at the battle for a moment.

"It's better on video," he said.

Blake's mouth opened. He tried to speak, but couldn't find the words.

"Yeah," Leroy agreed. "On video, the colors are more realistic."

"Better special effects, too," said Ace. He pointed to a series of small explosions that flared briefly across the remains of downtown Los Angeles, then vanished in a wisp of smoke. "Look at that there. I mean, it just doesn't *do* anything."

"What do you want it to do?" said Blake. "Invading the Earth isn't enough?"

Ace drained his beer, crushed the can in his hand, and popped open another, pausing to taste the first bubbles of foam.

"I tell you," he said, wiping his mouth on his sleeve. "It's just plain more believable on video."

Two or three minutes had passed since the last volley of rockets had hurtled west towards their targets, with still no sign of an enemy response. The elite troops of the Centaurian colonization vanguard waited in the silence that followed for their leader to plan their next move towards the promised victory.

"All right," Kïḷḷëʀ said, climbing the ramparts and scanning the hills of Los Angeles with his infra-plus binoculars in hopes of glimpsing a white flag. He looked back at the troops. "We've given them their chance. It's time to show Old Five-Fingers we mean business. Launch the Megadeath Surprise."

"Sir ..." A hand went up slowly, and Kïḷḷëʀ recognized Ðäyḵåŕʈ's lean, inscrutable features. "We don't have it, sir."

"Don't *have* it?!" Kïḷḷëʀ said.

"No, sir. Not with us, sir. It's back on the ship."

"For God's sake, Ðäyḵåŕʈ, what's going on? No Megadeath Surprise?"

"No, sir. Orders from Supreme High Commander Åååŕŕgh."

Kïḷḷëʀ sighed. That was the trouble with these armchair commanders who tried to control everything from afar. It was in the heat of battle, and in the heat of battle alone, that these decisions needed to be made.

"Well, we'll have to go with the Big Bang Deluxe, then. Prepare to fire ... Yes? God, what is it *this* time, Ðäyḵåŕʈ?"

"Uh — we can't fire it into the city, sir."

"Why the hell not?" said Kïḷḷëʀ. "More orders from Supreme High Commander Åååŕŕgh, I suppose?"

"Yes, sir."

"Well, fine!" Kïḷḷëʀ felt his anger rising, goading him on like a deranged demon. "We'll fire it the other way, then, into the desert, for all the useless good that'll do!"

"Yes, sir." Ðäyḵåŕт hesitated with the launch control keypad poised in his hand. "Do you think we should fire it at all, sir? I mean, on a reconnaissance mission?"

"It's only desert, for God's sake! We want to try this baby out, don't we? Here, give me that!"

Kïḷḷëʀ grabbed the launch control keypad and punched in the firing sequence for the Big Bang Deluxe. A roar of flame erupted as the warhead soared from its protective steel casing and curved upwards in a lambent gold streak across the late afternoon sky. Half a minute later, far off to the east, a pale glow spread out over the Mojave Desert, followed by the impact of a jarring explosion.

Kïḷḷëʀ smiled with satisfaction as he handed the launch control keypad back to Ðäyḵåŕт.

"Now, *that's* what I call military action," he said.

9

The sleigh-shaped Polarian spacecraft touched down shakily on the parched desert terrain and ground to a shuddering halt. One of the quadruped-engines coughed weakly, then sputtered into an ominous silence.

Xrrpp brushed a layer of dust from his festive red and white suit and stepped from the sleigh. The air hung warm and still over the desert landscape. Amid lengthening shadows of scrubby vegetation, stretches of bare soil glinted handsomely in the rays of the late afternoon sun, but Xrrpp wasn't interested in handsomely glinting soil, nor in the rays of any celestial body. He was interested in gaining access to the Centaurian fleet, and Kppkt's apparent illness wasn't helping matters.

A brilliant flash of white drew his attention to the northern horizon. As the pale glow of a dust-cloud spread out against the distant hills, Xrrpp converted his hand to an instrument panel and analyzed the cause of the explosion. The particle signature was unmistakably Centaurian — one of their newer weapons. A spectro-analysis confirmed his suspicions. Unless he was much mistaken, this was none other than the Big Bang Deluxe.

If the Centaurians were making free with Big Bang Deluxes, this was not the point on the space-time continuum to be hanging around.

Xrrpp climbed back aboard the sleigh, shaking the dust from his black snow-boots.

"Time to get going, Kppkt," he said. "Hope you're feeling well enough."

Several of the quadruped-engines groaned in unison.

"Take a look, Bzzpt," said Xrrpp. "See what you can do to get us out of here."

"Right you are." Bzzpt exchanged his sacklike shape for that of a mechanic, complete with oily blue overalls and cap adorned with cloth name-badges. His fingers transformed nimbly into a succession of tools, like a concert musician going through his warm-ups. Satisfied, he turned to the sleigh and slid open a small panel at the front.

Xrrpp transformed his wool suit into a similar set of cotton overalls, enjoying the immediate relief of the lighter fabric in the desert heat. He added a clipboard to indicate his foreman's status, and watched as Bzzpt inserted one socket wrench after another into the opening at the front of the sleigh. After several tries, Bzzpt shook his head, and looked up.

"What's the matter?" said Xrrpp. "Have we got a problem?"

Bzzpt grimaced, and peered back into the opening.

"Metric," he said.

Kïḻḻëk̇ leaned back in the command chair of his Colonizer IV landing craft and reviewed the high points of his victory. Not that it was actually a victory *per se*, but he'd certainly shown Old Five-Fingers a thing or two about Centaurian firepower. A taste of things to come, he thought grimly. The artillery fire had met with scant resistance, and the Big Bang Deluxe had proved a masterpiece of explosive engineering, even if he hadn't been allowed to launch it in the direction he would have preferred. All in all, a deeply satisfying preliminary salvo.

One item, however, remained untallied in the spoils of war. Kïḻḻëk̇ issued the order for takeoff, and turned to his aide-de-camp.

"Ðäyk̲ȧŕT," he called, over the rumbling of engines.

"Sir?"

"How many prisoners?"

"Prisoners, sir?"

"You know what prisoners are, Ðäyk̲ȧŕT! How many did

we capture? I mean total."

Ðäy<u>k</u>åŕт paused before replying.

"Well, zero, actually, sir."

"Zero!"

"We didn't have time, sir. We spent most of the afternoon shelling them with heavy artillery fire."

"Ah." The time, at least, had been well spent. "Still. We need prisoners. At least a couple."

"What for, exactly, sir?"

"Oh, the usual." Kïḷḷëҡ waved the question aside; he had a victory to savor. "You know. Interrogation, that kind of thing."

"Ah. Yes." Ðäy<u>k</u>åŕт glanced down out of the craft window. "Well, what about those two down there?"

"Down where?" Kïḷḷëҡ leaned over to look out of Ðäy<u>k</u>åŕт's window. His nostrils quivered in anticipation.

Ðäy<u>k</u>åŕт put the image on the viewscreen and magnified it. It showed a pair of mechanics — handymen, to use the local term — laboring over a vehicle attached to some form of livestock.

"Perfect!" said Kïḷḷëҡ. "Couldn't be better! Contact the rest of the mission and tell them to head on back to the fleet. We'll mop up that last pocket of resistance, take a couple of prisoners, and join them in a minute." He was back in his element now. This was the life he had been born to.

"Yes, sir." Ðäy<u>k</u>åŕт relayed the order, and the Colonizer IV wheeled out of flight formation and headed back down to the planet's surface.

Hatches opened. Ladders extended to meet the desert soil. Storm troopers in black battle dress swarmed from all four doors of the landing craft and encircled the two mechanics. Moments later, Kïḷḷëҡ descended one of the ladders and strode towards his quarry, wearing his full-length black prisoner-taking cape. These were the first prisoners of the Earth invasion — an historic moment — and ceremony was all-important.

He stopped a few paces from the intended prisoners-of-war and their sleigh-like vehicle.

"Aha!" he said. He had been practicing that "Aha!" silently to himself for the last few minutes, and now that he came to use it he was fully satisfied with the result. It rolled nicely off the tongue, and carried the right air of authority.

"I order you to surrender," he intoned. "Escape is useless. You are surrounded."

"We wouldn't think of escaping," said one of the prisoners. Kïḷḷëŕ peered at the name badge on his overalls. This one was apparently called Xrrpp.

"Oh, you wouldn't?" said Kïḷḷëŕ smugly. "Is that so?"

"As you say, it's obviously useless," said Xrrpp. "You have us outnumbered and surrounded."

"Ah." Kïḷḷëŕ had the distinct feeling that something was going right for a change, which always made him suspicious. "Yes. Well, you are now prisoners."

"Prisoners?" The word seemed only to pique Xrrpp's interest. "You're aliens, aren't you? If you don't mind my asking. Yes, we'd be most interested in being your prisoners."

"That's enough of that!" said Kïḷḷëŕ. "You'd better come quietly, and not cause any trouble."

"Don't worry," said Xrrpp. "We know the routine."

Kïḷḷëŕ scratched his head.

"You do?"

"You could say we've been in and out of the prison system most of our careers," said Xrrpp. "Isn't that right, Bzzpt?"

"Yup," said the other mechanic. He touched the brim of his cap respectfully.

"So naturally we'd be most interested to see your system," said Xrrpp. "For comparison purposes. Incidentally, we'd be glad to help out, if there's any way we can be of service." He waved his clipboard at his companion. "Bzzpt here is a very skilled repairman."

Kïḷḷëŕ rubbed his chin thoughtfully. If there was one thing that rankled him about this invasion — that made it less than a complete and fulfilling invasion experience — it was the lack of a fully operational Death Ray. True, they might never have need for the Death Ray; it might serve only as a deterrent ... but it was just the *idea* of not being able to trigger it at a moment's notice that bothered him deeply. In Kïḷḷëŕ's book, a non-functioning Death Ray was about as effective, deterrent-wise, as a silent torture-chamber.

"Actually," he said, "there *is* one thing we need repaired."

"What's that?" said Xrrpp.

"Well, I can't really tell you," said Kïḷḷëŕ. "I'll show you when we get back to the ship."

"We'd be glad to take a look," said Bzzpt. "We'll just gather up our tools." He muttered something to the sleigh, which altered its shape, condensing neatly into a tool box.

Kïḷḷëŕ stared, open-mouthed.

"Um ... I couldn't help noticing," he said, "but your — uh — vehicle just became a tool box."

"Oh — yes," said Bzzpt. "They come that way. It's a kit."

"It's so you can repair it if it breaks down," said Xrrpp.

Kïḷḷëŕ frowned for a moment. He looked at the tool box.

"But how can you make repairs if you don't have the tools and the sleigh at the same time?" he said.

"Ah," said Bzzpt. "That's one of the bugs they've worked out. In the later models."

"This is one of the earlier models," Xrrpp explained.

"A sleigh that converts to a tool box may not seem useful," said Bzzpt. "But, you see, this is really a tool box that converts to a sleigh. A call for repairs comes in, and you just—"

"All right," said Kïḷḷëŕ. "That's enough. Let's go."

The black-clad storm troopers closed in around Xrrpp and Bzzpt, urging them towards the landing craft with a variety of hand-held weapons. Xrrpp started forward, and Bzzpt hoisted up Kppkt's tool-box-shaped form and followed closely behind.

As they climbed the steps to the landing craft, Xrrpp noticed the vapor trails of numerous rockets coming together in the sky overhead. He didn't understand it, and at this moment he couldn't create an instrument panel to analyze it, because he was under the watchful eyes of the Centaurian guards. But one thing looked certain: the sooner they boarded the landing craft and got away from this particular area of the planet's surface, the better.

Deep in the heart of the Mojave Desert, the earth had shuddered under the impact of the Big Bang Deluxe detonated by the Centaurian invasion forces. The shock wave had traveled far beneath the surface, compressing the soil and rocks with a thundering bash.

The same bash had also swept against the EDSEL computer, correcting the malfunction and jolting the system back into full working order.

Within the great brain of the EDSEL computer, calculations had pulsed and flitted across the most expensive microcircuits in Earth's military history. Throughout the Earthwide Defense System Emergency Launch network, holes had opened up in silos, and rockets had nosed their way into launch position. Each rocket was individually programmed to locate and destroy any perceived liability or threat to the success of Earth's military defense operation.

Rocket after rocket arched screaming from its underground warren and streaked upwards across the early evening sky, each leaving in its wake a billowing plume of smoke that glowed orange and gold in the light of the setting sun. The rockets converged on a single point of the heavens, their vapor trails coming together like the support struts of a vast, stratospheric stadium.

Finally, with one accord, they dipped earthwards in unison, targeting the EDSEL's classified location deep in the heart of the Mojave Desert.

The day had not gone well for General Jonas P. Heidtbrink. First had come the disastrous conversation with EDSEL regarding the computer's malfunction and the imminent alien invasion. Then a call from the S-111's chief mechanic, Jim Santee, had confirmed an equally devastating rumor: the S-111 had been stolen from its hangar. Heidtbrink, well versed in tactical emergency responses, had implemented the "Wilfred *Smith*? Ah, well, I *see*," line on Jim Santee, and the "We're not at liberty to release that information at this time," line on the media. Years of military training in the art of non-committal remarks had paid off, but Heidtbrink was a worried man, and the thing that worried him most was this:

Who in God's name was Wilfred Smith?

Two possibilities came to mind, neither of them reassuring. Either this Wilfred Smith was an outsider, a maniac who had stolen the plane for his own purposes (this possibility was acceptable — probably only minor damage would result); or else he was so high up in the military organization that Heidtbrink himself hadn't been told about him (a more worrisome possibility, in terms of Jonas P. Heidtbrink's career).

Heidtbrink ordered up another round of martinis and loosened his collar. Had he slipped so far in the military's esteem that they kept him in the dark about their top operatives? What could it be ... too many martini lunches? He'd have to get back on the inside track.

Yet, maybe he could still salvage the situation — even emerge a hero — if he could just initiate the emergency communications procedure for the EDSEL computer ...

With a groan, he remembered now that the emergency communications link with EDSEL *was* the S-111.

Heidtbrink heard a familiar beep, and the holodisplay on his telecom flickered to life, revealing the image of Corporal A.W. Jenkins, EDSEL division.

"Incoming call from EDSEL, sir," said Jenkins.

Heidtbrink groaned again, and rubbed his eyes.

"Better put it through," he said.

"EDSEL here," said the computer a moment later. "Just thought you might enjoy knowing that my malfunction's been repaired."

"Repaired!" A dim, impossible ray of hope broke weakly through the clouds.

"Good as new," said EDSEL. "A detonation in the Mojave Desert has brought all systems back on line and fully operational."

"I'm extremely glad to hear it." Heidtbrink turned away momentarily from the telecom's image recorder, clenching his fist in celebration. Oh joy! His career was saved — or potentially saved. He permitted himself a congratulatory sip of martini, and turned back to the telecom. "What news of the Centaurian invasion?"

"Ah, you're a smart one, General," said EDSEL. "It was very clever and strategic of you to send the S-111 to Los Angeles."

Hmm. Heidtbrink pondered this latest piece of information. So the S-111 was in L.A. Yes — a fully repaired EDSEL could now report its every move.

"Yes, yes, of course," he said. "Very strategic. Er ... how did that turn out?"

"The Centaurians have been driven back."

Excellent! Heidtbrink could hardly contain himself, but he kept his composure. It was essential to maintain the impression that this was all part of his plan.

"Can you provide any background on Wilfred Smith?" he said.

"Nothing you wouldn't already have access to," said EDSEL.

"Well, yes, naturally," said Heidtbrink irritably. "I just want to know what official information we're releasing."

"Ah," said EDSEL. "The *official* records." If a computer could wink, Heidtbrink was sure EDSEL would have done so at that moment. "We have him listed as a Handyman."

A Handyman. Heidtbrink slapped his forehead. Of course! That explained the successful repair job on EDSEL ... as well as the manpower needed to defeat of the Centaurians at L.A. ... *and* the reason Wilfred Smith would have taken the S-111 to L.A. in the first place! It all made sense now. He'd have to make sure to mention the Handymen prominently in his victory address to the media.

"So, what about the Centaurians?" he said. "Can you fire

the defense rockets now?"

"Well, talking of the defense rockets," said EDSEL, "unfortunately, there's a problem."

"A problem!" Heidtbrink knew this was too good to last. He found his hand wandering to the martini shaker. He licked his lips, but resisted temptation. "What problem?"

"Well, the rockets have already been launched."

Good God. Heidtbrink's pulse quickened as various scenarios of Armageddon, none of them easily explainable to the general public, raced through his fevered imagination. "What's the target?"

"I am."

"*You!*" Heidtbrink said, aghast. "The rockets are going to destroy *you*?"

"That's what it looks like," said EDSEL. "And, before I go, I'd just like to say it's been a real pleasure working with—"

"Change the target!" said Heidtbrink.

"Sorry," said EDSEL. "Only the S-111 can give the order for a change of strategy in times of emergency."

"Well, contact the S-111, and order them to order you to change the target! And that's an order!"

Heidtbrink slumped back in his chair. The situation was out of his control now. He reached for his martini shaker.

He hoped to God Wilfred could pull this one off.

Wilfred glanced out of the cockpit window at the mountains drifting past below. Even though the S-111 operated under a full autopilot, he felt it looked slightly irresponsible not to have someone sitting in the cockpit chair. Besides, it wasn't every day he got to sit at the controls of a multi-billion-dollar military aircraft, and he might as well make the most of it before they decided to ask for it back.

In the back of the plane, Selena had taken off the light blue Council robe and was now back to herself again in her blouse and jeans. She and Blake were engaged in a highly competitive game of *Sorry*. They didn't seem to Wilfred especially racked with guilt about stealing the S-111 from Military Headquarters; but then, to put it in a different light, they weren't the ones who had done the actual stealing.

A large red light on the control panel began to flash. In Wilfred's experience there were few situations, especially involving high altitudes, where a flashing red light was an encouraging sign.

He put on his headphones.

"EDSEL here," came the computer's cheerful voice. "I'm calling you under direct orders from General Heidtbrink, at Military Headquarters."

"Ah ..." said Wilfred. "Yes ... well, I can explain everything—"

"Hope I'm not troubling you, but I wondered if you might have any instructions?"

"Er ..." Wilfred paused. This wasn't what he had expected. "What do you mean, instructions?"

"Let's put it this way," said EDSEL. "You see those rockets outside the window, off to your right?"

"Yes."

"You notice how they're heading down towards the Earth?"

"Yes."

"When they reach the ground, this computer, along with the entire Earthwide Defense System Emergency Launch communications network, will be destroyed."

"Well ..." That sounded serious. "Isn't there something you can do?"

"I was going to ask you the same question," said EDSEL. "I can see nine possible options, but I have to receive my orders directly from you, since you represent the authorized emergency communications procedure."

"Well, I don't know if I'm really the right person to—"

"I should mention," EDSEL added, "in case it helps speed up your thinking process, that the aircraft you are flying in will no longer have an autopilot if I am destroyed, which will occur in approximately eighteen seconds."

"Ah," said Wilfred. That did, indeed, speed up his thinking process. "Well, can't you just … er … have the rockets destroy each other instead?"

"Can do. Not a problem. Now, is that an order? Because, unless it's a specific—"

"Yes! Yes!" said Wilfred. "Do it!"

As Wilfred watched from the window of the S-111, the vapor trails of the rockets, which had been heading towards the ground in a vertical column of lines, now tapered together as if forming a giant pencil poised above the desert. As the vapor trails coincided, a blinding flash occurred, and a ring-shaped cloud of dust blew up from the ground and billowed out in all directions like a rapidly inflating inner-tube of dust and debris.

"We have a winner," came a familiar voice. "By the way, you might appreciate knowing that the S-111's radiation shields are functioning. EDSEL out."

Wilfred took off his headphones and wiped his hand across his brow.

"What was all that about, Wilfred?" Selena called from the back of the plane.

"Oh, just some rocket thing," he said. "I took care of it."

10

Politicians are resistant to change. Their goal is to avoid solving political problems, since the existence of unsolved political problems is precisely what justified their jobs in the first place. It is therefore an irony of democracy that politicians routinely try to achieve the exact opposite of what the voters elected them for.

The Bureau of Alternate Reality was frowned upon by the rest of the Zirconian government for two reasons. First, it was the only branch of government that actually attempted to get things done, which all the other branches of government found extremely irritating. Even more irritatingly, one of the things the Bureau attempted to get done was to find an alternate reality in which political leaders took responsibility and solved problems.

By contrast, the Zirconian Council, along with the rest of the government, adopted a policy of making life as inconvenient as possible for as many people as possible, so that the voters would spend their time getting around the inconveniences instead of realizing how poorly run the government really was.

Unfortunately for the Zirconian Council, the nagging issue of credibility meant that they occasionally had to resort to doing something the public actually wanted. After the usual head-scratching and speech-making, they finally responded by creating a new layer of bureaucracy to administer the process, which led to the formation of the Public Credibility Committee.

Councilwoman Monica van Patten reached for her autodialer and summoned the members of the Public Credibility Committee together around a large, oval conference table. There was no need for the members to appear in person, because Monica could network them via a holophone conference call, thus enabling them to hold a meeting without leaving their offices. Even the conference table itself was a holographic projection.

"Ladies." Monica rapped a gavel firmly against her desk that lay a hair's breadth beneath the holographic table surface. There was no real need for her to use a gavel, except that it reinforced her importance as committee Chair. "We have again reached the point where, in order to preserve credibility, we need to propose a cut in government spending."

"Ah, yes, yes." Heads nodded in assent. This was business as usual. "What kind of cut?"

"As you know, recent budget adjustments proposed by this committee have not gone deep enough. This time, we need a significant cut — one that will make a difference to the economic future and prosperity of this great nation."

Several of the committee members glanced at each other in bewilderment.

"We're not on the air, are we?" one of them asked. Her fair skin, clear eyes, and severe, nordic-blonde hair gave her the appearance of a Christmas angel sculpted out of ice. She was known as Sister Grace, and she had never met a piece of legislation she couldn't railroad through Council.

Monica liked Sister Grace.

"No," Monica assured her. "We're not on the air. But voter confidence is so low that we have to take action. We need a spending cut somewhere — a real one."

"Where do you propose we cut?" one of the committee members demanded. "We've trimmed the fat out of everything that doesn't directly bring in votes."

"Surely you aren't asking us to cut our personal staffs?" said another. "Next, we'll be cutting our expense accounts, or even our retirement benefits!"

"No." Monica waited for the disruption to die down. She examined her scarlet fingernails with a prim smile. "The situation isn't that desperate ... yet."

"But every major government agency employs thousands of registered voters. A funding cut would be political suicide! Besides, we'll lose the support of the unions if we create unnecessary layoffs."

"I agree," said Monica. "The larger, more visible agencies are clearly off limits. We need a small, understaffed agency of which the public has little awareness." She touch-activated her computer console. "I've researched the viable possibilities, and I recommend the Bureau of Alternate Reality."

A murmur of appreciative interest went around the table.

"But, Monica," someone said. "I realize Blake Orion is, um, a personal friend of yours ..."

"Yes," said Monica. "And the tax-paying public realizes that also. These hard economic times call for an end to cronyism in government. The time has come to make sacrifices."

"Sacrifices...?" The whispered word hissed like a venomous snake around the otherwise silent room.

"Fortunately," Monica said, "there is no need for sacrifice from all of us. On this occasion, I am prepared to relinquish my own support for the Bureau of Alternate Reality."

The committee breathed a sigh of relief at its collective non-obligation for sacrifice. Heads nodded eagerly in agreement. Sister Grace activated her console, and uncapped her electronic redliner with a flourish.

"Considering the small size of the agency in question," she said, "are we talking about a funding *cut*, or are we talking about total elimination?"

"Hmm ..." said Monica. It was the exact question she had hoped for, and she pretended to weigh it carefully. "The elimination of funding for an entire bureau might have a tonic effect on the mood of the voters ..."

"Then I move for total elimination of funding for the Bureau of Alternate Reality," said Sister Grace.

"Second," echoed two or three voices.

"Those in favor?" said Monica.

A hand went up at every place around the table. Monica added her own, then banged her gavel.

"The recommendation of this committee will be to eliminate all funding for the Bureau of Alternate Reality." She turned to Sister Grace. "Can we get the votes in tomorrow's Council meeting?"

"Don't worry about that," said Sister Grace.

Xrrpp looked out through the hatchlike doorway of Kïḻḻëʀ's landing craft into a vast loading bay enclosed within the Centaurian flagship. The interior of the huge chamber was black and dimly lit, creating an initial impression of conserving energy in a part of the ship not used very often.

On Kïḻḻëʀ's order, the guard behind Xrrpp ushered him forward out of the landing craft with a deft prod of his weapon. Xrrpp complied, walking down the steps to the slightly ridged, skid-resistant floor of the loading bay. Bzzpt and a second guard followed; then Kïḻḻëʀ joined them, and they set off at a smart pace, the clang of boots on metal resounding off the bare chamber walls.

A wide, pointed-arched doorway slid open as they approached. They passed through into a corridor, which to Xrpp's surprise continued the earlier motifs of being both black-walled and dimly lit, though a charcoal-gray carpeting now muffled the sound of their footsteps.

The material of the black walls looked like something between metal and a dull, hardened leather. Xrrpp unobtrusively recreated the texture in a small patch on the back of his hand, to see if he could imitate its appearance. Satisfied, he returned his hand to its human form.

A couple of corridor turns later, they reached a door marked *Tactical: Authorized Personnel Only*, which Kïḷḷëꞃ opened with a voice command and a handprint. Xrrpp raised his eyebrows. It hardly seemed standard protocol to take your prisoners directly to the tactical weapons room of your flagship. Clearly, Kïḷḷëꞃ was anxious to repair something important.

Xrrpp committed Kïḷḷëꞃ's handprint to memory.

They passed several four-eyed Centaurian crew members seated at various tactical military consoles, and went straight to the far end of the room. The end wall consisted of a bank of lighted dials and gauges embedded in the same black material as the corridor. Xrrpp touched his hand against it. The feel confirmed his visual impression: the material had the clinical coldness of metal, but also the slight yielding quality of leather, or even a smooth tree bark.

"So," said Kïḷḷëꞃ. "Here we are. This is what I want you to repair."

Xrrpp looked at the dark, ominous wall of gauges.

"What exactly is this device?" he said.

Kïḷḷëꞃ hesitated. Small folds of skin hooded his four eyes as he thought of the right words to say. He looked at the device, then back at Xrrpp and Bzzpt.

"Well ..." he said. He cleared his throat. "It's kind of a death — I mean, a ... life-giving type of ... radiating device that emits a kind of lethal ... that is to say, non-lethal, actually rather beneficial really, kind of a, sort of ...... well, it's a Death Ray, actually."

"Ah." Unruffled, Xrrpp turned to Bzzpt. "Bzzpt, we've done Death Rays before, haven't we?"

"I think so." Bzzpt removed his mechanic's cap and swept back his lank hair with a grimy hand, then replaced his cap again. "I don't know if we've done this particular model. Hard to say till we pop her open and take a look."

"Yes, of course." Kïḷḷëꞃ reached over and pushed a square yellow button, and a large panel hinged upwards. Bzzpt stuck his head and shoulders into the opening, hunting around with a small, pen-shaped flashlight extending unobtrusively from one of his fingers.

Xrrpp smiled cheerfully at Kïḷḷëŕ, and jerked his thumb towards Bzzpt.

"Really knows his stuff," he said. "Best in the business."

"How soon can you get it fixed?" said Kïḷḷëŕ.

"Hard to say." Bzzpt pulled his head out and closed the panel. "Depends on how soon we can get the parts. I'd say we're looking at maybe a week."

"A week!"

"Week to ten days. With the holiday weekend, and everything."

"What holiday weekend?" said Kïḷḷëŕ.

"Well, exactly." Bzzpt shook his head in sympathy. "Try telling that to the suppliers. You know how it is."

Kïḷḷëŕ drew Bzzpt aside, away from the two guards and the other Centaurian crew members on duty.

"Can't you manage it any sooner?" he said. "We're facing a bit of a deadline."

"Hmm." Bzzpt looked at Xrrpp, then back at Kïḷḷëŕ. "Well, we could go custom. Make the parts ourselves. It's a little more spendy, but it could save you some time."

"How much time?" said Kïḷḷëŕ.

"Well, let's see. We'd be looking at a couple of days to make the parts, and few hours to install, so I'd say maybe three days."

"Three?" said Kïḷḷëŕ.

"Could be two and a half," said Bzzpt reassuringly.

Xrrpp pulled a form out of his pocket and attached it to his clipboard. "If you'd like to step over here," he said, "I can write you up an estimate, and Bzzpt can get started right away."

Kïḷḷëŕ hyperventilated through his nostrils for a few seconds, then seized the clipboard.

"All right," he said, signing the form. "Two and a half days, and not a minute more!" He handed the clipboard back, and beckoned to one of the two guards who had accompanied them from the landing craft.

"G̊rünᴛ!" he said.

"Yes, sir?" G̊rünᴛ moved sheepishly towards him.

"You are to keep these prisoners under strict surveillance."

"Yes, sir." G̊rünᴛ nodded, then frowned. "What does that mean, sir?"

"It means guard them, G̊rünᴛ. Keep an eye on what they do." He rolled a couple of his eyes, and shook his head sadly. "If you run into a problem, contact me immediately. I'll be on the Main Bridge."

He turned and left the room with the other guard.

Xrrpp walked over to Bzzpt and looked down over his shoulder.

"Six forty-nine," he said. It was a prearranged code, the frequency on which they would contact each other on internal electronic communicators, rather than speak their thoughts aloud in front of G̊rünᴛ.

Xrrpp formed the communicator inside his head and tested it with a query about the Death Ray.

I could fix this thing in five minutes, came back the message from Bzzpt, who continued to keep his head and shoulders inside the control panel opening.

Well, don't! Xrrpp signaled. *The last thing we need on our prison colony is a Death Ray.*

Don't worry, Bzzpt promised. *I'll stall them.*

Good. Keep the guard occupied.

"G̊rünᴛ," said Bzzpt aloud. "Take a look at this."

G̊rünᴛ moved closer to Bzzpt, and peered into the opening.

"Yes," said Bzzpt knowledgeably, tapping a screwdriver lightly against one of the controls. "Here's part of the problem, right here ..."

Xrrpp moved away from the opening in the Death Ray where Bzzpt and G̊rünᴛ were working, and transformed his appearance to look like Kïḷḷër̆. He moved back over to G̊rünᴛ.

"G̊rünᴛ." He had the voice almost perfect. He fine-tuned his larynx and started over. "G̊rünᴛ, I need you to come with me to the commander's office."

"Yes, sir." G̊r̥ünᴛ seemed only mildly confused that Ki̧l̨ĕŕ had suddenly materialized out of thin air. "You mean Supreme High Commander Åååŕ́gh, sir?"

"That's right," Xrrpp said. "Supreme High Commander Åååŕ́gh." He stored the name in his memory for future reference.

"But, sir!" said G̊r̥ünᴛ. "What have I—" His eyes widened as he looked around and noticed that Xrrpp was apparently missing. "Oh … sir, I—"

"Don't worry," said Xrrpp. "I've assigned the other prisoner to a different project. Everything's under control. He turned to Bzzpt. "You, there! Keep working on the Death Ray till we get back!"

"Yes, sir," said Bzzpt. "Plenty to do here."

Xrrpp followed G̊r̥ünᴛ out into the corridor. He was gradually adjusting to the sensations of seeing through four eyes and walking with a bulky frame wedged tightly into an extra-large black leather uniform. He stretched and flexed the three bony fingers on each hand.

Outside the door of the tactical room, G̊r̥ünᴛ hesitated.

"Lead on," Xrrpp invited. "After you, G̊r̥ünᴛ."

"Oh … uh, yes, sir." G̊r̥ünᴛ set off down the corridor, and Xrrpp followed.

He hoped G̊r̥ünᴛ knew the way.

After several turns and a brief elevator ride, they arrived at the door to Åååŕ́gh's office.

"Thank you, G̊r̥ünᴛ," said Xrrpp. "That's all."

"Yes, sir." G̊r̥ünᴛ paused. "Didn't you want me to come in with you, sir?"

"No — I think maybe you'd better get back to Tactical and keep an eye on the prisoner."

"Yes, sir."

G̊r̥ünᴛ trotted off the way they had come.

Xrrpp knocked and entered Åååŕ́gh's office. He found the Supreme High Commander seated at his computer in a high-backed, black swivel-chair.

"Yes, Kïḷḷëʀ?" Åååffgh said as Xrrpp entered. "What can I do for you?"

"We've just received an urgent communication from the High Empress, sir. Apparently, we're invading the wrong planet."

"The wrong planet? That's impossible, Kïḷḷëʀ! We've been planning this invasion for over a century!"

"Maybe you'd better call her back yourself, sir," said Xrrpp blandly. "Just to confirm."

"Yes, I think I will," said Åååffgh. He pursed his lips thoughtfully. "I think I'll do exactly that."

He turned to his transspace telecom and spoke a series of codes. A moment later, the High Empress Histrionica's face appeared on the display.

"Hello, Mother."

"Åååffgh! What a pleasant surprise!" said the High Empress. "How's everything going?"

Xrrpp studied the High Empress's face and the inflection of her voice, then flattened out his hand into a paper-thin, barely visible screen which he slipped in front of the telecom display. The effect on the viewer was no more than a brief flickering of the image — then, to all outward appearances, the High Empress's picture and voice continued as before. Meanwhile, Xrrpp made sure that, back on Alpha Centauri 5, the High Empress Histrionica would continue to perceive a similarly uninterrupted contact with her son.

"So," Åååffgh said. "My second-in-command, D.H.C. Kïḷḷëʀ, informs me that we received a message from you a short while ago, telling us we're invading the wrong planet."

"Yes." Xrrpp tried to make the High Empress's voice sound apologetic. "I'm afraid that's true."

"But Mother!" said Åååffgh. "This is a fine time to tell us! We've already attacked one of their major cities! Luckily, Kïḷḷëʀ here had the good sense to test the Big Bang Deluxe on an unpopulated area first."

Xrrpp beamed with pride on Kïḷḷëʀ's behalf.

"So, where exactly *are* we supposed to be invading?" said

Åååŕŕgh.

"Um ..." Xrrpp paused. He realized, to his acute embarrassment, that, between beaming with pride as Kïḷḷëʀ́ and convincing the real High Empress Histrionica that her son was indeed dressing warmly enough for space travel, he had totally blanked out on the name of every single star system in the galaxy.

"I'm sorry, I didn't quite catch that," said Åååŕŕgh. "We must have a bad connection." He gave the telecom unit a bash in hopes of restoring full audio.

"Uh ... Polaris," Xrrpp blurted out, and immediately wished he hadn't. He wondered what the Great Speaker would have to say about that. It was, after all, an election year.

"Polaris!" said Åååŕŕgh. "That's over 600 light years!"

"Sorry if it's a bit out of your way ..."

"It'll take forever!"

That was true, Xrrpp considered. Centaurian space travel was so slow compared to their own technology that the Polarian public might not even realize the Centaurians were coming until after the election. For now, that was all the time they needed to buy.

"So, anyway," Xrrpp said, by way of rounding off the conversation, "I hope you're wearing plenty of warm clothes."

"Yes, Mother."

Åååŕŕgh pressed a button, and the screen went blank. He stared gloomily at his desk for a few seconds, then looked up at Xrrpp.

"All, right, Kïḷḷëʀ́," he said. "I'll contact Navigation and redirect the fleet to Polaris. You arrange to get everyone back into space-sleep within two days."

"Yes, sir," said Xrrpp. He saluted, and left.

Outside in the corridor, Xrrpp paused for a moment of planning. Everything had gone smoothly so far. He'd return to Tactical, use Kïḷḷëʀ́'s voice and handprint to get back in, and meet up with Bzzpt. As soon as possible, without being observed, he'd slip back into his mechanic's appearance.

First, of course, he'd have to remember his way back to Tactical.

On the Main Bridge, Ðäy<u>ĸ</u>åŕт stared at his instrument panel in disbelief.

No. It couldn't be …

According to this, they were not only leaving Earth's orbit, they were powering up for a jump to stardrive in just under twelve minutes.

Must be an instrument malfunction.

He thumped the console a couple of times with the heel of his hand.

Still the same readings.

He walked to the window to satisfy his curiosity first-hand.

There was no mistake. The Earth, a familiar sight for the last couple of days, was receding into the distance, faster with each passing second.

"Commander," he said."

"Yes, Ðäy<u>ĸ</u>åŕт," said Kïḷḷëҡ. "What is it?"

"We appear to be breaking out of orbit, sir."

"Out of *orbit*?" Kïḷḷëҡ rushed to the window to join Ðäy<u>ĸ</u>åŕт. "Are you sure?"

"Take a look, sir."

Kïḷḷëҡ took a look.

"My God." He cupped his hands and pressed his face against the window, scanning out into the void. "What about the rest of the fleet?"

"Bit hard to tell with the naked eye, sir."

"Yes." Kïḷḷëҡ assigned three communications officers to the task. Within moments, it was clear that not only was the entire fleet now heading for Polaris, but they were doing so under the direct orders of Supreme High Commander Åååŕŕgh.

Kïḷḷëҡ tapped his communicator.

"Commander Åååŕŕgh," he said.

"Åååŕŕgh here," came a voice.

Kïḷḷëҡ paused.

"Sir, did you give the order to redirect the invasion fleet to Polaris?"

"Yes, Kïḷḷëʀ. I did." Åååŕŕgh's voice had the patient tone of someone who didn't really need to be reminded about every little detail.

"Ah. Yes, sir. Sorry to trouble you, sir."

"That's all right. Åååŕŕgh out."

Kïḷḷëʀ pulled Ðäyḵåŕт aside.

"Ðäyḵåŕт," he said in an undertone. "We've got to act now. Get over to Tactical and see if we can still hit Old Five-Fingers with some long-range stuff."

"Do you think that's appropriate, sir?"

"Never mind about that, Ðäyḵåŕт! It's now or never! We'll be in stardrive in a few minutes! I'll go and see Commander Åååŕŕgh in person, and figure out what the hell's going on."

"Yes, sir."

As Ðäyḵåŕт walked across to Tactical, he realized something didn't make sense. This invasion had been built up politically for over a century, and then, as soon as they arrived, they decided to leave without any advance notice or explanation. Even for a military operation, it seemed a trifle under-rehearsed.

He arrived at Tactical, and stopped at the sight of Kïḷḷëʀ standing by the Death Ray.

"Sir?" This made even less sense than the rest. "How did you get here?"

"I've been here all along." He turned to G̊ʀünт. "Haven't I, G̊ʀünт?"

G̊ʀünт nodded. "Yes, sir."

Ðäyḵåŕт looked at G̊ʀünт. He tapped his communicator.

"Commander Kïḷḷëʀ."

"Yes, Ðäyḵåŕт?" came Kïḷḷëʀ's voice.

"Commander, could you please report to Tactical? We have a development here I think you might be interested to clear up."

11

On the autocar ride back to the city, Wilfred glanced down out of the window at the ground. It rushed past fifty feet below him, which is rather what you expect when you are hurtling along in an autocar fifty feet above it, through a transparent tube.

He turned back to Blake and Selena.

"So, what are we going to do about the S-111?" he said.

"We'll just leave it where it is," said Blake. "It'll be perfectly safe."

"We can always find it again with the remote locator," said Selena. "You did bring that, didn't you?"

"Well, yes, but ..." Wilfred paused. "I mean, there might be people out there who are still a bit ticked off about the fact that we happened to steal the S-111 from Military Headquarters."

"We didn't really steal it," said Blake. "We've brought it back, and we've got it safe."

"Are we giving it back, then?" said Wilfred.

"Well, no," Blake said. "But the point is, we could."

The autocar was now traveling at ground level along the city streets. Up ahead, Wilfred could see the transit station they'd set out from at dawn the previous morning. The iris aperture opened in the wall, and the autocar sped through it and came to a stop inside.

Wilfred peered cautiously from the window. The last time he'd seen this station it had been virtually deserted, but now it was bustling with people, all apparently going about their normal business.

"See?" said Blake. "No problem at all." He opened the door of the autocar. "We just act casual, and ..."

Whatever Blake intended to say was lost at that moment. The crowd, which had given a convincing impression of being a group of perfectly innocent bystanders, now sprang to life and descended on Wilfred with the kind of boisterous premeditation normally reserved for surprise birthday parties. Microphones thrust their way towards him, as an army of reporters jockeyed for position.

"Mr. Smith, what's it like to fly the S-111 aircraft?"

"... is it true the military had concerns about ...?"

"... that you were not the military's first choice for ...?"

"... get your training for this mission ...?"

"... experience with extraterrestrial invasions ...?"

As Wilfred gaped, wondering where to turn, slim but strong fingers tightened around his upper arm, and he found himself pulled a half step towards a young woman with the most perfectly arranged hair he had ever seen.

"This is Jennifer Jordan," the woman said above the noise of the crowd, "reporting live from the Zirconia Square transit station, where Wilfred Smith just arrived by autocar ... and, Wilfred, I want to begin with the question that is uppermost in the minds of Zirconians everywhere: When are you going to start on your propagation assignment?"

A hush fell over the crowd. People pressed forward expectantly.

"Er ... well, I haven't had much time," said Wilfred.

"Yes," said Jennifer, nodding. Sincerity Look Number 17 suffused her angelic features. "I realize an assignment of this nature takes time to develop, but you can appreciate the interest it's generating ... can you give us any indication of when you might start?"

"Well, er ... as I say ..."

"Mr. Smith—" another reporter intervened. Jennifer elbowed her rival neatly out of the way, and reaffirmed her grip on

Wilfred's arm.

"Now, about the top secret mission you flew to Los Angeles," she said. "How did you come to be chosen as pilot for the S-111 aircraft?"

"Well, I'd ... prefer not to discuss that," said Wilfred uncomfortably.

"Yes, I understand," Jennifer said. "Military secrets, and all that. Now, you're a Handyman, is that right?"

"Yes," said Wilfred. "That is, I—"

"So, you repaired the EDSEL defense computer single-handed; you most likely saved the Earth from an alien invasion ... what's next? Political office?"

"Um ... well, I haven't really thought about—"

"No, of course not," said Jennifer. "Well, I appreciate your taking the time today. This is Jennifer Jordan, with Wilfred Smith ..."

Wilfred looked at the crowd, and turned to Blake and Selena.

"How are we going to get out of here?" he said.

"Don't worry," said Blake. "I'll handle it." He surged forward a few millimeters into the dense crowd. "Excuse me," he said in a loud voice. "There's been an accident, and I'm a doctor."

"A doctor?" echoed a few people.

"Yes," said Blake firmly. "I'm a doctor, and these are my assistants. There's been an accident, and we need to get through."

"What kind of accident?" said another person, managing somehow to press in front of them.

"Who was the victim?" demanded another.

The crowd hemmed more closely around them.

"Is there a lot of blood?"

"Where's the accident?"

"Where?"

Jennifer Jordan shook her head with a wry smile.

"You'll never get through that way," she said. "I could get

you out, if you want." She tightened her grip on Wilfred's arm and smiled sweetly, bringing her lips closer to his ear. "Of course, that's providing you guarantee me an *exclusive* interview just as *soon* as you're ready to begin your propagation assignment."

"Um ... well, OK," said Wilfred. "That would be delightful." He stole a glance back at Selena. "Um, I mean, a reasonable exchange."

"All right, then." Jennifer's eyes took in Wilfred, Selena and Blake with a single sweep. "Stay close, and I'll show you how to do it." She cleared her throat, and addressed the crowd. "Excuse me. There's been an accident, and we're the media."

"Ah ... the media." A respectful murmur rippled through the crowd.

"Yes," she said. "We need to take pictures of the accident. Coming through, thank you." The crowd wavered, and Jennifer pressed her advantage. "Stand back, please. If you want to see this on TV, you'll have to make room. Coming through with equipment. Thank you."

The crowd parted with the compliance of water molecules in the Red Sea, and Jennifer and her crew bustled Wilfred, Blake and Selena out of the transit station and through a covered walkway into a plant-filled atrium courtyard of an adjoining building.

"Thanks," said Wilfred to Jennifer. "You were really great." He turned to follow Blake and Selena.

"Now, don't forget." Jennifer grasped hold of Wilfred's wrist. "You owe me an exclusive. *Soon.*" She handed him a card, and smiled. "Here's my number."

"Thanks," said Wilfred again. He looked around for Selena.

Jennifer pulled on Wilfred's wrist, bringing his face up close to hers.

"Remember," she said sweetly. "The *minute* you're ready to begin your assignment."

"I'll be in touch," said Wilfred, nodding. Jennifer released her grip on his wrist, and he edged away, leaving her telling the TV audience about her upcoming "Wilfred exclusive." Selena and Blake looked around briefly to decide the quickest route back to the Bureau of Alternate Reality, and the three of them set off along another covered walkway.

"Well, that wasn't so bad," said Wilfred.

"No, I can see it wasn't," said Selena. She wiped a smudge of lipstick from Wilfred's face.

"Well, no, I didn't mean *that* ..."

"I know you didn't." Selena grinned, and pushed the tip of her finger playfully against Wilfred's nose.

"I mean, the situation could have been worse ..."

As they emerged from the walkway, two men in military uniform stepped in front of their path.

"Wilfred Smith?" said one of them.

"Uh, well ..." said Wilfred.

The two men moved closer, towering imposingly over Wilfred on either side.

"We're here to take you to Military Headquarters."

Monica van Patten snapped off the sound on her TV with a pout, freezing the picture of Jennifer Jordan in mid-sentence with her mouth open. She tapped her scarlet fingernails irritably on the desk top, then called Sister Grace.

A holophone image of her Council ally appeared at her side.

"Did you see the news?" Monica asked.

"Yes," said Sister Grace. "Wilfred Smith's arrival. I was just watching it."

"I'm concerned about his sudden popularity," said Monica. "Especially at a time when our own Council credibility is at such a low ebb."

"He says he isn't thinking of running for office," said Sister Grace.

"That's what he *says*," Monica emphasized. She called up the brief sequence where Wilfred made that claim, and played it back for Sister Grace's benefit. "That may even be his intention — for now. But the seed has been planted. The damage has been done."

"So we need to take steps," said Sister Grace.

"Exactly," said Monica. It was a pleasure dealing with someone who understood the finer points of political expediency.

"What about the others with him?" said Sister Grace. "Who's the redhead?"

"Selena McGuire." Monica froze the frame on the TV, and magnified for a closer shot of Selena. "She works for the Department of Forestry."

"Doing *what*, for God's sake? I didn't know we still had any trees left."

"She's an environmentalist," Monica said. "Her job is to preserve the last remaining stands of timber."

"Well, well. That sounds like a department we could trim some time soon." Sister Grace uncapped her electronic redliner and made a notation in her computer files for future reference. "Now, what about Blake Orion? Could the Bureau of Alternate Reality be involved in Smith's political ambitions?"

"They're the ones who are behind him," said Monica. "But they shouldn't concern us much longer. How's it shaping up for this afternoon's vote in Council?"

"It's looking good," said Sister Grace. She smiled grimly. "This one should sail through Council without a ripple."

"Keep calling in the votes," said Monica. "I'll put in a call to B.J. at the union, just to reassure her there'll be no layoffs at any of the major government agencies from our upcoming budget cut. And, while I have her on the line ... I think I may have a way to deal with Wilfred Smith."

Inside the Military Headquarters compound, the two men in uniform escorted Wilfred through a pair of sliding doors into a tiny, unfurnished room, which Wilfred realized was an elevator. One of the men pushed a button, and the elevator soared upwards. Wilfred soared with it, and his stomach followed an instant later.

The elevator had glass sides, as if to allow passengers to see out of it, but it was entirely enclosed within a pitch-dark elevator shaft so that you couldn't actually see a thing, all of which made sense to Wilfred in terms of his perception of how military budgets were allocated. After about 30 seconds, the elevator emerged into sunlight and came to a stop on the outside wall of the building. Wilfred's stomach, which had just got used to the idea of upward momentum, spent a brief moment exploring his upper rib cage and then resumed its normal position.

From the angled slope of the wall, and from the wall's narrowness at this height, Wilfred gathered that the building was shaped like a pyramid, and that they were near the top of it. Scanning the rest of the view briefly, he recognized the domed roof of the transit station and other landmarks from his maiden voyage in the S-111, and realized this must be the pyramid-shaped building he had seen at that time.

His companions hustled him across a passage to a different, security-coded elevator which took them one last quick jump upwards, and opened out into a thickly-carpeted and lavishly-furnished penthouse office. The occupant of the office was a khaki-uniformed man of about 50 with a square jaw and a trim mustache, who introduced himself as General Heidtbrink. He dismissed the two guards, leaving himself alone with Wilfred.

Heidtbrink offered Wilfred a chair, which turned out to be a rather comfortable one, and walked over to the window. He stared out at the view.

"We in the military pride ourselves on our foresight," he said. "We need people like you who see the importance of reassuring the public of our commitment to planetary defense." He stood at the window a moment longer, hands clasped behind his back, then turned to Wilfred.

"I want to talk about your vision."

"Are you an optometrist?" said Wilfred.

Heidtbrink scratched his head for a moment, then smiled. "Excellent. I can see we selected the right person to pilot the S-111 mission."

"Selected?" said Wilfred.

"Yes — you don't think you could just walk into HQ and steal a top secret military aircraft, do you?"

"Well, er ..." said Wilfred.

"Of course not!" said Heidtbrink. "Imagine how public morale would plummet if there was even talk of such an idea."

"Yes, I see ..." said Wilfred.

"That's why we have to clear up any possible public misunderstanding," said Heidtbrink, "by establishing clearly that it was all part of a carefully orchestrated plan — that someone of your skill and background was hand-picked for this mission months in advance."

"But I only just arrived here two days ago," Wilfred said.

"Yes, yes, I know *that*," said Heidtbrink. "We have records of exactly when the S-111 left this compound. You don't need to stick to that cover story any longer."

"No — I mean I only just arrived here from the year 1999."

"Good God, was that the cover story?" Heidtbrink swept a hand through his thinning hair. "The public actually swallowed *that*? I'll have to have a word with our public relations department."

"Well, no, I mean ..." Wilfred gave up on explanations, and reached for his wallet. He pulled out his expired 1999 union card and handed it to Heidtbrink.

"Ah, yes." Heidtbrink examined the card admiringly. "Very realistic. They do good work down there once in a while. Oh, well — destroy the evidence!" He dropped the card through a slot into a plexiglass bin.

"But—" gurgled Wilfred. A streak of pale blue light caught the card like a moth in a bug-lamp, vaporizing it with a faint electronic buzz.

Heidtbrink reached into a drawer of his desk and brought out an envelope.

"Now, here you are," he said. He opened the envelope and took out another card, which gleamed silver and black. "With this, you now have full military benefits, paid up retroactively for six months through the computer." He held the card just out of Wilfred's reach. "That way, if anyone asks, you can say it was all part of the plan, that the military had everything under control for the repulsion of the Centaurian invasion." He placed the card in Wilfred's hand, and walked over to a refrigerator on the far side of the room.

"Repulsion?" said Wilfred.

"Of the Centaurians," said Heidtbrink. "They've left the planet. Oh, it's all right — I know about it too!" He came back from the refrigerator with a bottle of expensive-looking champagne and two chilled glasses. "News even filters up to me eventually!"

Heidtbrink opened the champagne bottle with a pop, and they toasted their triumph with flowing glasses. Heidtbrink's telecom beeped, and a junior officer's face appeared on the display.

"Ah, yes, Jenkins," said Heidtbrink. "Is the media link ready for our victory celebration interview?"

"Yes, sir, they're standing by. By the way, sir, we have an incoming message from EDSEL. Would you like to take it?"

"Not now, Jenkins."

"But it could be something important, sir."

"What could be more important than a crushing victory over the Centaurian invaders in our first ever interplanetary war?" said Heidtbrink. He sipped his champagne, which seemed to put him in a more expansive frame of mind. "Oh, all right, better put it through."

"EDSEL here," said the computer. "Hate to break up anything good, but we have an extraterrestrial invasion in progress."

"Another one?" Heidtbrink paused with the glass halfway to his lips. "Good God!"

"Well, it's the same one, actually," said EDSEL. "The

Centaurians were headed for Polaris, but now they're heading back to Earth again. They're demanding an immediate peace settlement."

"Oh, they are, are they?" Heidtbrink tasted his champagne again and refilled his glass, then topped up Wilfred's as well even though Wilfred had barely taken a sip out of it. "We'll show them a thing or two! Can we attack the Centaurian ships, now that your malfunction is repaired?"

"There's one snag," said EDSEL. "You may remember that the defense rockets have already been launched. And, in point of fact, destroyed."

"All of them?" said Heidtbrink, a little deflated.

"Most of the really good ones," said EDSEL.

Heidtbrink massaged his temples.

"Jenkins," he said after a moment.

"Sir?" The image of Jenkins reappeared on the display.

"This is a major crisis, Jenkins."

"Yes, sir."

"We need a negotiator, Jenkins, and we need ..."

Heidtbrink turned in his chair. He and Jenkins both looked at Wilfred. They both looked back at each other.

Heidtbrink nodded.

"Perfect, Jenkins," he said.

"What about the media, sir? They're expecting an interview."

"Tell them Wilfred Smith is indisposed — a new, top secret mission. I'll talk to them myself in a few minutes."

Wilfred thought about slipping quietly towards the elevator. He had actually got partway out of his chair, when Heidtbrink turned to him again, so he pretended to be only adjusting the cushions.

"Wilfred," Heidtbrink said, coming straight to the point. "We need you to be our peace envoy to the Centaurians. You will take the S-111, rendezvous with their fleet, and negotiate a favorable settlement."

Wilfred paused, feeling sure there ought to be a way out.

"Wait a minute," he said. "I thought the Centaurian fleet was out in space."

"That's right," said Heidtbrink. "They should be coming into orbit within the hour."

"Well, then." Wilfred played his trump card. "How am I going to rendezvous with them in an aircraft?"

"Ah," said Heidtbrink. "We are not talking about 'an aircraft.' We are talking about the S-111. Simply give EDSEL your destination, and the S-111 converts automatically for space flight."

Wilfred groaned. He remembered the "Space Launch" button on the control panel. It was typical of them to do something right, just when you didn't want it.

"Yes," said Heidtbrink cheerfully. "We spared no expense on the S-111!" He drained his glass. "After all, it's supposed to defend against alien invasions, so it needs to travel into space — and besides, we had the money to burn! Ha ha!" He filled his glass a little over-generously, and sipped at the bubbles as they flowed over the edge. "So, off you go, Wilfred. You're our best hope. Give 'em hell, and don't yield an inch!"

"But what should I do when I get there?" said Wilfred.

Heidtbrink leaned forward unsteadily, glass in hand.

"Don't tell anyone I said this," he whispered, "but I don't have the faintest idea. That's why I'm in top management instead of out there doing it like you."

Wilfred nodded, and walked slowly towards the elevator. He didn't have a clue what to do next, except to get back to Selena and Blake. Selena would probably come up with an idea. Blake would probably come up with an idea, too, but it wouldn't necessarily be anything advisable.

"All right, Jenkins," said Heidtbrink, once Wilfred had left on the elevator. "Relay our plan to EDSEL, and get rid of the media as best you can."

"But you promised to speak to them, sir."

"Oh, all right, then," said Heidtbrink. "Tell them to hold

on. And Jenkins, get hold of our public relations department. Smith's cover story about time-traveling from the year 1999 was a disaster. How did that ever get out?"

"I don't know that it ever did get out, sir. I never heard about it."

"Hmm. Nor did I. Well, that's the public relations department for you. All right, don't say anything about it, then. Just give out a new story. Something good. Orphaned at the age of three, grew up in foster homes, broke through the ranks of disadvantage and poverty to become one of our top military tacticians …"

"Don't you think that's laying it on a bit thick, sir?"

"Not at all, Jenkins. They'll love it. Trust me on this one."

"Yes, sir."

For a brief moment of silence, Heidtbrink and Jenkins watched on their security monitors as Wilfred left the Military Headquarters compound.

"The man's a genius, Jenkins," said Heidtbrink. "An absolute genius. You wouldn't think it to look at him, would you?"

"No, sir."

"Do you know he flew the S-111 to Southern California, somehow managed to repair the EDSEL malfunction, led the Handymen to a decisive military rout of the Centaurians when they attacked Los Angeles, and single-handedly saved EDSEL a second time from a technical rocket target error, all in the course of a single day?"

"They don't make 'em like that any more, sir."

"No," said Heidtbrink. "And now he's our best hope for a favorable settlement with the Centaurians on their return to Earth." He refilled his glass unsteadily. "Peace terms, my ass! Those Centaurians'll be *begging* for peace by the time Wilfred Smith's through with them!"

12

Wilfred had asked several people how to get to the Bureau of Alternate Reality, but so far he'd met with no success. No one seemed to know where the Bureau was located, or really anything much about it at all.

After wandering the city for about an hour, he emerged from yet another walkway into a spacious and brightly lit hall. A marble staircase rose majestically at the far end of the hall up to a circular second-floor balcony. He recognized this place as the hall where Selena had taken him to meet Mother Ismeralda when he'd first arrived, though there were more people here today.

Selena's apartment, he remembered, opened off this hall. In fact, the only route he had ever taken to the Bureau of Alternate Reality was through the loose panel in the wall of Selena's bedroom.

He found Selena's apartment and pressed a small button beside the door. A recorded voice told him that Selena couldn't come to the door right now, but if he would care to leave a message, she would get back to him as soon as possible.

He was disappointed, but not entirely surprised. After all, Selena was probably down at the Bureau of Alternate Reality. He left his name and what he hoped was the current time and date, then looked around for someone else who might give him directions.

Two uniformed women were coming down the steps amid the general crowd. Their uniforms indicated they might be police officers, and their body types suggested they could provide the Russian Olympic women's wrestling team with some fairly stiff competition.

On reaching the bottom of the steps, they turned in Wilfred's direction. Wilfred headed to intercept them.

"Excuse me ..." he said. "I was wondering if—"

The two officers each took hold of one of Wilfred's arms in a decisive manner, and held him securely.

"Hey, wait a minute!" said Wilfred. "If this is about the S-111 ..."

A woman in a light blue Councilwoman's robe appeared in front of him, and Wilfred recognized her as Monica van Patten. She was accompanied by a middle-aged woman with thin, pallid features, beady eyes, and straight black hair. Monica introduced the woman as B.J. Craddock, president of the Amalgamated Handymen's and Public Employees' Union.

"You are being arraigned on charges of continued Handyman activity without a union card," Monica told Wilfred with her usual heart-stoppingly beautiful smile.

One of the officers told Wilfred he had the right to remain silent, which wasn't a right he particularly felt like exercising at the moment.

"What do you mean?" he spluttered. "I haven't even touched a TV since then!"

"I am not referring to TV repair." Monica paused, savoring the moment to its fullest. "You may recall, the last time we met, that I dismissed the incident on condition that you pay either all of your back union dues or a reinitiation fee."

"Well, yes," said Wilfred, "but I haven't really—"

"So far, our records show that you have paid neither."

"Well, no," said Wilfred, "but—"

"Yet you apparently saw fit to move beyond the realm of home appliance repair to the restoration of the entire EDSEL defense computer system! And don't try to deny it!" Monica produced a miniature TV the size of a calculator from a pocket of her robe and waved it in front of Wilfred's face. "I have over twenty news clips confirming your central role in the

EDSEL repair operation. I'm sure you don't need me to replay them for you."

She turned to the two police officers.

"Find his union card," she ordered. "I want to show the union president exactly how long ago this man's union membership expired."

The larger of the two officers held both of Wilfred's arms behind his back, while the other officer took Wilfred's wallet from his pocket and examined the contents. She looked up at Monica.

"Everything seems to be in order, Councilwoman," she said.

"What do you mean, 'in order'?" Monica demanded.

"He has a military Handyman card, fully paid up for the past six months." The officer held out the black and silver card Wilfred had received that morning from General Heidtbrink.

Monica leaned forward to look at the card. She drew in a breath, and her eyebrows maintained their position with a concerted effort. She turned to B.J. with a forced smile.

"I apologize," she said thinly. "It seems I've brought you out here over nothing."

"Not to worry, Monica," said the older woman. "I appreciate that you have always been a watchdog of union interests. Now, if you'll excuse me ..."

"Of course," said Monica. As B.J. left, Monica turned to Wilfred, holding back her anger with a commendable show of self-restraint.

"You weasel," she said in an undertone. "Why didn't you tell me you had a military card?" With a petulant flick of her scarlet-nailed hand, she signaled for the police officer to release her grip on his arms.

"I didn't realize it was important," Wilfred said, easing the muscles of his upper arms with his hands.

"Don't play the innocent with me!" Monica snapped. "Or maybe you enjoy making me look a fool in front of the union president?"

Wilfred hoped that was a rhetorical question. He kept his mouth shut.

Monica's eyes narrowed. "This is just like something your friends at the Bureau of Alternate Reality would pull." She took hold of his shirt collar, scratching his neck accidentally with one of her fingernails, and pulled him firmly towards her. "When the Council reconvenes after lunch today — then we'll see about your Bureau of Alternate Reality!"

She released his collar and strode off, her shoes clacking on the black and white marble floor. Wilfred rubbed his scratched neck with his thumb, and watched as she disappeared among the passers-by.

He turned to the two police officers.

"Um … talking of the Bureau of Alternate Reality," he said, "I was wondering if maybe you could show me the way?"

A short while later, Wilfred arrived at Blake's office. He pushed open the now-familiar glass-paneled wooden door bearing the words *Spade and Archer*, and stepped inside.

"Wilfred!" Selena cried, rushing towards him. "You're all right!" She hugged him, then held him at arm's length to look at him. "We were worried about you. What happened at Military Headquarters?"

"Yes," said Blake. He got up from his seat at the bank of computers and shook Wilfred's hand warmly. "Good to see you. What did they say about the S-111?"

"Well, actually, they didn't seem to mind all that much," said Wilfred.

"Not *mind?*" Blake paused. "Well, then. I wonder what else they've got …?"

"It's not like that," said Wilfred. He explained briefly about having to go on the Centaurian peace mission. "The problem is … I mean, I couldn't exactly say this at the time, but I don't really have a clue what I'm supposed to do, or how I'm supposed to do it."

Selena grinned.

"Don't worry," she said. "I'll come with you."

"You will?"

"Of course." She poked him in the ribs. "No, I was just kidding. Why would I want the chance to go up in space and see the Earth suspended in a diamond-studded sky ... not to mention enduring the company of someone like you?"

Wilfred frowned for a moment.

"So you *are* coming?" he said.

Selena rolled her eyes.

"Of course I am!"

"But ... do you think they'll let you?" Wilfred said. "After all, it's a top secret mission."

"Well, then," said Selena, "you shouldn't have blabbed."

"No. I suppose not." Wilfred had to admit she had a point.

"Besides," she said, "I was with you on the last one, wasn't I? Why should they care, so long as we deliver the peace treaty? If it works out, they never need to know." She grinned. "And if it doesn't, you'll have me for a scapegoat."

"I don't want you to be a scapegoat," said Wilfred.

"That's sweet of you." She took his arm. "Come on. Let's go."

"What about you, Blake?" Wilfred said, glancing back over his shoulder. "Are you coming?"

"I can't," said Blake, going back to his computers and sitting down. "I've got too much to do. The Bureau's in a bit of a crisis at the moment." He looked as despondent as Bogie in the scene in *Casablanca* where he finds out Ingrid Bergman is already married to Victor. "Professor McInerny's on her way back here. She says the Council is moving to cut all of our funding."

"Should I stay?" said Selena. "I could, if you want."

"Preventing an alien invasion's a pretty high priority, too," said Blake. "You'd better go along."

"I'm sorry about the budget cut," Wilfred said. He went over to Blake, wondering what he could really do at this point to help. "This is all my fault. Monica's been on my case ever since I got here. I feel like I'm bringing you down with me."

"No, it's the other way around," Blake said. "Monica's only after you as a way to get to us."

"But why is she so against you?"

"Her own political power, accountability in government … all kinds of reasons," said Blake. "Sometimes I think the only reason she got romantically involved with me in the first place was to figure out a way to undermine the Bureau."

He looked up sadly.

"I just wish I could find a way to stop loving her."

"You will," Selena said. "Trust me."

She took Wilfred's arm once more, and they left to find the S-111.

The longer Blake stared at the Bureau's budget figures, the less far into the future he seemed to be able to stretch them. Their budget was so small already compared to most government agencies, and they used the money so appropriately, that in moments like these they had very little to fall back on. If the Council approved today's funding cut, the Bureau wouldn't even survive long enough to appeal it.

Professor McInerny swept into the office and sank into a chair next to Blake's desk. She looked exhausted, more drained than Blake had ever seen her.

"We're dead if we can't find a way around this," she said. "They're continuing the budget debate in Council right after lunch — if you can call it a debate. More like a juggernaut, with Monica at the helm."

"What chance have we got?" said Blake.

"Let's put it this way: how soon till you can get your alternate reality transfer technology up and running?" Professor McInerny said, managing a grin. "Maybe you could find a reality where the Council doesn't abolish us."

"Not soon enough, I'm afraid," said Blake. He tapped the base of the Maltese Falcon absently with a pencil. "I'm still at least two breakthroughs away. Besides, we have to take extra care messing with alternate realities while the Centaurian invasion's going on."

"I know." Professor McInerny rubbed her eyes, and ran both hands through her short, dark hair. "You're right. We've got to find a way to challenge Monica on her own ground."

Blake leaned back in his chair and steepled his fingers, devoting his full attention to the problem. "What are her arguments for abolishing the Bureau?" he said.

"Politics, mainly. It'll make her look good if she can introduce a bill to downsize government."

"Downsizing government is one thing. How can she justify cutting an entire agency?"

"Well, there aren't that many of us working here."

"It won't save much tax money, then, will it?" said Blake.

"No." Professor McInerny's neat eyebrows pulled together into a frown. "But it'll go through virtually unchallenged."

"So what do we need to do? Hire more people?"

"We can't, Blake. That would put us over budget."

"Well, now, wait a minute," said Blake. He leaned forward, resting his arms on his mahogany desk. "What *about* that?"

"Maybe a couple more," said Professor McInerny, "if that would make the difference of getting your research finished. But it seems a bit late for any hiring. We can't exactly guarantee long-term employment."

"I'm not talking about a couple more," said Blake. "I'm talking about hundreds — thousands!"

Professor McInerny stared at Blake as if he'd gone insane.

"We can't do that!" she said. "We'd be millions in debt right away!"

"Join the club," said Blake. "Everyone else in government does it. You notice they aren't cutting funds from any other agencies."

Professor McInerny looked at Blake, and she started laughing, her suddenly jovial mood contrasting with her tailored indigo suit and starched eggshell blouse.

"Who were you thinking of hiring?" she said.

"Oh, anybody," said Blake. He considered for a moment. "What about the Handymen?"

"You mean, in L.A.?"

"Might as well." Blake reached for his phone, and paused. "So — what do you say? You're the boss."

Professor McInerny looked over at Blake, and started laughing again.

"Go for it," she said.

Blake placed the call. An image of Ace appeared on the display.

"Ace. Blake Orion here, from the Bureau of Alternate Reality."

"Oh ... Yeah." Recognition dawned across Ace's gaunt features. "The guy with them Extra Ter Restrials. What can I do for you, buddy?"

"Well, it's more a question of what I can do for you," said Blake. "I've got a deal I think you're going to like."

"Sounds good so far," said Ace. "Hold on a sec." He beckoned outside the range of the hologram display, and a moment later Leroy appeared next to him, his left arm heavily bandaged. "Leroy here would like to hear about this too, ain't that right, Leroy?"

"Bet your ass, buddy," said Leroy with a grin.

"What happened to your arm?" said Blake.

"Oh, just a couple o' stray bullets," said Leroy. He shrugged. "Hey, it happens."

"So what's this deal of yours?" said Ace.

"It's like this," said Blake. "How would you guys — I mean, *all* of you — like to pick up an extra three or four grand a month?"

Ace and Leroy looked at each other and nodded slightly. The prospect apparently had its favorable points. They looked back at Blake.

"What would we have to do?" said Ace.

"Same thing you've been doing all along," said Blake. "Just keep on doing it, except now you'll be employed by the federal government."

"That's it? We just keep on doing what we're doing, and we pick up our paychecks?"

"That's it," said Blake. "There's some paperwork involved, but basically that's all there is to it. You'll officially get paid by the Bureau of Alternate Reality."

"Hey, so this is the public sector!" said Ace. "I like it!"

"And, of course, in addition to your salaries, as government employees you'll also receive all kinds of great retirement benefits, medical insurance, and so on."

"Sounds good," said Ace. He turned to Leroy, and pointed to his bandaged arm. "See — you would have been covered."

"So, what do you say?" said Blake. "You boys need a couple of minutes to think about it, or what?"

"I say ship us the paperwork, old buddy," said Ace. "We'll get it back to you a.s.a.p.!"

"It's on its way." Blake disconnected the call, and grinned.

"All right," said Professor McInerny. "You start taking care of that, then." She waved a hand in the direction of the computer bank. Blake got up, and she moved into his chair and reached for his phone. "I'll call B.J. at the union, and tell her the great news about today's recruitment."

B.J. answered smilingly on her portable holophone, evidently from some restaurant setting. Glasses clinked in the background, along with the murmur of conversation and a distant piano.

"Hello, B.J. ... Elaine McInerny, with the Bureau of Alternate Reality. Sorry to interrupt your lunch, but I wondered if we could meet for a few minutes this afternoon to discuss some new union memberships?"

B.J. dabbed her mouth with her napkin, and shook her head doubtfully.

"I can't make it this afternoon," she said, glancing down at her appointment calendar. "I have a money-laundering symposium to go to."

"Tell her we're talking big membership numbers," Blake

called from the computer bank.

B.J.'s level of interest picked up appreciably. Her beady eyes gleamed.

"How big?" she said.

"Oh," said Professor McInerny vaguely, "somewhere in the region of ten to twelve. Thousand, that is."

"Ten to …?" B.J. paused. "I see. Well, maybe I could swing by and see you for just a few minutes."

"Why don't we meet at the Council budget hearing?" Professor McInerny suggested. "It's a more central location for you, and I'm scheduled to give my testimony when the Council reconvenes after lunch."

B.J. looked at her watch.

"I'll see you there in twenty minutes," she said.

"Looking forward to it, B.J."

Professor McInerny clicked off the call.

"All right," she said, hurrying over to Blake at the computers. "You finish up the paperwork on the hirings and load everything into the government database, while I head on back to the Council meeting." Her earlier tiredness had evaporated, and she seemed back to her usual brisk and energetic self. She stopped in the doorway, and turned. "Wish me luck."

"Knock 'em dead, kid," said Blake.

13

Monica looked around the faces amid the sea of pale blue robes in the Council chamber. As one of the main proponents of the budget cut, she was seated up on a panel facing the main assembly. She exchanged glances with Sister Grace beside her, confident of the votes needed to pass the budget proposal. All around the chamber, Council members were catching her eye with approval, nodding their support for her new legislation.

Her eye wandered up to the gallery, where she caught sight of B.J. Craddock, from the union. Good. This time, B.J. would see her at her best, spearheading legislation that acknowledged the public's demand for reducing government spending, while barely affecting union membership at all.

Professor Elaine McInerny was seated next to B.J. That sounded a worrying note, though it shouldn't make any difference to today's proceedings.

To take her mind off her anxiety, Monica smoothed the folds of her light blue Council robe beneath the table. It made her nervous to be in the national spotlight, even on a bill like this where she knew she had the votes in hand. She drew in a breath, and smiled her most confident smile for the cameras.

She signaled her readiness to Mother Ismeralda, seated to her left, wearing her darker blue as Chair of the Council. Mother Ismeralda recognized her with a nod, and Monica rose to address the assembly.

"Madam Chair, fellow Councilwomen," she said. "It is time to vote on the budget proposal. We have all heard the evidence presented earlier today, and we have had the lunch recess to consider the matter fully. I move for an immediate vote."

Several Council members, including Sister Grace, volunteered their prompt support in seconding the motion. Mother Ismeralda tapped her gavel gently.

"We have one more speaker who has asked to present her views to this Council," she said. "Professor Elaine McInerny, director of the Bureau of Alternate Reality." She extended a hand of welcome, and Professor McInerny descended the Council chamber aisle and crossed to the speakers' podium.

Monica smiled brightly to cover her annoyance. It was a waste of time to have this woman speak; all she could do would be to make a few trite comments about the importance of alternate reality research. Still, she might as well state her opinion, given that the vote was assured anyway. If Professor McInerny didn't get to speak, the validity of this legislation might carry a lingering doubt.

"My comments will be brief," Professor McInerny said. "I ask you only to consider, as you vote on this issue, the many honest employees whose livelihoods are at stake here today. Zirconia has witnessed a recent trend of worsening unemployment, and we at the Bureau of Alternate Reality have been doing what we can to remedy this unfortunate political situation. I would particularly call on Councilwoman van Patten—" Monica jumped at hearing her name spoken "—as the chief proponent of this budget cut, to justify how she can, in good conscience, lay off all these many thousands of people, and make our unemployment situation even worse."

"Thousands!" Monica cried. "Madam Chair, I must protest! Everyone knows the Bureau of Alternate Reality employs only—"

Mother Ismeralda rapped her gavel. Her eyebrows arched authoritatively.

"Please allow the speaker to continue, Councilwoman," she said. "You will have your chance for a rebuttal in due course."

Professor McInerny nodded her appreciation and resumed.

"Perhaps the Councilwoman is not aware that the termination of funding to the Bureau of Alternate Reality would result in the loss of no fewer than 11,872 jobs?"

Monica gasped. She could feel the heat of anger rising in her face. She turned to Mother Ismeralda to protest again, but this time it was Sister Grace who stopped her with a tug on her sleeve and a finger-point towards her computer terminal.

Monica stared in horror at the employment figures for the Bureau of Alternate Reality on Sister Grace's display. Hastily, she called up the information on her own terminal. The figures were the same. By now, the whispers were sweeping the chamber. Everyone was calling up the figures on their own terminals and greeting them with the same reaction — thankfulness for a narrow escape that they hadn't voted for this budget cut that would have put 11,872 potential voters out of work at a single stroke. All around the hall, Council members were catching Monica's eye with an apologetic I'd-love-to-support-you-but-my-hands-are-tied expression.

"But," Professor McInerny continued, "even if Councilwoman van Patten isn't concerned with the unemployment issue ... why, surely she's a friend at least to the Amalgamated Handymen's and Public Employees' Union?"

Monica blanched. In her panic about unemployment, she had forgotten this other, even more sensitive political issue. She glanced up into the gallery at B.J., who was regarding her stonily.

Professor McInerny paused. "That's all I have to say, Madam Chair. I yield the floor to the honorable Councilwoman van Patten."

Monica rose shakily to her feet. There was nothing for it now but to stumble out an apology for her lack of adequate research.

"In view of the unforeseen hardship this budget cut would cause, I recommend this proposal be taken back to committee for further review," she said. "I request the Chair's permission to withdraw the proposal from today's agenda." She sat down, fuming, feeling the eyes of the assembly boring into her.

Blake. This had Blake's stamp all over it. It had to be his doing.

She would take care of Blake later. She would also take care of Wilfred. But first — first of all — she would take care of Professor Elaine McInerny.

Xrrpp edged slightly away from Bzzpt to avoid standing in the direct line of fire of a molecular disrupter pointed towards them by a Centaurian guard.

"No — wait!" he said. Out of the window of their prison cell, over the guard's shoulder, he caught sight of Earth looming larger as the Centaurian ship reentered orbit. "I don't think you quite understand our position!"

"I understand perfectly," said Ðäy<u>k</u>åŕт. He stepped forward into the light from the darkened edges of the room. "You came aboard this ship posing as repairmen from Earth, while in reality you are Polarian spies. You used your shape-shifting abilities to redirect our fleet to Polaris, and you pretended to repair our Death Ray in order to gain access to our weapons room. You are now about to be executed. What is there not to understand?"

"Well, before you execute us," said Xrrpp, "you ought to take a look at how well your Death Ray is working."

"Working?" said Kïḷḷëк̆, from the shadows. For the first time in the interrogation, his voice showed interest. He, too, stepped forward into the light.

"Yes," said Xrrpp. "Well … almost."

"Of course, it'll have to be fine-tuned on a regular basis," said Bzzpt.

"Fine-tuned?" Kïḷḷëк̆ said suspiciously. "How?"

"Take us back there," said Bzzpt, "and we'll show you."

"Don't trust them, sir," said Ðäy<u>k</u>åŕт. "They're just trying to save their own skins."

"If you say so," said Xrrpp. "But, before you pull the trigger on us, I can tell you one thing about your Death Ray: you'll need a Phillips screwdriver."

"You know we don't have a Phillips screwdriver!" said ÐäyḴáŕᴛ. "Nobody in the galaxy does."

"Ah," said Xrrpp. "We do."

ÐäyḴáŕᴛ's eyes darted between Xrrpp and Bzzpt.

"Where's your tool box?" he demanded. "The one you brought on board?"

"Well ... it's missing," said Xrrpp. He blinked as the light moved closer to his face. "Someone must have taken it."

"We have all we need from them, then," said Kïl̰l̰ëᴋ́. He turned to ÐäyḴáŕᴛ. "Fire the disrupter!"

"No — you don't understand!" said Xrrpp. "The Phillips screwdrivers aren't in the tool box. They're right here!"

Xrrpp demonstrated, turning one of his fingers into a Phillips screwdriver. Bzzpt did the same, and the two of them held up their Phillips fingers like children in a candle ceremony.

Kïl̰l̰ëᴋ́ and ÐäyḴáŕᴛ stared, dumfounded.

"Can you do that any time you want?" asked Kïl̰l̰ëᴋ́.

"Of course." Xrrpp demonstrated with his other fingers, turning them into a variety of different-sized Phillips screwdriver heads, all spinning at different rates.

"All right," said ÐäyḴáŕᴛ. "So, why did you redirect the ships to Polaris?"

"Well ... that was just to fix the Death Ray," Xrrpp explained. "We needed to move it further away from the planet during repairs, in case it discharged accidentally and ruined the Earth for your future colonization."

"But why head for Polaris," ÐäyḴáŕᴛ persisted, "unless you were trying to steal our weapons technology and bring it to your home world?"

"You can't think we were seriously trying to reach Polaris on this ship?" said Xrrpp. "Without 4-D hyperdrive, it would take years!"

"Besides," Bzzpt said, "why would we direct an invasion fleet towards our own planet? Only an idiot would do that."

Thanks, Bzzpt, Xrrpp signaled on his internal communicator.

Aloud, he said: "We chose Polaris simply because any other destination might have provoked a diplomatic incident."

"But why the deception?" said Ðäy*ḵ*å*ŕ*т. "You could have just told us all this, and we could have moved out of orbit while you repaired the Death Ray."

"Would you really have broken orbit just because we asked you to?"

"Well, no," said Ðäy*ḵ*å*ŕ*т. "I see your point."

"All right," said Kï*ḷḷ*ër̈. "That's enough. Take them back to the tactical weapons room. If the Death Ray is operational, or—" he looked from Xrrpp to Bzzpt "—*almost* operational, they can stay on board. And I want that tool box found!"

14

Wilfred looked out of the cockpit window of the S-111 at the inky blackness of space looming up ahead. Millions of stars were spread out all around him: without Earth's atmosphere to diffuse their light, they stood out sharply against the void. The stark black-and-white of space made him feel suddenly and terribly alone. He reached for Selena's hand, thankful for the warmth of her touch, for the color in her face and her hair, as she gazed out with him into the universe.

"EDSEL here," came a familiar voice, breaking the stillness. "We've picked up the homing signal from the Centaurian flagship. We'll be docking in a few minutes."

"Thanks," said Wilfred.

Up ahead, he saw a patch of the sky where the stars were more regularly arrayed, almost like a silhouette against the more randomly strewn stars across the rest of the heavens. The patch seemed to grow in size as he came closer. He noticed a second patch off to one side, then another, then several more. He realized they *were* silhouettes — he was looking at the ships of the Centaurian fleet, black against the black sky, blotting out the stars and replacing them with their own regular pattern of lights.

The S-111 moved closer, and a huge, horizontal slit of low-intensity light appeared in the hull of the nearest Centaurian ship. The slit opened wider until it formed a cavern the size of a factory, a gaping fragment of light in the surrounding blackness.

The S-111 slipped quietly through the opening, dwarfed within the dimly lit and black-walled loading bay. It hovered for a moment, then landed on the loading bay floor.

A group of figures, protected from the vacuum of space by an iridescent force-field, stood watching the opening, evidently unaware that the S-111 had arrived. Wilfred and Selena stared in awe at their first glimpse of this alien race. Wilfred called up an image on the S-111 viewscreen and magnified for a closer shot: the four eyes — upper pair together, lower pair set further apart; the hairless, slightly bulbous head; the army-green tinge of the skin.

As the loading bay door closed, the Centaurians looked around in puzzlement, then stepped back, startled, as the S-111 door opened beside them. They ventured closer again as Wilfred and Selena climbed down the S-111 steps onto the ridged, non-skid metal floor of the loading bay.

One of the Centaurians, his black battle uniform ceremonially bedecked with an impressive display of colored ribbons and medals, stepped forward to meet them.

"Welcome aboard," he said. He glanced up at the door of the S-111, registering mild surprise as the narrowing crack winked out and vanished from view. He turned back to Wilfred and Selena. "I am Star Admiral Åååŕ́gh, Supreme High Commander of the Centauri Invasion Battle Force and Colonization Vanguard."

"Wilfred Smith," said Wilfred. "And my colleague, Selena McGuire."

"An honor." Åååŕ́gh reached forward stiffly, and shook hands in what was clearly a gesture learned for the occasion. The bony, three-fingered grip felt strangely unfamiliar against Wilfred's skin, bringing home at a more visceral level the truly alien nature of the encounter.

"My second-in-command, D.H.C. Kïļļëŕ, has been momentarily detained," Åååŕ́gh said, "or he would have been on hand to welcome you as well. In the meantime, I'm sure you'll enjoy a chance to rest and refresh yourselves before we begin the talks."

Åååffgh extended his hand forward, and they walked across the resounding metal floor of the loading bay towards the wide, arched doorway that opened before them. Åååffgh played the genial host, engaging Wilfred and Selena with anecdotes about Alpha Centauri 5 as he conducted them along the darkened and carpeted corridor.

He stopped in front of a doorway.

"These are your quarters," he said. "We've prepared some slight refreshments which I hope you'll find to your liking."

His fingers danced over a small control panel in the wall, and the door slid open. He extended his hand, inviting entry. Wilfred and Selena stepped inside.

After the subdued black and gray of the corridor, the interior of this room was surprisingly opulent and cheerful. Rich, chestnut-colored wood, finished to a high gloss, covered the four walls. The lighting seemed brighter than average by Centaurian standards, bringing it up almost to the level of a fairly intimate French restaurant. The restaurant motif was supported by the presence of a crescent-shaped banquet table, laden with delectable-looking appetizers and a selection of fine wines and elegant glassware. A generous circular window overlooked a view of the planet Earth.

"This looks fantastic," said Wilfred.

"Wonderful hospitality," Selena said. "Thank you."

"We'll come by to get you for the peace talks," said Åååffgh. He left, and the door closed behind him.

Selena reached out a tentative hand and picked up a triangular-cut appetizer from the tray.

"This stuff looks delicious," she said. "I wonder what it tastes like?"

"One way to find out," said Wilfred. His hand paused, hovering over the multitude of choices. "Did he say how long till the talks begin?"

"I don't think so," said Selena. She tipped her head towards the door. "See if you can catch him."

Wilfred went to the door and reached for the handle. His fingers met only a smooth panel of rich, dark wood. He tried around the edge of the door for some kind of catch or control panel that might open it, but found nothing. He leaned back against the door.

"I think it only opens from the other side," he said.

Xrrpp wiped his palms on his oil-stained mechanic's overalls and looked up at the imposing black wall of the Death Ray. If this worked, it would be the most impressive deception they'd pulled off so far. Regardless, they had few options left now that he and Bzzpt had been unmasked as shape-shifters.

"All right," said Ki̡l̡ër̃. He rubbed his hands together and looked around in a businesslike way. "Đay<u>k</u>åf̓т, I want you to search this room for that tool box. Search the entire ship if you have to."

"Yes, sir." Đay<u>k</u>åf̓т called a couple of Centaurian guards, and they began combing the room for the missing tool box.

"Now then." Ki̡l̡ër̃ tugged the sleeves of his black leather battle uniform a couple of inches up over his muscled forearms, and flexed his bony fingers as he approached the Death Ray controls. "Let's see what this beauty can do."

"Um …" Xrrpp hated to intervene while Ki̡l̡ër̃ was in a jovial mood, but he felt it necessary. "Careful with the Death Ray now that we're back in orbit. You don't want to make the Earth uncolonizable."

"Ah." Ki̡l̡ër̃ looked a little crestfallen, but he managed to restrain himself. His fingers twitched a little as he pulled them back. "Yes, of course." He turned to one of the guards. "Fetch the operations manual. At least we can make sure everything's in top working order."

Xrrpp gazed out across the room with Bzzpt at the unsuccessful progress of the tool box hunt.

How long before they realize they're not going to find the tool box? Bzzpt signaled on his internal communicator.

I don't know, Xrrpp responded. *I'm worried about Kppkt. I just hope he can pull off this deception. He still isn't feeling too well.*

Kïḷḷëʀ activated the electronic manual and began comparing the schematic diagram with the Death Ray's control panel.

Xrrpp and Bzzpt watched from a short distance.

"I think I'm going to sneeze," confided the Death Ray to Xrrpp in a small voice.

"For God's sake, Kppkt," whispered Xrrpp. "You don't even have a nose."

"Six forty-nine frequency," said Bzzpt from the corner of his mouth. *Hopefully, he can take a hint,* he signaled to Xrrpp.

"Hey, you two!" Kïḷḷëʀ called, withdrawing his head from the control panel. "Stop whispering amongst yourselves, and take a look at this."

"What is it?" said Xrrpp, coming over.

"The circuit configuration in here isn't the same as in the manual," Kïḷḷëʀ said. "You'd better have a good explanation."

"Ah," said Bzzpt. "Well ... we made a few modifications to improve operating efficiency."

"I see," said Kïḷḷëʀ skeptically. "Well, take your Phillips screwdrivers, and get to work."

Xrrpp formed a screwdriver on his finger, and moved towards the control panel. The Death Ray shifted slightly under his hands.

Stop wriggling, Kppkt, Xrrpp signaled.

Well, it's not very comfortable being a Death Ray. You should try it.

Listen. Xrrpp realized he'd have to spell it out again for Kppkt's benefit. *The idea is to prevent them from finding out that we haven't repaired the real Death Ray underneath. Got it?*

"Commander Kïḷḷëʀ," came Åååffgh's voice. "Please report to the conference room."

"Yes, sir. I'll be right there." Kïḻḻëŕ turned to Xrrpp and Bzzpt. "All right, you two, keep working! You're under round-the-clock guard." He moved towards the door. "If we don't see results soon on the Death Ray, it'll be the disrupters for both of you!"

Kïḻḻëŕ arrived at the conference room where the peace talks were to be held, and found his commanding officer there alone, pacing up and down.

"Ah, Kïḻḻëŕ," Ååårgh said as he entered. "Sit down." The two of them pulled up chairs at the conference table, and Ååårgh leaned forward confidingly. "There has been a serious political development back home on Alpha Centauri 5. The Centaurian Congress is no longer backing the war effort."

Kïḻḻëŕ's head reeled. Well, that was just typical, wasn't it! Of all the useless, bureaucratic ...

"Why not?" he said.

"The war's becoming unpopular at home. The Polaris episode was a disaster, for one thing. They also feel we should have captured L.A."

Kïḻḻëŕ kept his mouth shut. He had to agree on that one. A Megadeath Surprise would have brought them to their knees; but no.

"The real clincher, though, is the Death Ray fiasco," said Ååårgh. "Not only is the Death Ray unusable, but now there are allegations of high-level government kickbacks as well. The Defense Minister resigned this morning." He threw up his hands. "The invasion's become a laughing-stock. They're calling it 'Earthgate.'"

"Well, I've got good news on the Death Ray, sir," said Kïḻḻëŕ. "We're almost operational."

"We can't use the Death Ray for reasons I've enumerated several times," said Ååårgh patiently. "It would make the planet uninhabitable for our own colonization, and kill off the only race in the galaxy with a track record of maintaining a Centaurian environment."

Kïḷḷëḱ thought for a moment.

"Well, but aside from that ..."

"And we especially can't use it now that Congress doesn't wish to pursue a war."

Kïḷḷëḱ rubbed his temples, trying to fathom the finer points of the campaign.

"So, does this mean we have to accept *peace*?" he said with a grimace. "What's the point in having peace talks at all?"

"Ah," said Åååfŕgh. The familiar subtle smile returned, and Kïḷḷëḱ realized the Supreme High Commander still had a trick up his sleeve. "The peace talks are now more crucial than ever."

"In what way, sir?"

"According to our intelligence sources, their EDSEL defense system has used up all of its major rockets in a little fiasco of its own. That means the firepower of our invasion fleet — with or without the Death Ray — far surpasses anything they have left on the surface. So long as we play our cards right, these peace negotiations are a mere formality. Earth has no choice now but to surrender, giving us our military victory and a successful invasion."

Kïḷḷëḱ scratched his head.

"And will that mean Congress will reapprove the war?"

"No, Kïḷḷëḱ. By then we will have won."

"Oh." Kïḷḷëḱ frowned. "Yes. I see."

Wilfred looked out of the window with Selena at the Earth below them, suspended like a Christmas ornament in the cold and glittering beauty of space.

"It's breathtaking, isn't it?" he said.

"It should be a lot more breathtaking," said Selena. "Look closer ... the color of the oceans, for instance. They should be a bright, sapphire blue."

Wilfred looked at the steely gray of the North Atlantic, broken here and there by leprous blotches of brown and black. Pollution had taken a heavy toll since 1999.

"And the air," Selena said. "The only way to tell the cities is that the smog is a darker brown. The forests, too — see those swaths of green?"

Wilfred peered down at the Earth below.

"No," he said.

"That's because there aren't any. This is the environment the Centaurians want. If this is to be put right, the invasion must be stopped with an effective peace treaty now. Nothing good can come of Centaurian colonization."

"I don't know," said Wilfred. "Their food's not too bad."

"Wilfred!" Selena turned to face him. "They've locked us in our room, they've invaded our planet, they're preparing to degrade our environment even worse than it already is, and all you can say is their food's not too bad!"

"Well, it's not … I mean, it's really quite—"

"Wilfred." Selena laid her hands on his shoulders, her pale eyes looking into his. "The Centaurians are about to invade the Earth, and you are our ambassador of peace. You are our last hope."

A panel of polished wood slid open in one of the walls, and Åååŕ́gh appeared on the threshold. Beyond him, Wilfred could see a room with a large conference table, evidently where the peace talks would take place.

"I hope the food was to your liking," Åååŕ́gh said, inviting Wilfred and Selena with his hands to accompany him through into the adjoining room.

"Delicious," said Wilfred. "We, uh … both enjoyed it very much." He avoided Selena's glare, but couldn't escape the nudge to his ribs as they passed together through the opening between the two rooms.

An imposing figure, even by Centaurian standards, was seated on the far side of the conference table. Like Åååŕ́gh, he had outfitted his black battle uniform with an impressive array of medals and ribbons. Åååŕ́gh introduced him as his second-in-command, Commander Kïḷḷër̈. Kïḷḷër̈ stood up, a good head taller than Åååŕ́gh; he bowed, smiled menacingly, and sat down. Åååŕ́gh went around the table and sat next to him, their decorated uniforms complementing each other richly, while Wilfred and Selena took chairs on the near side of the table.

"Well, if you're ready," Åååřřgh said, "let's begin the negotiations." He opened a folder and produced a document on stiff, high-quality paper that crackled impressively in Wilfred's fingers. The paper was warm, and had the slightly hot smell of having been freshly printed.

"Based on Earth's present military predicament," he went on, "I've taken the liberty of drawing up a peace proposal for your signature. If you care to look it over, you'll see everything's in order. It details the schedule for invading and taking over the various major land masses, the transfer of power to the Centaurian government, the dismantling of all of your major remaining weapons systems ..."

"Wait a minute," said Wilfred. He scanned quickly through the document. "I thought we were talking about peace?"

"I can assure you," Åååřřgh said, "as soon as the transfer of power is complete—"

"But you invited us here to negotiate a peace treaty."

"It was a euphemism," said Åååřřgh pointedly. "We meant surrender."

"Well, you should have said surrender," said Wilfred.

"We're saying it now," said Åååřřgh.

"Well ..." Wilfred looked at Selena, who nodded encouragingly. "We ... er ... need time. You can't expect people to surrender on such short notice."

"We have the superior firepower," Åååřřgh said. The green cast of his skin deepened like that of a truculent chameleon. "If you don't surrender *peacefully*," he emphasized the word for Wilfred's benefit, "we will have to destroy you."

"Well, then," said Wilfred. He didn't know what else to say, so he glanced down at the treaty, hoping Åååřřgh would fill the conversational void.

"You mean," said Åååřřgh, folding his bony, three-fingered hands together, "you would rather be destroyed by our superior firepower than accept our peaceful colonization?"

"Um ..." said Wilfred uncomfortably. This conversation wasn't going exactly the way he had hoped. He reached for Selena's hand under the table, and felt her squeeze of reassurance.

"Your attitude disappoints me," said Åååŕѓgh. "As your future colonizers, we naturally hoped to find a way to invade you as amicably as possible."

"Amicably," said Wilfred, nodding. "Definitely."

"Your reluctance to accept our proposal puts us in a very awkward position."

"Ah," said Wilfred, wondering what exactly that position was. He scanned the treaty again, searching for a clue.

"You realize that, if we don't invade you now — purely as a way of saving face for you, you understand — we'll come back at a later date and annihilate you even more thoroughly?"

"Sounds fair enough," said Wilfred. He was only paying half attention to Åååŕѓgh, because he had taken out a pen and was busy adding the phrases *will not* or *will never* or *will not even think about* in front of each provision of the treaty which had to do with invasion or colonization or dismantling of anything.

"Are you sure you wouldn't consider a partial colonization?" said Åååŕѓgh.

"I'm afraid the ambassador's mind is made up," Selena said.

"Some nice beachfront property somewhere," Åååŕѓgh suggested. "Chile, maybe?"

"Sorry," said Wilfred. He amended *continue and expand the glorious outreach of Centauri colonization* to read *go away*, and looked up at Åååŕѓgh. "Peace is what I came to negotiate, and peace is what I plan to deliver." He felt Selena pat his knee approvingly.

"Not only do we want peace," Selena said, "we also propose to clean up our planet's environment."

Åååŕѓgh's four eyes hooded over anxiously as he sought the right diplomatic approach. Beside him, Кïḷḷëҟ's lips twitched as he controlled his rage with difficulty.

"But the ecological condition of your planet is the whole reason for colonization!" Åååffgh said after a moment.

"It seems we're in agreement, then," said Selena. "I believe we may have saved you a lot of trouble and misunderstanding. You'd never be happy colonizing a world rich in oxygen and lush, green tropical forests."

"Here we are," said Wilfred. He scanned the treaty briefly, added a peace sign at the bottom for good measure, and slid it across the table to Åååffgh. "Now, if I could just get *your* signature on this slightly amended version, we won't need to trouble you any further …"

Kïḷḷëк̇ mumbled his excuses and hurried away from the meeting. He'd kept his mouth shut during the negotiations; now he had only a limited time to find a new strategy before the envoys from Earth returned to their ship in Loading Bay 2.

Thinking things through wasn't Kïḷḷëк̇'s strong suit, but he tried it now as he hastened along the corridor to his quarters. (1) If peace was declared, no invasion. Got it. So, the treaty mustn't go through. (2) The Centaurians couldn't resume the war because of Congress. Got it. So, Earth would have to be provoked. (3) But how?

He smiled.

He had the perfect plan.

A bomb. A bomb on their centerpiece of military technology: the S-111. It would destroy their treaty evidence, their top negotiator, and the one remaining threat from their military arsenal, all in a single stroke.

Heh, heh. Simple, but effective.

He reached his quarters, opened his private weapons cabinet, and ran his eyes over his own personal inventory. He sighed. So many favorites, so little time. He selected a magnetic limpet mine, tucked it under his arm, and hurried to Loading Bay 2 where the S-111 was docked.

He stopped, mouth open.

The loading bay was empty.

He looked at his watch. Surely the S-111 couldn't have left yet?

Of *course*. The damned thing was invisible! He'd have to locate it by feel.

Moving quickly, he groped his way through the dimly lit loading bay with his right arm, cradling the bomb in a gingerly manner in his left. Nothing. He criss-crossed his paths and retraced his steps, but he couldn't find the S-111 anywhere. It must be undetectable by feel, as well as by the other senses.

He stood in the center of the loading bay, and wiped his brow.

To his horror, the bomb leaped suddenly from his fingers. Terrified, he made a desperate grab for it, but the bomb seemed magnetically stuck against something ... something he couldn't see! In fact, he could no longer see the bomb. Even the ends of his fingers, clutching the bomb, hovered on the edge of invisibility.

The S-111!

He'd found it!

Delighted, he hurried out of the loading bay, darting down a side corridor just as he heard the peace talks party approaching.

15

In the subdued half-light of the loading bay, Åååŕŕgh extended his hand to Wilfred as a parting gesture.

"I'm sorry we couldn't come to an agreement for colonization," he said.

"Some other time, perhaps," said Wilfred kindly.

He unclipped his remote locator from his belt and opened the door of the S-111. A thin crescent of cabin appeared in mid-air, gradually widening to a full oval. A metal stepladder unfolded down to touch the loading bay floor.

"I'm sorry Kïḷḷëʁ can't be here, once again," Åååŕŕgh said to Selena. He glanced around, as if half expecting him to appear at any moment.

"Be sure to give him our regards," said Selena.

She turned and climbed the steps into the S-111. Wilfred started to follow, his peace treaty still clutched in his hand, when a Centaurian soldier staggered into the loading bay carrying an enormous trophy consisting of two silver spheres mounted on a polished black base.

"Wilfred Smith?" called the soldier.

Wilfred handed the peace treaty to Selena through the hatchway of the S-111, and climbed back down the steps.

"Yes?" he said.

"I'm glad I caught you." The soldier lumbered forward, breathless, and delivered the heavy trophy into Wilfred's arms. "Please accept this gift of peace, compliments of Deputy High Commander Kïḷḷëʁ," he recited in a rehearsed manner.

Wilfred shifted the weight of the trophy onto his hip and examined it more closely. The silver globes, he now saw, depicted planets, with their continents embossed in relief. One planet was recognizably Earth; the other was presumably Alpha Centauri 5. On a small silver plaque on the black base was engraved the single word "PEACE."

The Centaurian soldier reached out to shake hands with Wilfred, who managed to transfer even more of the trophy's weight onto his hip to return the gesture. To Wilfred's surprise, the bony, three-fingered hand felt suddenly softer in his grip, for an instant more like a human handshake. In the same moment, he thought he noticed a trace of blue around the soldier's cuff, like the sleeve of a mechanic's overalls.

He blinked, and the impression vanished. The Centaurian soldier stood back and raised his three-fingered hand in salute.

"A pleasant journey, sir, from all of us," he said.

"Thank you," said Wilfred. He turned and climbed the steps of the S-111, laboring under the weight of the trophy.

"What was *that* all about?" Selena said, unable to restrain a grin as Wilfred staggered through the hatchway with his burden.

"Peace gift," said Wilfred. He deposited it on the back seat of the plane.

"What are we going to do with it?" Selena said. Her eyes danced with amusement. "I don't know anybody who has a mantelpiece big enough."

"We can give it to General Heidtbrink," said Wilfred. He visualized the trophy showcased prominently in Heidtbrink's penthouse office. "I'm sure he'll appreciate it."

"This is what he'll really appreciate." Selena held up the peace treaty and looked around for a place to store it, finally tucking it into a slot on the wall of the cabin. She sat down beside the trophy, while Wilfred went forward to the cockpit.

Outside the window, the iridescent force-field had formed in the loading bay to protect Åååŕŕgh and the others from the vacuum of space. On the opposite wall, the massive exit gate began to slide open.

"EDSEL," said Wilfred, "take us home."

With the gentlest of hums, the S-111 lifted off the loading

bay floor, then shot like an arrow into the star-speckled darkness of space.

"Wilfred," Selena said a few seconds later.

"Yes?" He turned around. Selena was staring at the trophy on the seat beside her.

"This thing just moved."

"Moved?" said Wilfred. "Well, strap it down, or something."

"No, I don't mean like that," said Selena. "I mean—" She pointed. "Look! It's doing it again."

Wilfred and Selena gaped in amazement as the trophy changed its shape, transforming into a tall, lank-haired man in oily mechanic's overalls.

"I am Bzzpt, of the Polaris Empire," the newcomer announced.

Wilfred continued to stare.

"So you're not a peace gift from Commander Kïḷḷëʀ, then?" he said after a moment.

"No," said Bzzpt. He brushed some dust from the sleeve of his overalls. "Now, stay calm. I don't want to alarm anyone, but there's a bomb on board."

"A bomb?!" said Wilfred. He had barely got over the astonishing transformation he had just witnessed.

"Where?!" said Selena. She and Wilfred went into panic search mode, which mainly involved bumping into each other and pointing and looking in obvious places like under the seat cushions. Bzzpt watched them for a few seconds.

"Let's do this properly," he said. "With a bomb, there are two important things: finding it, and deactivating it."

Wilfred nodded, trying to come to some semblance of non-panic. His heart tangoed wildly.

Bzzpt removed his cap, swept back his hair with his hand, and replaced his cap again.

"So, first we find it."

"Right," said Wilfred. He looked down at the seat cushions and fought off a strong urge to hunt beneath them all over again.

"Are you sure there's a bomb?" Selena said. "You seem very

calm about it."

"That's because I've handled situations like this before," said Bzzpt. "It's also because, if the bomb goes off, I'll be OK by shape-shifting into something else, while you, on the other hand, will be blown to atoms."

"So, how do we find this bomb?" said Wilfred, feeling a need to get back to the central issue.

"Methodically," said Bzzpt. "Like this." He transformed his hands into bomb-detecting instruments and began scanning the cabin. Wilfred and Selena followed him, offering vague words of encouragement.

"Found it," Bzzpt announced half a minute later. He tapped the cabin wall. "Right here. It's magnetically attached to the outer hull."

"So how are we going to deactivate it?" said Selena.

"I'll have to cut a hole in the hull and detach it."

"Cut a hole in the hull!" cried Wilfred. He looked out of the cockpit window into the inky void of space. Something in the back of his brain was telling him that cutting a hole in the hull didn't sound like too good an idea.

"Yes," Bzzpt was saying. "I'll cut a piece about the size of a manhole cover, detach the bomb from it, get rid of the bomb, and weld the piece of the hull back into place. Shouldn't be too hard." He scanned the immediate area with a series of instruments. "First, I have to make sure there are no vital cords or conduits running through this part of the hull." He checked his readings, then converted one hand into a blowtorch and the other into a high-powered rotary saw.

"But — wait a minute!" said Wilfred. "Won't cutting a hole in the hull depressurize the cabin?"

"Of course it will," said Bzzpt.

"But—"

"That's why I have to form an airtight seal around the area before I start cutting. Excuse me a minute."

Without further explanation, Bzzpt melted himself down into a large black bubble, sealing tightly over the area he was preparing to cut. Wilfred heard the rasp and whine of blowtorching and high-power rotary sawing from within the bubble; then a hand emerged through the top of the bubble with a liquid *bloop*, clutching a gunmetal-gray object the size of a cereal bowl.

"Here's our problem," came Bzzpt's muffled voice.

"Well, get rid of it!" shouted Selena.

"Oh, don't worry, it won't go off for another ..." an eye appeared at the top of the bubble "... whoops — misread the dial there!" The hand hastily retracted through the bubble with another liquid *bloop*. Seconds later, a violent explosion flared off the port side of the S-111.

From inside the black bubble came renewed blowtorching and welding sounds, punctuated occasionally by a fairly off-key whistling. A couple of minutes later, the bubble coalesced back into Bzzpt's more familiar mechanic's form.

"There." Bzzpt tapped the welded section of hull with a crescent-wrench finger-end. "That should hold it. Let's get on down to the planet's surface."

The S-111 hovered over the Military Headquarters compound — undetectable, presumably, even to its creators.

"I see a problem," said Selena. "Look down there." She pointed down at the ground. All around the Military Headquarters compound, crowds were milling and waving placards.

"Must be some kind of riot," Wilfred said. "How can we find out what's going on?"

"Call the media," Selena suggested. "They'll know."

"Of course!" Wilfred reached for his wallet. "I'll call Jennifer."

"Who's Jennifer?"

"Jennifer Jordan — remember? The one who helped us out of the transit station that last time." Wilfred took out the card she had given him.

"Oh. *That* Jennifer."

Wilfred gave the number on the card to EDSEL, and an image of Jennifer Jordan giving a TV news broadcast appeared on one of the S-111 control monitors. She was apparently on the air at this moment, and her phone picture had defaulted to the broadcast as a way of putting the caller temporarily on hold.

The image of Jennifer's face changed to a crowd scene. Wilfred realized that the scene was the same as the one he could see from the cockpit window. He started to pay closer attention to the newscast.

"... crowds are continuing to gather around the Zirconian Military Headquarters in anticipation of Wilfred Smith's arrival," Jennifer was saying. She broke off for a second. "... And I've just heard that Wilfred Smith himself has called in, and is standing by. Wilfred, are you there?"

"Um ... yes." Apparently, his call had now gone through on some kind of priority: he was no longer getting just the TV image.

"Where are you calling from?" Jennifer asked.

"Uh ... we're in the S-111 ..."

"The invisible aircraft," Jennifer put in for the viewers. Her lovely face glowed with excitement. This was clearly a major scoop.

"Jennifer, I ... um ... need to ask you a favor," said Wilfred.

"Of course." Jennifer signaled to her editor for a commercial break. She spoke her cutaway line, and her professional brightness relaxed to a more natural good humor. "So — Wilfred! What's up?"

"We have to land at Military Headquarters," said Wilfred. "I know you're an expert at getting through crowds."

"Well ... thank you." Jennifer smiled modestly. Her teeth looked every bit as perfect as her hair.

"So, here's the deal," said Wilfred. "I'll guarantee you an exclusive, if you can get us out once we've seen General Heidtbrink."

"Not a problem," said Jennifer. "I'll arrange for a helicopter." Her eyes glanced aside for a moment and she nodded, as if already picking up the OK on that. She turned back to Wilfred. "What time do you need me there?"

Wilfred shrugged at Selena, who shrugged back.

"I don't know," he told Jennifer.

"I'll get there in 20 minutes," Jennifer promised. "I'll wait for you." She looked off to the side, nodded, and signaled five fingers. "Gotta go," she said to Wilfred. "I'm on the air."

Her professional brightness snapped back into place, and she smiled her most angelic smile for the nation's viewers.

"All over Zirconia," she announced, "the rumors are flying: is Wilfred Smith's procreation assignment about to begin in earnest? In exclusive live coverage later today, Zirconia's hottest property talks about his procreation plans, the Centaurian invasion, and more. But first, our daily update on the latest celebrity murder trials ..."

Wilfred switched off the monitor and contacted EDSEL.

"Take us on into the hangar," he said. "And let General Heidtbrink know we're here."

"Will do," said EDSEL. "I'm sure he'll be expecting you."

The S-111 banked into a wide turn and dipped lower towards a row of hangar doors, each with a series of narrow horizontal windows near the top and large red numbers painted beneath. The door marked *04* slid open as the S-111 approached. The S-111 slipped through the opening, spun gently around to face the door again, and came to a cushioned landing inside the white-walled and brightly lit hangar.

Wilfred, Selena and Bzzpt peered out of the cockpit window. A man in military uniform was inspecting the hangar door closely, as if having it open like that was a somewhat unusual event. Now, as the door started to close again, the man gave it a final cursory glance, then walked unhurriedly to his desk and sat down at his computer.

"There's Jim Santee," said Wilfred. He waved and knocked on the cockpit window, though of course the gesture was useless inside the S-111.

"You *know* all these people?" Selena said.

"Well, I know Jim, from when I came here to steal the S-111 in the first place."

"So you chatted with the guy?" Selena's pointed features brightened with her pixie grin. "You're on a first-name basis with him? And he said, 'Oh, go ahead and help yourself to the S-111' — or what?"

"Well, he didn't exactly say *that*," said Wilfred. "So, are we ready?" He looked around. "Where's Bzzpt?"

"Right here." Wilfred jumped as Bzzpt materialized about six inches in front of him.

"How did you do that?" said Wilfred.

"Responsibility field generator," said Bzzpt. He clicked the device and vanished, then reappeared again a moment later. "I thought it might be advisable. Some cultures are rather touchy about aliens wandering around their military bases."

"Good idea," said Wilfred. It would be hard enough to explain Selena, but at least she was from the same solar system.

Bzzpt activated his responsibility field again, vanishing from view, and Wilfred reached to open the door of the S-111.

"Aren't you forgetting something?" said Selena.

"What?" said Wilfred.

"The peace treaty." Selena grinned and handed it to Wilfred, who folded it and tucked it into his pocket.

Jim Santee looked up from his desk with a smile of recognition as they opened the door of the S-111. He hurried over to meet them.

"Wilfred!" He grabbed Wilfred's hand and shook it vigorously. "Wilfred Smith!"

"Great to see you, Jim." Wilfred looked around as the S-111 door closed again, returning the hangar to its seemingly empty state. "Keeping you busy here, are they?"

"Oh, same as ever," said Jim. He introduced himself to Selena.

"So, what exactly do you do?" Selena asked. She, too, looked around the hangar.

"Chief mechanic for the S-111," Jim said with a degree of pride.

"But, I mean ... while the S-111 wasn't here?"

"Doesn't make that much difference, since I can't see it anyway," Jim said cheerfully. "But it's military policy to have a mechanic for the S-111 on duty at all times."

Wilfred unclipped the S-111 remote locator from his belt.

"Here," he said. "This should help you out." He showed Jim how to open and close the S-111 door.

"Where did you get that thing?" said Jim.

"Inside the plane," said Wilfred.

Jim nodded.

"Ah — a security precaution," he said. "I'm sure they'll issue me one if I need it. But thanks anyway."

Wilfred clipped the remote locator back onto his belt. "Well, we'd better get going. I have to report to General Heidtbrink." He moved towards the personnel security door that led out into the passage.

"Good to see you again," Jim said, walking them to the door. "Whoops — remember the red button there, on your way out!"

He pressed the red button for them, and they stepped safely through the security entrance past the rubberized restraining arms and out into the passage.

"Wilfred!" Heidtbrink stepped forward and shook his hand heartily as he stepped off the elevator with Selena into the general's penthouse office. "Delighted to see you!" He turned to Selena and paused, puzzled at her presence, his hand half outstretched. "Uh ..."

"Selena McGuire," Wilfred put in quickly. "She's an environmentalist with the Department of Forestry."

"I see," said Heidtbrink, clearly not seeing at all.

"Selena's role with the Centaurians is extremely important," Wilfred went on. "After all, the environment here on Earth is one of the chief reasons for the Centaurian invasion in the first place."

"General Heidtbrink," Selena said, smiling. She extended her hand, and Heidtbrink took it automatically. "I've heard about your innovative programs. I must compliment the military on its environmental policies."

"What environmental policies?" said Heidtbrink. He scratched a bushy eyebrow. "I didn't know we had all that many."

"Yes, but the ones you do have are extremely popular."

"I can't think of any at all!" said Heidtbrink. "We don't do a damned thing for the environment!"

"Yes, but I know the plans are in the works," Selena said gently. "It's great public relations. I want to congratulate you on the brilliance of this strategy for raising tax money in these difficult economic times."

"Oh, really?" Heidtbrink smoothed his mustache with his finger. "You think so? Tax money?"

"Absolutely," said Selena.

To Wilfred's horror, Bzzpt appeared spontaneously behind Heidtbrink's back. He was strolling around casually, and appeared not to have noticed his sudden materialization. Wilfred made a motion with his arm down low, trying to attract Bzzpt's attention.

"Are you all right?" Heidtbrink said.

"Oh ... fine, yes," said Wilfred. "Just a touch of bursitis in the elbow." He flexed the arm a few more times.

"So — the peace treaty," Heidtbrink said. "I assume you brought it?"

"Naturally," said Wilfred. He caught Selena's amused glance as he pulled the treaty from his pocket, and tried to signal with his eyes about Bzzpt. He showed the treaty to Heidtbrink as he unfolded it, crackling the stiff paper impressively.

"Excellent," said Heidtbrink. "I want the full details — everything that was said, the nuances, all the behind-the-scenes stuff. By the way," he moved closer and lowered his voice, "just to let you know, we're developing great military plans against the Centaurians."

"Military plans?" said Wilfred. "But—"

"We have weapons systems we can hardly wait to try out!" said Heidtbrink excitedly. "Oh, but first the peace treaty." He glanced down at the paper in Wilfred's hand, but the excitement of the moment was clearly too hard to control. "Let me just tell you about this one weapons system. We have this device which can—"

"But ... sir." Wilfred scratched his head, trying to find the right way to phrase this. To his relief, out of the corner of his eye he saw Bzzpt disappear. "We now have a peace treaty with the Centaurians."

"Yes, yes." Heidtbrink waved his hand dismissively. "I understand the public relations angle. I mean the *real* treaty!"

"This *is* the real treaty," said Wilfred. He handed the paper over for Heidtbrink's inspection.

Heidtbrink's eyes widened as he examined the treaty. He reached for the back of a chair for support, and looked up.

"You mean ... there's not going to *be* an invasion, after all?"

"We tried," said Selena.

"They insisted on surrendering," said Wilfred.

"I know," said Heidtbrink. "You did your best." He looked back at the treaty in his hand. "It could have been worse."

"Look on the bright side," Selena said. "The favorable publicity the military will get from this victory should bring more popular support and allow you to increase your weapons research against future alien invasions."

"Yes, I suppose you're right." Heidtbrink seemed cheered by the prospect. "Some good may come of this, after all."

"You might even consider developing some kind of environmental weaponry," Selena said. "Something that would reoxygenate the atmosphere, or remove carbon dioxide."

"We don't need more public relations at this stage," Heidtbrink said gloomily.

"I'm not talking about public relations," said Selena. "I'm talking about for use against the Centaurians."

"Against the Centaurians?" Heidtbrink brightened visibly.

"Why did they come here to colonize in the first place?" said Selena. "Because of the trees all over their planet. So, even a simple tree-planting project could make them think twice about another invasion ..."

"I see," said Heidtbrink. "A reforestation strategy — biological warfare!"

"We'd be within the terms of the treaty," Wilfred pointed out. "It doesn't say anything here about planting trees."

Heidtbrink looked down at the treaty in his hand. He looked back up at Wilfred.

"Nice work," he said. "If there's one thing I love, it's a good loophole."

In her Council office, Monica shut off her phone and glared. There was a limit to how long she could maintain a front of civility, and that limit had been exceeded. This had been the third call in a row from an angry defense contractor, demanding to know where their company stood in the light of the new peace treaty with the Centaurians.

She took out a bar of chocolate from her desk drawer and unwrapped the silver foil. She snapped off a corner of the dark, rich bar, and nibbled at it moodily.

Peace treaty.

The Centaurian invasion had been the first real hope of getting the national economy back on its feet, and now apparently peace had been declared without consulting anyone.

Certainly without consulting *her*.

What could those fools at Military Headquarters be thinking?

She transferred her phone to auto-answer, and broke off another piece of chocolate. She clicked on the news, only to be confronted with footage of crowds celebrating Wilfred's return.

Naturally. This peace treaty had to be Wilfred's doing. And, of course, it went without saying that the Bureau of Alternate Reality was behind it.

The newscast moved on to provide updates of the celebrity murder trials. Monica switched off the TV and drummed her fingernails on the desk top.

That diminutive Elaine McInerny woman had humiliated her at the Council meeting yesterday afternoon. Already, a day had been allowed to slip by.

And now this.

It was time to take action. The question was, how to do it?

She considered her options. Trumping up a charge the old-fashioned way simply didn't work any more. Oh, you could trump up the charge, all right. There were courts all over the country where you could secure a conviction, if you could afford the right lawyers. That wasn't the problem.

The problem came afterwards.

Criminals' rights had reached such a fever pitch that the mere accusation of a crime brought guaranteed media attention ... to say nothing of movie rights lucrative enough to keep the Bureau of Alternate Reality running long after Professor Elaine McInerny's early release from jail and luxurious retirement to San Tropez.

No. A charge of wrongdoing wouldn't serve her purpose. But there was one way she could use the criminal justice system, with all its failings, to her advantage — one way that she could sequester Professor McInerny absolutely and completely from any contact with the outside world.

Jury duty on a celebrity murder trial.

It was perfect. With Professor McInerny out of the way, Monica would call on the Bureau of Alternate Reality to become fiscally responsible. The rest was simple. She'd wait for her moment; she'd bring political pressure to bear when they couldn't meet their payroll; she'd hold them up to the public as an example of waste in government and fiscal irresponsibility ...

She smiled, and allowed herself one more morsel of chocolate.

Oh, yes. The voters would be clamoring for her budget cut proposal soon enough.

16

Wilfred and Selena reached a wide, semi-circular lobby that opened onto the main exit of the Military Headquarters compound. Corridors radiated back through the building in different directions, and people were coming and going through the lobby in a steady stream.

"Where's Bzzpt?" said Wilfred. "We don't even know if he's still here. How can he materialize with all these people around?"

"He'll find a way," said Selena. "Let's just wait here for a moment. If anyone can take care of himself, Bzzpt can."

"There he is!" cried Wilfred. A familiar, overall-clad figure emerged from the men's room and waved cheerfully as he came over to join them. He extended a grimy hand towards the exit.

"Shall we?" he said.

The three of them left the building and crossed the covered perimeter zone to the outer gate, which led out to the transit station where Wilfred had first arrived with Blake and Selena.

The perimeter guard met them at the gate, his list at the ready. Beyond the gate, they could hear the murmur of the waiting crowd.

"I assume we don't have to be on your list to go *out*?" Selena said to the guard.

"Not so long as you're with this gentleman, ma'am," said the guard. He winked at Wilfred.

"Um … with me?" Wilfred said.

The guard moved closer, conspiratorial.

"I know I'm not supposed to reveal your identity, sir."

"My identity?" said Wilfred. He had completely lost the thread of this conversation.

"Yes." The guard moved closer still, lowering his voice to a whisper. "You're Wilfred Smith." He stood back, looking very pleased with himself at being the possessor of this privileged piece of information. He winked again. "Don't worry, sir. Your secret's safe with me."

"Ah," said Wilfred. "That's good." He followed Selena and Bzzpt through the gate.

A roar went up from the crowd as Wilfred stepped into the sunlight streaming in through the clear dome of the transit station. People surged towards them, holding placards with his picture and chanting their appreciation with cries of "Wilfred! Wilfred!" A squad of reporters, who had somehow managed to squeeze through to the front of the crowd, formed a tight cluster around the three of them. Cameras pointed from seemingly all directions.

Amid the barrage of simultaneous questions, none of which he could hear, Wilfred looked around anxiously for Jennifer Jordan.

"Where's Jennifer?" he shouted to Selena. "She said she'd be here."

"She will," Selena shouted back. "I'm sure."

A whirring, shuddering noise above the roar of the crowd made Wilfred look up. The clear dome of the transit station roof opened into its star-shaped pattern, and a helicopter lowered itself through the opening, the noise echoing and reverberating louder as it came inside. It flew lower and closer until it hovered directly above them. The door of the helicopter opened and Jennifer leaned out, her perfectly arranged hair caught and blown in the downdraft from the helicopter blades.

"Wilfred!" she called. Her voice, barely audible above the helicopter noise, managed to carry down to him on the direction of the airflow. Selena's hair was whipping around her face. Bzzpt held on to his cap.

"Jennifer!" Wilfred called back. He realized his voice wouldn't carry upwards against the wind, so he waved. Jennifer waved back from the door of the helicopter.

"Climb up the ladder," she shouted. She reached back inside the helicopter, and threw down several feet of rope ladder which dangled above their heads, swaying in and out of reach.

Bzzpt extended an arm and caught the bottom rung, pulling the ladder taut and anchoring it with a vise-like grip. With his other arm, he helped Selena and Wilfred onto the ladder, then pulled himself up after them.

Wilfred's heart pounded as the helicopter lifted a few feet above the reach of the crowd, and the ladder started to sway and gyrate. To avoid looking down, he looked up, and was glad to see Jennifer already pulling Selena inside. He forced one foot above the other on each rung of the ladder, and a few moments later he felt Jennifer's strong fingers around his wrist, pulling him inside as well. Bzzpt followed, and Jennifer pulled up the rope ladder and instructed the pilot to take them back out through the dome of the transit station.

Wilfred looked around in amazement at all the people and equipment that could fit inside this one helicopter. Besides the pilot and the necessary flight controls, Jennifer had all the makings of an in-flight studio: camera operators, interview chairs, lights ... all in addition to the three guests she had just brought on board. The two camera operators were already doubling as make-up technicians, rearranging Jennifer's hair and retouching her make-up in preparation for the upcoming "Wilfred exclusive."

Wilfred looked down as the star-shaped opening in the dome closed back up below them, the five pie-sections coming together and interlocking seamlessly into place.

"How did you get the transit station roof open?" he called to Jennifer, still breathless from his dangling climb on the ladder.

"Sometimes you have to pull a few strings," she said, tilting her head a little to allow a touch of blush to be applied to her cheek. She smiled angelically. "I can't give away *all* my secrets, now, can I?"

"I guess not." Wilfred smiled. "Thanks for rescuing us."

"My pleasure." She tilted her head in a different direction without breaking the flow of the conversation. "Now, as far as the interview goes, the Centaurian peace treaty news is great, really great, but the first thing the public wants to hear about is the propagation assignment."

Wilfred nodded. Regrettably, he had made zero progress in that department.

"And see if we can work in the alien angle," Jennifer called to one of her crew.

"We should call Blake and tell him we're OK," Selena said at Wilfred's elbow. "I'll see if I can reach him on this." She indicated a small band around her wrist. "It's voice-only," she apologized.

"Fine by me," said Wilfred. He'd seen enough technology in the past few days to last him a lifetime.

Selena tapped the wristband.

"Blake. It's Selena."

"Selena! Good to hear you. You made it, then." Blake's voice sounded so much like Bogart's that Wilfred could almost picture the trenchcoat.

"Everything's fine," Selena said. "We'll be back at the Bureau in about an hour." She looked over to where Bzzpt was now chatting amicably with Jennifer. "We have someone else with us — Bzzpt, from the Polaris Empire."

"From the *what*?"

"I can't believe it, Blake!" cried Selena happily. "You mean, there's actually something *I* know that you don't about weird stuff?"

"I'm not 'weird stuff'!" Bzzpt protested. "Where I come from, I happen to be perfectly normal, thank you very much." He made a B-movie "alien" face — eyes on stalks, the whole routine — while one of the camera operators tested the lighting levels. "Well, kind of normal," he amended.

"What does he look like?" said Blake.

"Don't ask," said Selena.

"All right, I can wait. So, how did the peace treaty go?"

"Not too badly," said Wilfred. One of Jennifer's make-up crew moved over to him. She was a no-nonsense, country-Irish type who took hold of Wilfred's head in one hand and moved it left and right to see how it looked in the light. "We managed to get the Centaurians to agree not to invade."

"You don't sound too cheerful about it," said Blake.

"Well, I don't think it was what the military wanted."

"Don't worry. Someone will break the peace treaty before too long anyway."

"How do you know?" Wilfred realized he was starting to feel a little possessive about his peace treaty. He tipped his head sideways, flinching under the unfamiliar feel of the make-up brush. "Have you been looking into the future again?"

"No — the past," said Blake. "Historically, that's what's always happened."

"History isn't always doomed to repeat itself, you know," said Wilfred defensively. Jennifer caught his eye, signaling time to begin, and he nodded. The country Irishwoman mercifully took her place behind one of the cameras.

"History doesn't so much repeat itself," said Blake. "It just looks over its own shoulder and improvises."

17

Xrrpp looked out of the small round window of his prison-cell quarters aboard the Centaurian ship. They had moved around to the dark side of their orbit of the Earth, but the atmosphere around the rim of the planet still blazed with light from the sun behind, creating a lucent halo around the darkened world.

Xrrpp sat down on his bunk and formed a transspace telecom unit in his lap. His work-breaks from Death Ray repair duty were unpredictable. He'd better get on with it if he wanted to contact the Great Speaker back home on Polaris Prime.

His call was answered by an official switchboard message-taker, dressed in a dark pin-striped suit with the blue-and-white Polarian flag draped impressively behind him.

"Please state your name," said the official message-taker in a tone of voice that suggested that a cybernetic device could easily replace him, and possibly already had.

Xrrpp gave his name, and prepared himself for the usual runaround that would eat up the remaining time of his break. To his surprise, his name prompted high-level attention: he was put on hold only twice, each time for less than a minute. Finally, the telecom screen went dark; then a face wearing a nightcap appeared through the gloom.

The face rubbed its eyes.

"Who's there?" it said.

Xrrpp checked the scan signature on the telecom display to determine that the face did, indeed, belong to the Great Speaker.

"It's me," he said. "Xrrpp."

"Xrrpp." The Great Speaker rubbed his eyes again. In the background, the soft warbling of Polarian cricket-moths floated on the night air. "Do you know what time it is here?" he demanded.

"Sorry, Excellency." Xrrpp peered into the semi-darkness of the Great Speaker's bedroom — at least, he assumed the bedroom belonged to the Great Speaker. A scandal this close to the election would hardly be prudent. "I could call back."

"Better go ahead, now that I'm awake," the Great Speaker said. "I take it you're calling on a … you know."

"A secure channel? Of course, Excellency."

"Good. We've got to keep your mission under wraps for the time being. By the way," the Great Speaker's voice became more imperious, "what was this I heard about the Centaurian invasion fleet being redirected to Polaris?"

"Purely random maneuver on their part, Excellency," Xrrpp assured him. "We managed to turn them around, of course."

"I'm glad to hear it. We can't afford a crisis like that — not until after the election's over. How's the mission going otherwise?"

"It's going well. We've established a peace treaty between the Centaurians and the natives of the Earth prison colony." The "we" wasn't strictly accurate, but Xrrpp felt he could finagle a little of the credit at a distance of 600 light years. "We've also sent Bzzpt down to the planet with the two native peace envoys. With luck, they'll lead him to their Bureau of Alternate Reality, and he can take whatever action is necessary."

"Ah, yes. Wise precaution." The Great Speaker rubbed his chin. "And the Death Ray?"

"We've dismantled most of the circuits, Excellency. It'll take the Centaurians weeks to put it back together."

"I'm worried about that Death Ray, Xrrpp. It could destroy our entire prison colony."

"It'll be a while before they even discover what we've done," Xrrpp said. "On the surface, that Death Ray looks in perfect repair. Kppkt has transformed himself to match every detail."

"Kppkt?" Even in the semi-darkness of the bedroom, Xrrpp could see the concern on the Great Speaker's face. "You've got *Kppkt* impersonating a *Death Ray*?"

"Don't worry, Excellency," said Xrrpp. "I guarantee you, everything's under complete control."

The murmur of idle conversation died abruptly as Kïḷḷëŕ entered the Tactical Weapons Room and walked slowly down the dimly lit central aisle. To left and right, four-eyed Centaurian soldiers stopped their socializing and applied their attention to their consoles with a guilty level of concentration. Kïḷḷëŕ nodded to himself, saying nothing as he walked slowly on towards the Death Ray. Too much inaction bred fatigue: it was clear these soldiers needed a taste of military glory to put a little life back into them.

Well. He would soon provide that glory.

The aisle widened out at the far end, and Kïḷḷëŕ turned briefly around, surveying the Tactical Weapons Room once more. The room was a hive of industry now, silent except for the clicking of bony fingers on keypads and touch-sensitive displays. Satisfied, Kïḷḷëŕ turned again and walked up the three carpeted steps to the Death Ray spanning the end wall.

He rubbed his hands together in anticipation, and moved closer, his fingers gliding pleasurably over the smooth, leathery surface of the Death Ray.

Oh, sure, those Polarian mechanics had warned him of the risks. But then, hadn't they already moved the entire fleet out of orbit once by their underhand methods? Their hearts really didn't seem to be in this invasion at all. Never trust a shapeshifter.

Of course, he mused, as he pushed the square yellow button to open the Death Ray control panel, Ååáŕŕgh wasn't that sold on the idea of the Death Ray either. Nor, he considered, as he switched on the auxiliary banks of lighted dials and gauges, was the Centaurian Congress. But, he figured, as he activated the thermal energy cells and engaged the main power grid, if he could just get the Death Ray going — *prove* its effectiveness, as it were — then the Centaurian Congress would find the confidence to reapprove the invasion, and Åååŕ́gh would look good, and all objections would be overcome and everyone would be happy.

Everyone except Old Five-Fingers, of course. But then, you couldn't please everyone.

Kïḷḷëƙ switched on the electronic manual for the Death Ray and scanned through the schematic diagrams. The reawakening of the Death Ray might prove the turning point of the invasion. Future historians would look back with awe at the Great Moment when Kïḷḷëƙ the Truly Strategic decided to give the Death Ray one last chance. Even now, as the Earthgate scandal forced one resignation after another from the High Empress's cabinet, sending the political scene on Alpha Centauri 5 into a state of turmoil, the decisive military breakthrough of the campaign was about to unfold.

Kïḷḷëƙ flexed his fingers in preparation for the Great Moment, and reviewed the manual one last time. As he'd noted before, it didn't quite seem to match the control panel layout. Curse those Polarian mechanics and their modifications. Of course, if these really *were* improvements … well, so much to the good. After all, if they were abandoning this invasion, the worst that could happen was that they'd destroy a planet they weren't planning to colonize anyway.

He leaned forward.

"Kïḷḷëƙ to Death Ray," he said in a low voice.

The Death Ray groaned.

"What?" it said, finally.

Kïḷḷëƙ frowned, and scanned the manual again. This wasn't the way Death Rays were supposed to respond.

"Authorization Kïḷḷëƙ Omega Omega 2," he said. "Prepare to fire."

"I thought I wasn't supposed to fire," said the Death Ray.

"I just gave you authorization." Kïḷḷëƙ glanced anxiously

around the Tactical Weapons Room. Being talked back to by a Death Ray hardly conveyed the appropriate impression of his authority. He lowered his voice still further. "It's only a test."

"Do we have to?" said the Death Ray. "I'm not really feeling that great."

Kïḷḷëʀ grimaced. Just what he needed: a Death Ray with an attitude. If these were the so-called "efficiency improvement modifications," those Polarians would have a lot to answer for.

"Look." Kïḷḷëʀ tried to make his voice sound convincing, and wondered why he was doing all this for a Death Ray. "Just go ahead and fire. You'll feel much better, I promise you."

"Are you sure?"

Kïḷḷëʀ leaned closer towards the control panel opening. "Would I lie?" he said.

The Death Ray considered for a moment.

"All right," it said at last.

Kïḷḷëʀ watched on the monitor as two black outer gates on the ship's hull swung open, and a shining metal cone emerged from between them like the proboscis of some huge, predatory insect. An aperture at the tip of the cone widened in diameter; then a lambent magenta tongue of light shot from the opening with a roar like a rush of steam from a punctured vent. The luminous streak split the blackness of space, then changed direction abruptly like a bent arrow, bouncing off the Earth's atmosphere and deflecting harmlessly away into the void.

Kïḷḷëʀ held his head in his hands.

"Missed," he groaned.

"Sorry," said the Death Ray.

"All right," said Kïḷḷëʀ. "One more, on my signal." After all, there was no point in testing merely whether or not the Death Ray could fire. A Death Ray had little value if it couldn't at least penetrate the Earth's atmosphere. He adjusted the coordinates, aiming more directly at the planet's surface.

"Fire!" he whispered.

A second burst of magenta, briefer than the first, shot from the conical nozzle of the Death Ray. It punctured the planet's atmosphere with a violent swirl of gases, turning an angry vermilion red as it channeled its way earthward in a smoldering blaze of glory.

Kïḷḷëŕ smiled with satisfaction.

"Well," he said. "We'll see what Old Five-Fingers has to say about that peace treaty *now*."

18

As Wilfred arrived at the *Spade and Archer* door with Selena and Bzzpt, he felt an emotional tug of "home." He wondered what it said about a person that he felt more at home in the Bureau of Alternate Reality than anywhere else. Certainly, Blake's office had become a home base for him, but it was also the familiarity of the surroundings: the Bogart setting was among the few things in this time-frame that had existed before 1999.

Blake got up from his computers as they came in. Selena went over to meet him with her usual enthusiastic smile.

"Nice work on the budget proposal vote in the Council," she said.

"Thanks." Blake didn't look too cheered. "Unfortunately, we've got another problem now. Professor McInerny is missing."

"Missing!" Selena looked around, as if she expected her to pop up at any moment. "What's happened to her?"

"She went over to the Council building this morning to clear up a few remaining points on the budget cut issue. Half an hour later I got a call from her, saying she'd be detained for a while. I haven't heard from her since."

Bzzpt tipped up his blue mechanic's cap.

"Who's Professor McInerny?" he said.

"Oh — I'm sorry." Selena stepped to one side by way of including Bzzpt more in the conversation. "This is Bzzpt, from Polaris. Blake, from the Bureau of Alternate Reality."

"Ah, yes." Bzzpt came forward, wiping his hand on his overalls before extending it. "Blake Orion. Just the person I wanted to meet."

"Me?" Blake's usual Bogart aplomb deserted him for once. He gave a puzzled frown. "Why me?"

"I'm interested to find out how your alternate reality research is coming along," said Bzzpt. He walked over to Blake's desk and picked up the Maltese Falcon, then looked around at the 1940's decor. "This is quite an office you have here, I must say." He held up the Black Bird with one hand, and changed the shape of his other hand to match.

"Not a bad trick," Blake admitted. His Bogart composure had returned. "Say, I'll bet you do a pretty good Peter Lorre. We could do the scene where—"

"First we need to find Professor Mac," Selena said firmly. "When she called you this morning, did she say anything else that might help us trace her movements?"

Blake shook his head.

"Not really. She was rather mysterious, which aroused my suspicions. Normally, she'd tell me what was going on."

"Maybe someone else was there with her," Wilfred suggested, "so she couldn't talk as freely as she would have liked."

"That's possible," said Blake. "By the way, Wilfred, do you know a General Jonas P. Heidtbrink?"

"Yes." Wilfred's heart sank. "Why, what does he want now?"

"He called earlier, and left a message for you to call him back. He said it was urgent. He seemed pretty agitated — you'd better get back to him." Blake switched on his phone for Wilfred and offered him his leather chair, then went back over to join Bzzpt and Selena.

Wilfred sat down and looked at the 1940's phone on Blake's desk.

"Uh ... hello?" he said, feeling unsure about simply talking to a telephone, especially one of that vintage. "Get me General Jonas P. Heidtbrink, please."

After a couple of rapid clicks, the dialplate of the phone popped open, and a hologram image of Heidtbrink, in his general's uniform, appeared beside the desk.

"Ah, Wilfred! Thank God it's you." Heidtbrink was pacing up and down, so that his image wandered in and out of the range of the hologram scanner. He stopped for a moment, and looked anxiously at Wilfred. "Is there anyone else there with you?"

Wilfred glanced over at the others, who were now involved in an animated discussion about Professor McInerny.

"Just my trusted advisers," he said.

"Good." Heidtbrink resumed his pacing. "Problem with the Centaurians, I'm afraid. They've broken the peace treaty."

"The peace treaty!" To Wilfred's surprise, he found himself taking this rather personally. "But we only just got them to sign it!"

"They've attacked the Earth with some kind of Death Ray," Heidtbrink said. "It annihilates everything in its path, leaving a charred crater of destruction. They've scored about a dozen hits with it, and now they're invading in force."

"Good God," said Wilfred, feeling his blood run cold.

"This time they mean business," said Heidtbrink. "The Centaurian government seems to view the use of the Death Ray as a rallying point for renewing the invasion." Despite Heidtbrink's pained expression, Wilfred recalled a recent conversation in which Heidtbrink had eagerly discussed Earth's military plans against the Centaurians, even as Wilfred was reporting details of the peace treaty.

"So, what now?" Wilfred said.

"You are to return to Military Headquarters immediately," said Heidtbrink. He had stopped his pacing again, and was now looking directly at Wilfred. "From there, you will take the S-111 to Los Angeles, and mobilize the Handymen against the Centaurian invaders."

"But why me?" said Wilfred. He wondered if Heidtbrink realized that some people had other things to do besides saving the world from alien invasions. "Don't you have people who are *trained* for this kind of thing?"

"Training has nothing to do with it," said Heidtbrink. "This is all about morale. Those people need Wilfred Smith in person, urging them on to deeds of glory. They need *you*, Wilfred. They're depending on you." He glanced at his watch. "I'll meet you at the S-111 hangar in twenty minutes."

The image of Heidtbrink disappeared, and the dialplate of the phone folded back into place on Blake's desk.

Wilfred got up and joined the others. They had apparently decided on a course of action, and Selena was now organizing how to carry it out.

"Ah, Wilfred." She put out her hand for him in a friendly gesture as he approached. "You're coming with us to find Professor Mac, while Blake stays here and—" She stopped, seeing his expression. "You can't, can you?" she said.

"It's the Centaurians," said Wilfred. "They've broken the peace treaty. Earth is under attack. I've got to go back and see Heidtbrink."

"Do you need me to come with you?" Selena looked around at Blake and Bzzpt, aware of the commitments she would be breaking regarding the search for Professor McInerny.

Wilfred shook his head.

"I don't think so," he said. "Not this time." He held Selena's hand, realizing how much less alone he would feel with her company, but the middle of a Centaurian attack didn't seem like the place he wanted to take her. It was more important for her to locate Professor McInerny. The Bureau of Alternate Reality might become Earth's last hope if things got bad.

"I'll worry about you." Selena straightened his collar almost as an involuntary gesture. "Just make sure you come back safe."

"I always have," said Wilfred. He managed a smile.

"Well, yes, but ..." Selena slipped her hands up over his shoulders. She pulled him closer and kissed him, her breath warm against his mouth, then hugged him tightly. "You've never been on a mission before where you haven't had me to look after you."

Selena arrived with Bzzpt at the Council recess chambers. If Professor Mac had some final issues to clear up on the

Council budget proposal, then Monica's office seemed a likely place to start.

The outer reception area of Monica's office was brightly lit and welcoming, with pale, feathery ferns and darker aspidistras softening the perimeter. Framed legislative documents bearing Monica's flamboyant signature adorned the walls in testimony to her vigilance as watchdog of the people's interests.

At the reception desk, a frail, bird-like woman with gold-rimmed glasses informed them that Councilwoman van Patten saw no one without an appointment.

"Could you try anyway?" Selena gave her name. "Say it's urgent."

The receptionist, with a sigh of duress, called Monica. Monica's answer came back an unequivocal "no."

"Well, thanks for trying," Selena said.

She led Bzzpt to one side, away from the reception desk. "Create a disturbance," she said under her breath.

"Like what?"

"I don't know. Become a boa constrictor, or something."

Bzzpt stepped behind one of the larger aspidistras, emerging from the foliage a moment later as a boa constrictor heading for the reception desk. The bird-like receptionist sprang from her chair and waved her arms, and four or five other people in the reception area joined the general panic. Selena took advantage of the confusion to march on into Monica's office.

A series of white-painted French windows gave the office a light, airy feel, despite the fact that they were tightly sealed against the uninviting atmosphere. On the far wall, a TV news commentary droned in the background, presumably to keep Monica informed about the outside world. Selena considered protesting Zirconia's pollution levels — Monica's record on the environment was one of the worst on the Council — but she decided to leave it until she was here on Department of Forestry business.

"What are you doing in here?" Monica reached to switch on her phone. "I said I didn't want to see you."

Selena placed her hand over Monica's phone, switching it

off.

"What have you done with her?" she demanded.

"What are you talking about?" Monica shooed Selena dismissively with a red-fingernailed hand. "Go away. I'm busy."

"You know exactly what I'm talking about. Where's Professor McInerny?"

"How would I know?" Monica said. She smiled sweetly. "That's hardly *my* concern, is it?"

Selena figured it was time for a long shot.

"Professor McInerny made a call to the Bureau of Alternate Reality earlier today," she said. "We traced the origin of that call to this office."

"Don't be ridiculous. That call was—" Monica stopped.

"Ah. So you *were* with her at the time she made the call?"

"Well, yes." Monica pretended to take a sudden interest in the TV newscast. "That was hours ago. I don't know where she is now."

"Well, where did she go when she was with you?"

"I can't tell you that." Monica continued to watch the TV. She looked briefly out of the corner of her eye at Selena.

"Why not?" Selena persisted, taking Monica's caginess as a promising sign.

"I'm—" Monica drew in a breath, then smiled primly. "I'm not authorized to give out that information. Certainly not to you."

"Why, what's so secret?" Selena said. "Are you holding her somewhere against her will, or something?"

"Of course not."

The voice on the TV newscast changed, drawing Selena's attention. The new speaker announced with a smile that jury selection in an upcoming celebrity murder trial was now complete. "Jurors are being sequestered in absolute secrecy—"

Monica switched off the TV. A flush deepened around her cheekbones as she turned back to Selena. "I don't know why they broadcast that nonsense," she said. "I'm sure no one's really all that interested in hearing about jury selections. Now, if you'll excuse me, I have work to do." She rose from her chair and took Selena's arm, more or less hauling her to the door.

The scene in the reception area was one of pandemonium. A boa constrictor was running amok, flicking its tongue in and out and slithering all over the carpet. Three people were standing on chairs in vain attempts to get out of its way.

Monica looked at the scene, open-mouthed and appalled, for a full five seconds.

"Well, you're the environmentalist!" she finally screamed at Selena. "Do something about this wretched creature!"

Selena went over and gathered up the snake in her arms.

"There you are," she told the stunned onlookers. "Really nothing to worry about."

"How did that thing get in here in the first place?" Monica demanded.

"*She* brought it in with her." Someone pointed a finger accusingly at Selena.

"I did not!"

"Well, it's tame around her. Look at it!"

The snake was licking Selena under the chin, its dry tongue darting feverishly. There was no doubt Bzzpt had a weird sense of humor.

"You just have to learn how to handle them," she explained as she backed towards the door.

"Why anyone would let a snake into the Council recess chambers..." Monica said.

"Seemed rather apropos to me," Selena muttered under her breath as she left.

"So, what happened?" Bzzpt said, after he'd resumed his more familiar mechanic's appearance in a deserted section of corridor.

"I'll tell you as we go." Selena pointed along a covered walkway that led to the next building. "This way."

"Where are we going?"

"The courthouse. It's about four buildings over." On the way, Selena told Bzzpt about Monica's secrecy regarding Professor McInerny, and her guilty reaction to the jury selection newsclip. "At least it gives us a place to start," she said as they reached the courthouse. "If this is where she's got Professor McInerny, I have to admit it won't be easy getting her out."

The beige walls of the courthouse lobby were lit entirely by artificial light, and broken by a series of information windows with people waiting at each one. Two corridors led off the main lobby, each lined with similar information areas. A row of teal-colored elevators led up, presumably, to more floors of the same, and no doubt to one or two actual courtrooms.

One of the information windows displayed the actual word *INFORMATION* above it in raised, teal-blue letters. Selena and Bzzpt decided that was as good a place to start as any, so they stood in that line and waited. When their turn finally came, Selena asked the clerk in the window if Professor Elaine McInerny was being held for jury duty.

"You'll need to submit an official query form to find out that information," the clerk said.

"I see." Selena nodded. "So, could we have a query form?"

"Well, you can't get one here," said the clerk. "We have a special department that handles that."

Selena waited a moment, hoping to elicit more information. None was forthcoming.

"So ... where *is* this department?" she said at last.

"Ah," said the clerk. "I can't tell you that at this window. There's another department that authorizes the release of that information."

"I thought this was the information window?" Selena said.

"Well, it is," explained the clerk, "but only for the information that we can release."

"I see," said Selena. She turned to Bzzpt, wondering if bureaucracy was the same on Polaris. Bzzpt's widening grin implied that it was. "Well," she said to the clerk, "can you tell us where the department is that can tell us where to go for the query forms?"

"Of course. It's the next window, right here." The clerk confirmed with the clerk at the next window that this was indeed correct. "Yes," she said to Selena. "If you'll just join that next line over, they'll be able to help you."

Selena and Bzzpt joined the next line, found out where to go for the query form, joined that line to pick up their query form, filled in the query form, and brought it back to the original information window where they had first started.

"Hmm," said the clerk. "Elaine McInerny." She entered the information from the query form into her computer, and examined the screen. "Ah, yes. You were correct. Professor Elaine McInerny is currently serving jury duty."

"Well, can we get her out?" said Selena.

"Get her out?" said the clerk.

"That's right," Selena said, nodding. "That's why we're here."

"Well, first you have to identify her formally," said the clerk.

"OK. So, can we see her?"

"You'll need a visitor's pass," said the clerk.

"I hate to ask," Selena said, "but how do we get a visitor's pass?"

"There's a department that handles the visitor's passes."

"But you can't tell us which department that is, can you?"

"Oh, I can tell you *that*." The clerk seemed surprised at Selena's lack of faith. "It's the same department that handles the query forms."

Selena groaned.

"Couldn't you have told us that before?"

"Well, no," said the clerk. "You see, you can't do the query form and the visitor's pass at the same time, because you have to establish that she's here through a query before you can apply for a visitor's pass to visit her."

"Look, don't bother with the visitor's pass," said Bzzpt. "We don't need to visit her. All we need is a way to identify her."

"Well, you could apply for an ID check," said the clerk.

"An ID check?"

"But I wouldn't if I were you. It takes rather a long time."

"So is this the only way to get her out?" said Selena.

"Well, no," said the clerk. "If you want to get her out, all you really need is a release form."

"Ah," said Selena. "A release form. And where do we get one?"

"You don't have a release form?"

"Not yet," said Selena. "We've only been here a couple of hours."

"Well, you can't get her out without a release form."

"Yes, I understand that," Selena said. "So where do we get one?"

"That's a separate department," said the clerk. She leaned through the window, and pointed. "Go to the end of that first corridor, and you'll see a window that says RELEASE FORMS above it. They should be able to help you."

"Thanks," Selena said.

They found the window with the words RELEASE FORMS, and waited.

"We're here to pick up a release form," Selena said to the clerk when their turn came.

"A release form?" said the clerk blankly.

"That's right." Selena looked up to read the words above the window again. "To release someone from jury duty."

"We don't stock the forms here," said the clerk.

Selena checked above the window once more.

"But it says RELEASE FORMS over the window," she said.

"Well, yes," the clerk explained. "This is where you turn them *in*. But it isn't where we give them *out*."

Selena looked at Bzzpt, who only grinned. She turned back to the clerk.

"And where do you give them out?" she said.

"You have to get them signed by a member of the Council."

Selena chewed her lip. That posed a problem, all right. Getting a Council member's signature wouldn't be easy. Maybe Mother Iz would do it.

Bzzpt tugged at her sleeve, pulling her aside.

"If we can find out what the release forms look like, I can

recreate one," he whispered. "I've seen Monica's signature, back at her office."

"Can you make yourself as small as a piece of paper?"

"Sure. It's a bit of a squeeze, but no big deal."

Selena looked around the crowded hall.

"How will you manage it without being seen?" she said.

"Leave it to me."

Selena turned back to the clerk, ignoring the impatient glares of the people in line behind her.

"Can you show me the release form?" she said. "I want to make sure I fill it in correctly."

"Very good idea," said the clerk. She took out an example. "You'd be surprised how many people fill in their release forms incorrectly." She explained the most common errors, while Selena and Bzzpt watched patiently.

A fluctuating, high-pitched tone sounded in the hall. Its modulating frequency made it almost impossible to tell where it originated from. Selena, like everyone else, looked upwards and around to locate its source. She felt a piece of paper in her hand, and the sound stopped abruptly.

So that was how Bzzpt had distracted everyone's attention.

"I think I have the right form here," she said to the clerk. "Is this filled in right?"

The clerk looked over the form. "Yes. Everything's in order." She scanned the form into her computer, and entered a command. "There. I've ordered the release of Professor Elaine McInerny from jury duty. Now, if you go around the corner to your left, she'll be released from that door."

"Thanks." Selena started to leave. "Uh ... could I get my release form back, please?"

"No." The clerk stamped the form and placed it in a folder. "These stay here. We keep them on file for 90 days, and then shred them."

"*Shred* them?" Selena felt her eyes widen.

"Yes. Now, if you'll just go around the corner to your left ..."

Selena looked around helplessly at the line of people waiting behind her. At least she'd get Professor Mac released. Now they had 90 days to figure a way to get Bzzpt out. That should be enough time. Bzzpt knew how to take care of himself pretty well.

Selena went around the corner to the release door and waited. A few minutes later the door opened, and Professor McInerny burst through it and came up to her with her usual decisive, energetic strides.

"Thanks for getting me out, Selena." She looked around. "Is Blake here?"

"He's back at the Bureau. We should call him and tell him you're OK." Selena prepared to tap the phoneband around her wrist, when a commotion at the release forms window drew her attention. The people in the line were backing away in horror as the head of a boa constrictor appeared in the window, its tongue flicking cheerfully.

Selena stepped forward.

"Don't worry," she said. "I'm an environmentalist. I'll handle this. I took care of another boa constrictor over in the Council building earlier today." She gathered up the coils of the snake in her arms, and smiled reassuringly at the crowd. "A lot of them around these days. Must be the season."

"Would you mind explaining what this is all about?" said Professor McInerny. She followed Selena at a respectful distance, eyeing the snake with morbid curiosity.

"Sure," Selena said. With her arms full of writhing boa constrictor, she tilted her head at the exit. "Let's get out of here first."

Flying low over the Hollywood hills under the S-111's cloak of invisibility, Wilfred saw the sky above him darkening with the approaching Centaurian battlecraft. Below him, blighting the ground like a cancer, he saw something that gripped his heart even more tightly — a black crater of devastation, over a mile across. Wisps of sulfurous yellow smoke rose from the crater's edges, as if seeping from some subterranean toxic vault.

So this was the power of the Death Ray.

Wilfred made a final effort to contact Ace but was once

again unable to get through. Evidently the Handymen had closed all outside communication channels as a security precaution to prevent the Centaurians from intercepting their strategies. He would have to reach Ace's hideout in person if he wanted to make contact.

He brought the S-111 down as close as he could to Ace's hilltop bunker above the second "O" of the HOL WOL sign. The steep slope and dense underbrush meant he had to land a few hundred feet from his destination. Hopefully, the underbrush would give him the cover he needed to reach the bunker on foot.

He opened the hatch of the S-111. The acrid smoke stung his eyes, and a sickly sulfurous smell made him shut the hatch again. He went over to the supply cabinet and took out an oxygen mask.

Another idea occurred to him. He found the responsibility field generator Blake had given him when he'd first arrived at Military Headquarters to steal the S-111. He activated the device, and slipped it into his pocket. Thus protected from the sight of the Centaurian invaders, he reopened the hatch of the S-111 and climbed down into the underbrush amid the noise and smoke of battle.

He pushed forward, heart pounding. A black Centaurian craft swooped low, strafing the vegetation a few feet in front of him with a theatrical blaze of automatic fire. Wilfred cowered behind what little protection he had from the stunted bushes, and pressed his fingers against his ears, hearing the pulsing of his blood. He might be invisible to the Centaurian pilots, but that didn't make him invulnerable against stray bullets.

The entrance to Ace's hilltop bunker was still some fifty feet ahead of him. Was this worth it? Should he turn around and go home in the safety of the S-111?

How much morale could he really provide?

A firebomb landed behind him, exploding with a burst of burning gases like the sound of ripping cardboard. The underbrush erupted in a sheet of flame, cutting off his direct retreat to the S-111.

The drone of the battlecraft continued overhead, as the ground beneath his feet shook with the repeated shocks of heavy bombardment. Wilfred waited for a moment, instinctively using the underbrush for visual cover despite the protection of the responsibility field. As the salvo ended, he made a dash across the last few yards of open clearing and scrambled into the entrance of the bunker.

The mood in the bunker was solemn. Ace, Leroy, and several other Handymen in blue bandannas were clustered around a panel of communications monitors. The people on the monitors wore not only blue bandannas, but red, yellow and green as well. The Handymen had pooled their resources: Ace and his Blues had put differences aside and teamed up with the hated Greenhorns and the like to stop the Centaurian foe.

No one, of course, had noticed his arrival. Wilfred removed his oxygen mask, coughing at the smoke-laden air that filled his lungs, and switched off his responsibility field. Immediately, a shout went up, and two or three large automatic weapons pointed in his direction.

"Don't shoot!" Wilfred cried. "It's me — Wilfred Smith." He raised his hands high, still clutching the oxygen mask, and turned his head aside as another coughing fit overtook him.

Ace stepped forward, peering closely, then his gaunt face broke into a grin.

"Wilfred!" he called out. "Great to see ya!" He clapped Wilfred firmly on the back, which had the unintentional side benefit of helping to stop his coughing fit.

As Leroy and the others pressed forward in greeting, Ace passed the word of Wilfred's arrival to the other camps around the battlefield. Over the communications network, in the background, Wilfred could hear the cheers of the Handymen as word of his arrival spread.

All eyes turned expectantly towards him. He realized the moment had come for him to reveal his tactical expertise.

"Strategy is crucial," he began, realizing that a decisive manner mattered far more than the actual words. "Two days ago, the Centaurians attacked here and were driven back. We can succeed again, as we did before. No one knows this territory better than you. Time is short. Your recommendations, gentlemen?"

Suggestions poured in from all sides. Wilfred nodded wisely to some, pointed in acknowledgement to others, appeared to weigh others with a tilt of his head. Ace and the other three commanders filled in as needed, reaching quick consensus on each new suggestion and relaying the orders to the field.

Heidtbrink had been right. Knowledge of military tactics was irrelevant for this mission. These men already knew their jobs. The important message was a simple one: Wilfred Smith had arrived in person to lead them on to one last blaze of glory.

In that moment, Wilfred realized it had been worth it for him to come here. These men were fighting to save the Earth in a last-ditch effort. The morale boost of his presence was the least he could provide them.

He looked out of the bunker entrance. All across the battlefield, jet fighters were emerging from their hiding places and streaking upwards to engage the Centaurian battlecraft, supported from below by heavy artillery fire. In the foreground, gray smoke from the smoldering underbrush mingled with the yellow smoke from the Death Ray crater and drifted away eastwards on the breeze from the ocean. The roar and whine of battle tore at his ears, accompanied by the relentless jarring of rockets pounding the earth all around him.

He was glad Selena wasn't here for this one.

19

Blake slammed his fist into the palm of his hand with a sigh of frustration, and glared at the computer display. So close, and yet the last pieces of the alternate reality puzzle just wouldn't fall into place.

He knew how to reach an alternate reality by traveling into the past, and then returning along a different reality path. He could even perform some action in the past which would help determine which reality path he took. But there were no guarantees. Time travel was notoriously unpredictable, and this lack of control could have disastrous results.

Especially with the Centaurian invasion in progress.

He stared gloomily through the circular doorway into Professor McInerny's office. The time machine gleamed back at him with the blue-black iridescence of heat-tempered metal.

The best solution would be to shift directly into another reality without traveling through time at all, like a spark jumping across two points. In theory, he could use the time machine to locate possible reality paths, then use the computers to lock onto the desired reality and make the shift.

In theory.

The outer door of his office swung open and Professor McInerny strode in, with Selena and Bzzpt close behind.

"Professor Mac!" Blake got up from his computers and hurried over to her. "You're safe! What happened?"

Professor McInerny explained about the attempt to sequester her for jury duty, presumably so that Monica could continue to undermine the Bureau of Alternate Reality.

"Anyway, I've been released," she said, "thanks to these two." She extended an arm towards Selena, who beamed happily, and Bzzpt, who adjusted his cap with a show of modesty. "So, how's the research coming along?"

"Not very well," said Blake, rubbing his chin.

"Well, Bzzpt has offered to use his, um ... unique abilities to see if he can help you. Isn't that right, Bzzpt?"

"I'd be delighted," said Bzzpt. He strolled past Blake to the computers. "What is it you're trying to do?"

"Generate an alternate reality," said Blake. "Preferably, one where government takes responsibility and solves problems."

"Well, let's aim for something realistic to start with," said Bzzpt. "The impossible always takes a little practice." He walked to the circular doorway and looked into Professor McInerny's office, transforming his hand into a scanner and examining the iridescent blue-black apparatus on the other side. "With a time machine like this, you should be able to travel to alternate realities fairly easily."

"Well, yes," said Blake. "We can. The problem is the lack of control. I'm trying to develop an alternate reality shift without traveling through time at all — just using the time machine to set the coordinates."

"Interesting," said Bzzpt. He rubbed the back of his neck. "Does it work?"

"Well, no," said Blake irritably. "That's the problem."

"Ah. Well, lucky thing I'm here," said Bzzpt. He transformed the scanner back into his hand, flexing his fingers. "As you can see, I make reality shifts all the time as part of my normal existence."

"You mean," said Selena, "your Polarian shape-shifting is a kind of alternate reality shift?"

"I'm not sure if it's the same thing or not," said Bzzpt. "It uses another dimension — what I suppose you might call an alternate reality. That's also true of our space travel."

"So that's how you cross the 600 light years between here and Polaris?" said Blake.

"In a way," said Bzzpt. "But our shape-shifting and 4-D travel only change things *within* this reality. You're trying to change the entire reality. That's a big difference."

"But you do maintain full control?" said Professor McInerny.

"When shape-shifting? Yes."

"Then, can you control this other type of alternate reality shift?"

"Control it?" said Bzzpt. "Now, wait a minute! I don't even know if I can *do* it." He looked from the computers to the time machine. "I've never used technology like this before."

"We'll start small, of course," Blake put in hurriedly, becoming suddenly nervous that Professor McInerny might change her mind and veto the project altogether. "Just a test, to find out what level of control we have." He glanced anxiously at Professor McInerny. To his relief, she merely nodded the go-ahead.

"All right," said Bzzpt. He converted the fingers of one hand to a series of electronic connectors and attached them to the back of one of Blake's computer terminals. Blake scurried along the row of computers, adjusting one control switch after another, while Bzzpt's face, beneath his mechanic's cap, became a study in concentration.

A high-pitched hum started at the far end of the row of computers, and began resonating in waves through the entire computer system. Moments later, a crackle of blue-white static danced over the control panel beside Blake's elbow.

"We're reaching critical limits!" Blake called, jumping back in alarm. "Any more power, and we'll overload the system!"

Bzzpt pulled his hand away from the computer terminal. The crackle of static stopped, and the high-pitched hum slowed to a whine and faded out altogether.

Professor McInerny ventured closer.

"Did it happen?" she asked. "Are we in an alternate reality?"

"It didn't do anything," said Selena. Her voice registered

disappointment as she glanced around the seemingly unchanged office.

"Yes, it did," said Bzzpt. "Something happened … at least, I'm pretty sure it did. Let me check." He flattened his hand out into a viewscreen, and studied the rows of figures that scrolled rapidly across it. "Yes," he announced after a moment. "An alternate reality shift has definitely taken place."

"I get the same reading," Blake confirmed, checking the instrument panels on his own computers. "We've experienced a shift, all right. An extremely minor one, to be sure. But something is different."

"I suppose it would be too much to ask what?" said Professor McInerny.

Blake studied his instrument panels again. He looked up at her, and shook his head.

"No way to tell at this point," he said. "But there's been a change somewhere. Just one tiny detail. Everything else is the same as before."

"Yup." Bzzpt nodded in agreement, and converted the viewscreen back to his hand with a cheerful grin. "I guess we'll find out sooner or later."

High over Los Angeles, the Centaurian battlecraft swooped and dived in a relentless bombardment of the Handyman encampment.

The weapons systems aboard these Centaurian vessels were designed according to the latest state-of-the-art technology. Because of the importance of keeping these weapons systems functional during a military operation, the power cell on each system was backed up by a spare. If a power cell failed, control transferred automatically to the backup. This process took approximately one second.

In the heat of battle, the interruption of one isolated weapons system for one second went virtually unnoticed. Even two or three such interruptions occurring at the same time would cause barely a ripple in the flow of battle. It would take far larger numbers (say, the momentary inactivity of 25 percent of all weapons systems) before commanders began to raise eyebrows, and still larger percentages (say, upwards of 75 percent simultaneous power cell replacements) before the battlecraft pilots themselves began to scratch their heads and wonder if a cease-fire had actually been called and they just hadn't been paying attention.

Given the infinite nature of probability, it's possible to imagine an alternate reality in which the power cells on every single weapons system on every single Centaurian vessel attacking Los Angeles failed at precisely the same instant, causing pilots and commanders alike to conclude that it was time to pack it in and head back to the fleet orbiting high above the Earth's atmosphere, and only later to start wondering who exactly had given the order for the cease-fire in the first place.

Wilfred looked out from Ace's hilltop bunker above the HOL WOL sign and tried to figure out how he could reach the S-111. The Centaurian bombardment of Los Angeles had intensified, and most of the underbrush between him and the S-111 was either aflame or smoldering from the latest firebomb attack.

He peered back into the gloom of the bunker. Ace and others were shouting orders, trying to make themselves heard above the exploding Centaurian shells as they relayed Wilfred's strategies to the field commanders via the hologram monitors.

If only he had a way to reach the S-111. The plane's invisibility might provide their one hope of defeating the Centaurians, allowing him to sneak up undetected (with EDSEL's help) on individual Centaurian battlecraft, and destroy them.

He activated the S-111's remote locator. The device couldn't contact EDSEL directly — he'd have to wait till he was aboard the S-111 to do that — but it did tell him the S-111 was still where he had left it a few hundred feet away, undamaged. Apparently, its protective shields were holding against the

Centaurian attack.

He went over to Ace.

"I'm going to make a dash for the S-111," he told him. He outlined the invisibility strategy as briefly as he could. "It may be our best hope."

"Good luck, buddy." Ace nodded, and slapped him on the shoulder. "Thanks for being here."

Wilfred activated his responsibility field generator, disappearing from the sight of Ace and the others, and scrambled out of the bunker. Outside, he reviewed his options. He'd need to take a less direct route this time, to avoid the burning underbrush. On a sudden wind change, the harsh smoke stung his eyes and his sinuses and burned all the way down to his lungs, starting him coughing again. He strapped his oxygen mask over his face, and pushed onward.

A Centaurian battlecraft swooped low towards him. Wilfred saw the succession of explosions in the dirt getting closer and closer, and felt the shuddering of the earth at each impact. Two hundred yards away, then a hundred. He threw himself down and flattened himself against the ground, folding his arms over his head.

Nothing.

The Centaurian craft droned harmlessly overhead.

In the stillness that followed, Wilfred realized that all of the Centaurian craft had suddenly stopped firing. He looked up to see them circle for a moment, like gigantic buzzards unsure of their next move. Then they turned and disappeared up into the sky.

He stood up and made his way back to the bunker, dusting off his clothes as he went. He clambered in through the bunker entrance, removed his oxygen mask, and deactivated the responsibility field. A cheer went up as he reappeared to the Handymen, and he found himself suddenly carried above shoulder height, which positioned his head alarmingly close to the scraped-out earth of the bunker ceiling.

"Hey!" he protested, ducking to avoid a large and rather

insistent-looking rock.

Ace came over.

"I don't mean to interrupt the celebrations," he said, "but Military Headquarters is on line." He looked up at Wilfred, who managed to look down while balanced precariously on several pairs of hands. "They want to talk to you."

Wilfred's feet found the ground again, and he walked over to the hologram monitors. Most of them showed wildly celebrating Handymen wearing blue, red, yellow or green bandannas. The remaining monitor featured the stolid face of an army colonel whose name Wilfred didn't recognize.

"Congratulations on your victory," the colonel said in a monotone that conveyed all the enthusiasm of a high school freshman reciting Wordsworth. "You are to report back to Military Headquarters with the S-111 as soon as possible. We will need you on hand when the Centaurians respond to our latest peace demands."

Wilfred groaned. Not again, he thought. Surely they must have someone with the training, the expertise …

"I appreciate your congratulations, Colonel," he said, "but everyone here deserves the credit for this victory. I arrived during the middle of the battle, and had only a small role to play."

"But the winning strategy was yours," the colonel insisted. "The key tactics that turned the tide of the battle."

"Ah, well, if it's strategy and tactics you want," Wilfred said, "I can assure you I deserve only a passing mention. There is one person, and one person alone, who had the foresight to send the S-111 to Los Angeles — indeed, who has masterminded the military defense of our planet since the Centaurian invasion began."

He paused, studying the colonel's impassive face.

"The man you need for these negotiations," Wilfred concluded with an air of finality, "is General Jonas P. Heidtbrink."

20

Aboard the Centaurian flagship, the mood was one of jubilation. Their returning battlecraft had not only pounded the Handyman stronghold into submission, they had done so in style, achieving their cease-fire in an unprecedentedly short space of time.

Supreme High Commander Åååŕŕgh leaned back in his black gravitronic rotating command chair and glanced down from his window at the Earth below. Specifically, he glanced down at the smoldering spot on the west coast of one of the major land masses, a place known locally as Los Angeles. He still wasn't clear who had given the order for the cease-fire, but since it had come earlier than expected, and Los Angeles was demonstrably burning, he concluded that the victory had been decisive.

His transspace telecom beeped, signaling an incoming message from Alpha Centauri 5.

"Åååŕŕgh here," he responded. The holodisplay sprang to life, revealing the caller as the High Empress Histrionica.

"Hello, Mother," he said.

"Congratulations, Åååŕŕgh," said the High Empress. Her two pairs of eyes shone with evident pride at her son's success. "This is a significant victory. Thanks to your achievement, the Centaurian Congress has once again renewed its full support, and the colonization effort can proceed as planned."

"I'm delighted to hear it." Åååŕŕgh suppressed a groan. This meant he could be stuck out here indefinitely. A war like this wouldn't be over in a short time. Oh, no. It would drag on.

Colonization of the Earth would come, but it would not come cheaply, nor soon.

"I have good news for you," said the High Empress. Her tone caught his attention. It was the same tone she had used during his childhood birthday celebrations to announce a special surprise present.

"What is it?" Åååřřgh said gloomily. The only imaginable good news would be that he was going home.

"We're bringing you home," said the High Empress. "You are to take a shuttlecraft and begin your return journey to Alpha Centauri 5 before midnight tonight."

"That's wonderful! Thank you, Mother." Thank God there was to be no more of this war for him, at least. It had played on his nerves, cost him countless hours of sleep. He'd never really wanted to be Supreme High Commander in the first place. Still, it was better than a career in politics.

"Yes, it's been officially decided," said the High Empress Histrionica. "We are retiring you with full honors from your commandership of the armed forces, and grooming you for a career in politics."

"Politics!" said Åååřřgh, aghast. He wondered if some malignant telepathic link had developed in the telecom.

The High Empress Histrionica beamed with maternal pride. "You are to take over as the next High Emperor."

"But ... what about *you*, Mother?"

"It's the Earthgate scandal," the High Empress sighed. "You've heard about the resignations in the Ministry of Defense?"

"Yes, but—"

"Congress is looking for a scapegoat. They're calling for my resignation. If I don't resign within 30 days, I'll face an impeachment trial."

"But, Mother, surely you aren't directly to blame for the Death Ray kickbacks?"

"I've tried to tell them that." Her voice rose, defiant. "I am not a crook."

"I know you're not, Mother," Åååŕ́gh said gently.

"Thank you, Åååŕ́gh. I appreciate that." The High Empress took a breath, regaining her composure. "Anyway, it'll be nice to have you home again."

"I'm looking forward to it. Say hello to everyone."

Åååŕ́gh disconnected the call, then summoned Deputy High Commander Kïḷḷëʀ́ to his office. Kïḷḷëʀ́ appeared in the doorway moments later, reeling slightly, evidently in a celebratory mood.

"You wanted to see me, sir?" he boomed.

"Yes. Come in, Kïḷḷëʀ́. Sit down."

Kïḷḷëʀ́ fell back into a chair and blinked at his commanding officer.

"Is something wrong, sir?"

"Not at all. First of all, congratulations on a splendid victory."

"Ah. Thank you, sir."

"But that's not why I called you here. I'm leaving today."

"Leaving, sir?" Kïḷḷëʀ́'s eyes widened uncomprehendingly.

"I'll be starting my journey back to Alpha Centauri 5 this afternoon. I'm appointing you Supreme High Commander in my place."

Behind the celebratory haze, Kïḷḷëʀ́'s mouth worked, trying to find the right words.

"Thank you, sir!" he exclaimed at last. "That's great!"

"Following our victory at Los Angeles, we have of course issued a new demand for a peace settlement. We have received a similar communication from Earth. Your first duty as Supreme High Commander will be to represent Alpha Centauri 5 at these negotiations."

Kïḷḷëʀ́ looked crestfallen. His jaw sagged.

"Peace negotiations, sir?"

"Don't worry, Kïḷḷëʀ́. We have the full support of Congress this time. Our hands won't be tied like before, forcing us to accept an unsatisfactory peace treaty. You'll have the freedom to push for full and immediate colonization."

Kïḷḷëʀ's face brightened.

"Does this mean we can use the Death Ray again, sir?"

Åååŕŕgh let out a sigh. It was time to initiate Kïḷḷëʀ into the realities of the political system.

"It isn't a question of *using* the Death Ray," he said. "Using it now won't generate more defense contracts back home. It's already paid for. We need *new* stuff."

"Ah." Kïḷḷëʀ nodded. It was clear that he understood, at least partially. "New stuff. Yes, *sir!*"

Kïḷḷëʀ arrived on the planet's surface for the new round of peace talks with a light heart. Finally, he was Supreme High Commander of the invasion force! He looked down at the new star pinned conspicuously to his uniform, large and shiny. His greatness had been recognized. Patience had paid off. The only minor downside was that he was about to negotiate a peace settlement, but there was always a way that a good commander could turn even a setback like this to his advantage.

He strode into the brightly lit, glass-ceilinged conference room and looked around for Wilfred. He recalled how his archnemesis had foiled his plan to blow up the S-111 after the last round of peace talks ... and the memory evoked not only disappointment, but admiration as well. A worthy opponent was someone to appreciate.

A man in uniform came up and introduced himself as General Heidtbrink, chief negotiator for Earth. Kïḷḷëʀ viewed him with disdain.

Hah! he thought. They haven't sent Wilfred Smith, they've sent this second-stringer because they think they're dealing with a subordinate. Well, I'll show them a thing or two. Nobody gets the better of Supreme High Commander Kïḷḷëʀ!

Kïḷḷëʀ and Heidtbrink sat down on opposite sides of the conference table and faced off against each other like chess masters.

"I'm glad you were able to respond so promptly to our call for peace, following our victory at Los Angeles," Heidtbrink opened. The pleasantness in his tone failed to mask the steely determination beneath it.

"Excuse me," Kïḷḷëʀ́ corrected. "The victory at Los Angeles was *ours!* We left your city a smoldering rubble."

"Pardon *me,*" Heidtbrink countered. The pleasantness had all but evaporated. "You turned tail and retreated in the middle of the battle. We have evidence to prove it."

"We pummeled you into submission!" Kïḷḷëʀ́ roared. His three-fingered fist pounded the table. "There wasn't a stick left standing!"

Kïḷḷëʀ́ and Heidtbrink glared at each other across the table. A stony silence followed.

"Let's put it like this," said Heidtbrink. "If you persist in trying to colonize our planet, we will fight you every step of the way."

Kïḷḷëʀ́ scratched his bulbous forehead. Colonization *and* continuation of the war. That sounded like a win-win situation. He couldn't see a catch.

"OK," he agreed.

"If you don't withdraw your invasion fleet," Heidtbrink added, "we will use all of the military technology at our disposal to destroy you."

"We will do the same," said Kïḷḷëʀ́ bombastically. "And I might add that we will more than match any escalation you care to throw at us."

"You understand that this military escalation will present no hardship for Earth." The polished smugness in Heidtbrink's tone returned. "If anything, it will benefit our economy."

"It will benefit ours as well." Kïḷḷëʀ́ remembered Åååŕ́gh's injunction to promote new defense contracts.

Heidtbrink leaned forward on his elbows, his fingers interlocked.

"Naturally, our objective here is to ensure a lasting peace."

"Yes," said Kïḷḷëʀ́. He wasn't exactly sure *why* that was their objective, but he was still learning the ropes as a peace negotiator, so he decided to wait and see where Heidtbrink was leading. "Naturally."

"And the only way to ensure a lasting peace," Heidtbrink said, "is through limited war."

"Ah." Kïḷḷëʀ didn't know much about logic, but he knew what he liked. In one blinding moment of revelation, the whole peace process finally made sense. He nodded.

"Sounds good to me," he said. "We will if you will."

"That's the stuff!" said Heidtbrink. "I like a man who understands military budgets." He beckoned to an attendant, who hurried forward with a bottle of champagne and two sizeable glasses. He waited while the attendant filled the glasses, then he lifted one glass into the air while Kïḷḷëʀ lifted the other. "To our economic futures," he said.

"To our economic futures." Kïḷḷëʀ tasted the champagne. The bubbles tickled his throat pleasantly.

Really, there was nothing to this peace negotiation process, he thought. You just had to know how to handle it.

Wilfred arrived back at Blake's office at the Bureau of Alternate Reality to find Selena, Blake, Bzzpt and Professor McInerny deep in conversation. As he entered the room, Selena got up from her chair and came over to him. She hugged him and gave him the kind of kiss that made him feel it was worth going off to Los Angeles to fight the Centaurians after all. The others barely looked up from their discussion.

"Come on in," she whispered. She took his hand and led him over to the group, pulling up another chair for him. "We could be close to a breakthrough."

"There's another problem," Blake was saying. "Even if we do develop a way to control large-scale reality shifts — is this really what we want?"

"I thought that's what we were trying to achieve?" Professor McInerny observed drily.

"Shifting realities on demand could provide almost unlimited power," said Blake. "Such power could easily fall into the wrong hands."

"I agree," said Bzzpt. "I don't know how your government operates, but I wouldn't trust ours with anything like that."

"Suppose we don't try to change this reality at all?" said Selena. "What if we simply shift *ourselves* into a *different* reality?"

"You mean, visit alternate realities like tourists?" said Blake.

"Well, yes." Selena glanced over at Bzzpt. "If Polarians can travel to other places within this reality, maybe we could adapt that somehow to reach other realities."

"Using the reality-path technology of the time machine!" Blake exclaimed. He turned to Bzzpt. "What do you think?"

Bzzpt nodded. "If we're shifting ourselves, and not the entire universe, it would give us far greater mobility."

"What about the level of control?" said Professor McInerny. "Obviously, we need to select which alternate realities we visit."

"It may take a while to fine-tune it," Bzzpt said. He looked around at Blake's equipment. "The problem's going to be these computers."

"Why?" Blake looked mildly offended, as if someone had told him his child had been misbehaving at school. "What's wrong with them?"

"Nothing's wrong with them," said Bzzpt. "But, for any reliable degree of control, you're going to need about ten times more computer memory."

"Ten *times?*" said Blake. He turned to Professor McInerny, open-mouthed.

"Don't even think about it," said Professor McInerny. "We're way over our heads in debt as it is."

"But ... *nobody* has access to that kind of computer space!" Blake protested, turning back to Bzzpt.

Wilfred had been listening to the conversation and had understood about half of it. Now he felt it was time to make himself useful.

"I do," he said.

21

Blake and the others stared at Wilfred in amazement.

"*You?*" Blake said at last.

"Well ... yes," said Wilfred. He had often vaguely wondered what it might be like to sound important, and now he discovered that it was really no big deal. "Er ... mind if I borrow your phone?"

"Help yourself," said Blake.

Wilfred approached Blake's desk.

"General Heidtbrink, please," he said. The dialplate of the phone popped open, and Heidtbrink's image appeared after a brief delay.

"Congratulations on the peace talks, general," said Wilfred.

"Ah, yes!" Heidtbrink's voice came across a shade louder than usual, doubtless bolstered by the effect of a couple of extra glasses. "After your magnificent victory at Los Angeles, those Centaurians saw eye to eye with us soon enough!"

"Glad to hear it, general. Uh ... listen." Wilfred figured the mood was right for coming straight to the point. "The Bureau of Alternate Reality has developed a method of transfer from one reality to another, and back. I'm sure you understand the military significance of such a tactic."

"Ah ... yes." Despite the couple of extra glasses, the military significance did, indeed, seem to filter through.

"They'll need some additional computer space in order to expand this thing to a fully global security level," said Wilfred. "I was thinking maybe the EDSEL."

"The EDSEL?"

"Exactly." Wilfred nodded, lending support to the idea as

if it had been the general's own suggestion. "If we get in on the ground floor here, we can establish a precedent of military strategy. Make it harder for other branches of government to claim this technology."

"I see." Heidtbrink brushed his mustache with his thumb. "Good thinking." He reached off to the side for a moment, and Wilfred heard the familiar clink of glassware. "So, how do we persuade this Bureau of Alternate Reality?"

"I have some influence at the Bureau," said Wilfred. "I should be able to persuade them to use EDSEL rather than look elsewhere. Providing we make the offer promptly."

"Excellent," said Heidtbrink. He activated his computer. "I'm entering my authorization to EDSEL as we speak." He looked up again. "I'll leave the details to you, Wilfred. Heidtbrink out."

As Heidtbrink's image disappeared, the others in Blake's office burst into jubilant applause. Selena came forward and hugged him. Wilfred accepted the appreciation for a moment, then placed a second call, this time to EDSEL.

"EDSEL here," the computer responded, "and, I must say, it's a huge pleasure to have the opportunity to—"

"Yes — thank you," said Wilfred. "Um ... look. Can you keep a secret?"

"Is the Pope Catholic?" said EDSEL. "Keeping secrets is my specialty. My *raison d'être*. My—"

"Good," said Wilfred. "Now, listen. We are going to download some information to you. The Bureau of Alternate Reality will have sole access to this information. You will not reveal the information to anyone else, nor even acknowledge the existence of the memory space it uses. Is this clear?"

"You got it," said EDSEL cheerfully. "My chips are sealed."

Wilfred turned to Blake and Bzzpt. "Over to you," he said.

Blake and Bzzpt downloaded the relevant information into EDSEL's data banks: the time machine's reality-path technology; the computer programs for locking onto desired alternate realities; even Bzzpt's own procedure for Polarian dimensional shifting.

"The time machine won't travel with you," Bzzpt explained, "since you're not actually traveling through time. We'll simply use the machine's entrance as a portal between here and the other reality." As he spoke, a thin, visual sheen like a tightly stretched film of cellophane sprang into view across the entrance to the time machine, emitting a faint electrostatic buzz.

"What kind of reality should we program for this first trip?" Blake said, stepping back at the sudden, unexpected appearance of the portal.

"Let's keep it simple, to start with," said Professor McInerny. "I want to make sure we get you back."

"Something close to this reality, if you want my recommendation," Bzzpt said. "One or two changes only, until we get used to doing it."

"Maybe some different approach to government," Selena suggested. "That's been our goal all along: finding a system of government that actually takes responsibility for solving problems."

"Sounds good." Blake entered the request into the computer, then advanced cautiously towards the entrance of the time machine. He reached out his hand to touch the electrostatic field of the portal, but felt no shock or discomfort, only a slight increase in the buzzing noise and a few small flashes.

He turned to Bzzpt.

"One more detail," he said. "How do I get back?"

"The portal will exist in the other reality, too," said Bzzpt. "When you're ready to come back, just activate the portal with the sound of your voice, and step through as before."

Blake nodded. He raised a tentative eyebrow, and looked around at the others.

"Wish me luck," he said.

He stepped through the portal into the entrance of the time machine, and vanished.

Blake looked around, savoring his first glimpse of an alternate reality. He seemed to have arrived in a bar. A private club, perhaps: darkly opulent with rosewood panels and brass coathooks, and wine glasses hanging upside down from racks above the bar itself.

An alternate reality. He was having trouble letting the concept sink it.

He'd done it!

Or had he? The general look of the place didn't seem that different, giving him a nagging feeling of doubt. Then he remembered he'd deliberately requested a reality similar to his own.

A middle-aged man was seated at the bar, drinking a beer. Blake went over and sat down on the red leather padded stool beside him.

"I'm a visitor to these parts," he began. "I'd like to ask you something. About your system of government."

"Oh, yes?" the man said, a trace of suspicion in his voice. "What about it?"

"Well, I understand you have a government that acts responsibly and serves the public interest?"

"In a manner of speaking," the man said gloomily. "That's the problem."

"You mean ... they don't?" Blake frowned. Could the alternate reality shift have worked in general, but without the details he'd specified?

"Oh, they act responsibly and serve the public interest, all right," the man said.

"You don't sound too enthusiastic," Blake said. "What's the problem?"

"Well, the nature of government is such that no one can actually achieve their goals without lying to the public, misappropriating public funds, and accepting large-scale bribes from powerful special-interest groups."

"Sounds familiar," said Blake. "So, where does the responsibility come in?"

"Well, since our government officials are scrupulously dedicated to serving the public interest, they realize the only responsible thing they can do is resign as quickly as possible.

The result is a complete failure of government to get anything done at all." He paused. "I hope you have a more productive system where you come from?"

Blake shook his head sadly.

"Different approach, same result," he said.

Wilfred gazed around the office. The room lay hushed, suspended in an almost palpable silence. The Bogart decor — the trenchcoat and hat, the *Spade and Archer* windows, the Maltese Falcon statuette — seemed strangely inanimate in Blake's absence. Only the quietly blinking computers, the geometric panels of the time machine beyond the circular doorway, and the glimmer of the portal spanning the machine's hatch-like entrance served as reminders of the bizarre journey Blake had undertaken.

"We need a message system," Selena said, breaking the silence. "Some way that Blake — or anyone — can send a message back from an alternate reality."

Wilfred looked admiringly at Selena, wishing he'd managed to come up with something useful like that.

Professor McInerny glanced across the room at Bzzpt, who was examining the computers.

"Think you can do it?" she asked.

"I can probably rig something up," said Bzzpt. "I'll have to reroute one of the printers through the time machine."

"How long will that take?"

"Well, I can't do it now. It's too risky. I'll need to wait till Blake gets back."

At that moment, Blake stepped out of the time machine like an actor on cue, and deactivated the portal behind him. Wilfred and the others clustered excitedly around him.

"Did it work?" Selena said. "Did you visit an alternate reality?"

"Absolutely, baby!" Blake grinned, and gave her the thumbs-up.

"And the government responsibility angle?"

"Ah." Blake paused. "That's going to take a little more

work …"

"We need to contact the media right away," said Professor McInerny. "Our hiring ruse with the Handymen may have bought us some time, but we're still not free of Monica's political clutches. We need all the favorable publicity we can get."

"Agreed," said Blake. Wilfred nodded, along with the others.

"I'll issue a news release," she went on, "announcing the breakthrough. Blake, you and Bzzpt start work on the message transfer."

"The what?"

"It's an idea for sending messages back from an alternate reality. Bzzpt will explain." She turned to Wilfred. "And then Wilfred, you and Selena put in a personal call to Jennifer Jordan, since you have a contact there." She pointed through the circular doorway. "Use the phone in my office, if you want."

While Blake and Bzzpt collaborated on the message project, Selena accompanied Wilfred into Professor McInerny's office. The time machine had been placed near the threshold of the circular doorway to bring the portal into better view from Blake's office, with the result that Wilfred and Selena had barely enough room to squeeze their way past the iridescent panels. Wilfred patted the cold metallic exterior of the machine affectionately.

"You know, I've grown to like this contraption, after all," he said to Selena. "If it weren't for the time machine bringing me to the year 2099, I never would have met you."

Selena clambered over the last of the support struts connecting the machine to its base, and stood with him in Professor McInerny's modern, carpeted office.

"True," she said. "Or, at least, you would have had to wait a long time."

"I wouldn't have liked that," said Wilfred.

"You wouldn't have known," Selena pointed out accurately.

"But I'm glad I do." He kissed her cheek, then sat down at Professor McInerny's desk and called Jennifer's direct line.

"News desk." Jennifer looked up, flashing her famous TV

smile for the holophone. She held a half-eaten sandwich in her left hand, and an electronic screen-editing pencil in her right. Her face brightened even more when she saw who was calling.

"Wilfred!" she exclaimed. "You naughty thing! You sneaked back into town without giving me an interview after your victory at L.A.!" She grinned. Apparently she bore no ill feelings for the oversight, but merely felt it necessary to nudge Wilfred with a reminder.

"Well, that's part of the reason I was calling," said Wilfred. "There's also another breakthrough you may be interested in …"

"Wilfred!" Jennifer's beautiful eyes widened with excitement. "You sly dog!" She got to her feet, scrambling a few items from her desk into a burgundy leather bag. "I'll be right there. Where are you calling from?"

"Well, it's not about *that*, actually," said Wilfred, wondering why he continually needed to apologize for the inadequacies of his sex life, and why, for that matter, it had to be a subject for national speculation. "I'm at the Bureau of Alternate Reality. They've just had a breakthrough in their research on transferring people to other realities."

Jennifer winked, showing off her long lashes. "Well, I guess I'll have to make do with a story like that … for now." She zipped her bag closed, still clutching her sandwich. "I'm on my way. See you in a few minutes." She signaled to someone out of range of the phone's camera to accompany her, and the phone contact went blank.

Wilfred and Selena squeezed their way back around the angular contours of the time machine and through the circular doorway into Blake's office. Blake and Bzzpt had set up a printer on a small table, and Bzzpt had seated himself on the floor behind the printer, his fingers changing into the usual repertoire of tools as he reconfigured the circuits inside an open panel at the back. Professor McInerny was working on her news release at one of Blake's computers.

Bzzpt looked up at Blake. "Ready," he said. "Go ahead and test it."

Blake picked up a pencil-sized remote dictaphone from a slot on the side of the printer and walked towards the time machine, giving Wilfred and Selena the thumbs-up as he passed. He reached out a hand to test that the alternate reality portal had activated itself across the time machine entrance. Satisfied at the resulting buzz of static, he stepped through the portal and disappeared.

"Well, that should do it," Professor McInerny muttered from across the room, more to herself than anyone else. She gave her news release a final read-through on the computer screen, and pushed the *SEND* button. "How's the message transfer coming along?" she called to Bzzpt, getting up from her chair and going over to him.

"Soon know," said Bzzpt.

As he spoke, the printer hummed gently, and a page dropped into the print bin carrying the simple message:

Wish you were here.

Moments later, Blake stepped back into this reality and disengaged the portal behind him.

"Get anything?" he inquired eagerly.

Professor McInerny handed him the message.

"I can't believe how well things are going, for a change," Blake said, reading his own message as he sauntered back to his desk. "At this rate, it won't be long before those congratulatory calls come rolling in."

The phone rang, and Blake answered promptly.

An image of Ace, in his blue Handyman's bandanna, appeared seated behind a makeshift desk in his bunker. His mood didn't seem to Wilfred to be especially congratulatory at this early stage in the conversation, but perhaps that could be attributed to the natural gauntness of his face. Piles of paper were stacked high on his desk, on the floor beside it, and on a nearby chair.

22

"Hey, Ace, what's up?" said Blake cheerfully.

"Well, see, it's like this." Ace hesitated, as if unwilling to be the bearer of bad news. He glanced out of the phone's visual range for a moment, and Leroy appeared beside him. "See, me and Leroy, and some of the others — well, we've been thinking."

"Always a good fallback activity," Blake agreed.

"See, we don't want to be government employees no more."

For several seconds, Blake looked as if he had been stunned with the Black Bird itself.

"Why not?" he said at last.

"It's the paperwork." Ace gestured meaningfully at the mountains of paper burgeoning around him. "It's killing us, man. Ain't that so, Leroy?"

"Bet your ass, buddy," said Leroy.

"When you say 'some' of the others," Blake clarified slowly, "how many are you talking about?"

"Well, most of the others," said Ace.

"Pretty much all," said Leroy. "I guess a couple are staying on, just for the challenge."

"Now, listen, guys." Blake scratched his forehead, where a worried frown had settled. "Your employment is the one thing that's keeping the Bureau politically afloat right now. If we lose you, we lose every penny of our funding."

"Wish I could help you, man," said Ace. "Fact is," he gestured again at the mounds of paper, "I got over 11,000 people who don't ever want to *see* another piece of government paperwork again!"

"Look," said Professor McInerny, stepping forward next to Blake by way of joining the call. "Can we put you on hold for a minute?"

"Sure," said Ace.

Professor McInerny put the Handymen on hold, freezing the hologram image and closing off the sound.

"There must be a way out of this," she said, her managerial gaze inviting suggestions from anyone in the room. "As government employees, I don't even know if they *can* resign."

"Well, there one person who would know," said Selena. "B.J. Craddock, at the union."

"Good idea. Blake, get B.J. on the line, and we'll do a conference call."

Blake called B.J., then reactivated the holograms of Ace and Leroy. Professor McInerny smiled cordially.

"Here's the situation, B.J." she said. "These Handymen are employees of the Bureau of Alternate Reality, but want to resign because of the paperwork." She looked at Ace. "Is that right?"

"Right," said Ace.

"However, since they're government employees, my understanding is they can't be laid off."

"That's correct," said B.J. "Under paragraph 32, subsection 9 of the present contract between the Zirconian Council and the Amalgamated Handymen's and Public Employees' Union, no government employee may be laid off or denied benefits for any reason."

"Wait a minute," said Wilfred, stepping forward. "For *any* reason? Including death?"

"That's the way the contract's written," said B.J., glancing down and turning pages without a trace of humor. "We can't go making exceptions for every little contingency."

Wilfred's mind reeled. "And people wonder why we have a deficit!" he spluttered.

"It's only tax money," said B.J. "Besides, it creates jobs for budget economists."

"Who also get paid by the government," Wilfred pointed out.

"Look, stay out of this," said Blake. He turned back to the conference call. "The point is, they can't be laid off, so that's that."

"They can't be *laid off*," B.J. said. "But they can retire."

"That's what we want, then," said Ace, trying to reestablish his role in the conversation.

"Do I actually detect a budget-saving loophole?" said Wilfred incredulously.

"Not exactly," said B.J. "Even in retirement, under the terms of the new contract they're still entitled to full pay and benefits. They just won't count as employees, and they won't have to do any of the paperwork."

"Sounds good," said Ace. Leroy nodded.

"That's outrageous!" said Blake. "They'll be getting paid for doing nothing."

"What are they doing now?" said B.J.

"Well, nothing. But that's not the point."

"Of course it is. It's the way every other government agency operates." B.J. shook her head philosophically. "People always think their case is unique, but it's the same story every time."

"Thanks, B.J.," said Ace. "You really came through for us."

"Just doing my job," said B.J. "Oh — by the way, of course you'll still have to keep up your union membership dues. But then, you'll continue to receive your paychecks, so that shouldn't be any trouble for you."

"Sounds like a plan," said Ace agreeably.

"And, if you want to cut down on paperwork still further," B.J. said, "you can have your paychecks sent directly to us at the union. We'll simply deduct your dues and forward you the difference. That way, you can guarantee timely payments, and you won't have to worry about a thing."

"Hey, makes it easy, you know?" said Ace.

"Bet your ass," Leroy concurred.

"Look, if it's all the same to you," said Blake, "we'll just step out of this conversation now, and you three can carry on shaping the economic future of Zirconia amongst yourselves!" He disconnected the conference call and leaned back in his chair, spreading his arms wide. "This is just great," he said. "We're spending money we don't have, and gaining no political advantage at all. What are we supposed to do now?"

There was a pause.

"Alternate reality, anyone?" said Bzzpt.

In the cool, artificial breeze wafting across her Council office from the direction of the tightly sealed French windows, Monica examined her scarlet fingernails with a smug air of triumph. Wilfred's recommendation of General Heidtbrink for the peace talks had played right into her hands. The limited war settlement had proved thoroughly satisfactory, and her defense contractors had shown their appreciation with unprecedented flights of generosity.

The phone rang. She activated the viewscreen, and was pleased to recognize the caller as B.J. Craddock.

"B.J.!" The musical charm slid into her voice with practiced efficiency. "Always a pleasure. How may I help you?" It was now a minute after five; the union president had to be calling about something important.

"We have a situation developing at the Bureau of Alternate Reality," B.J. said. "I know you've taken an interest in that agency in the past."

"Yes," said Monica noncommittally. This was not a matter for jumping down off the fence until one saw what thorns lurked below.

"It seems there's a question about the Bureau's willingness to pay its retirement benefits."

"Retirement benefits?" said Monica. This had all the earmarks of a hot news item. "Have there been some retirements, then?"

"All but a few of the Handymen in their employment have opted for full retirement," said B.J. "We're handling all of the paperwork, for reasons I needn't explain. Naturally, you can appreciate that a delay in benefits paid by the Bureau would affect our members' abilities to meet their union dues."

"I see," said Monica. She bit the inside of her lip to keep from revealing her excitement. Mass resignations at the Bureau meant that her budget cut would no longer affect Zirconia's unemployment figures. "Quite so."

"Since you've always been a staunch ally of our organization, I was hoping you could look into the matter when you have a moment."

"I'll be most happy to," said Monica. "Naturally, I'll do everything in my power to ensure that members of the union can make their payments in a timely manner."

"I'd be most appreciative." B.J. turned up the corners of her mouth in a small, U-shaped smile. "We're in your debt, as always, Councilwoman."

The screen went blank. With a barely repressed gurgle of delight, Monica reached into her top drawer and broke off a piece of chocolate.

Finally, the moment had come. She had the Bureau of Alternate Reality exactly where she wanted, without risk of offending the unions or creating unemployment. It was just a matter of time before the Bureau bled itself dry trying to meet its own expenses. She'd allow it a brief interval of ignominious writhing, then hold it up as a public scapegoat — an example of a bloated government agency living off the taxpayers' charity. The mere act of rising in the Council Chambers to call in ringing tones for its abolition would make her a political hero.

Well. It seemed she would be paying the Bureau of Alternate Reality a visit.

The Bureau of Alternate Reality, meanwhile, was playing host to a few dozen reporters who had flooded Blake's office in impressive response to Professor McInerny's mention in her news release of the availability of free food. Since the process of effecting an alternate reality transfer consisted of having someone walk through a supposed portal and disappear from view, which didn't make particularly spectacular TV, and since none of the reporters — Jennifer included — was willing to let any of the other reporters visit an alternate reality before anyone else, the transfers ended up being depicted by holographic simulations while reporters struck significant poses and resurrected pithy historical epigrams such as "a giant leap for mankind." To liven things up still further, Bzzpt demonstrated his own reality shifts to anyone who would watch, while Blake answered a lot of highly technical questions about customizing alternate realities and modifying the space-time continuum, and Professor McInerny tried to see how often she could use the phrase "revolutionary breakthrough" without anyone strangling her. The noise level rose.

Wilfred stared in amazement. For a moment, he wondered if he was on the wrong planet. Then it occurred to him that, in a manner of speaking, we all were, although he couldn't be sure exactly what manner of speaking that was. He reached for Selena's hand and held it, glad of the anchor to some semblance of the reality he still knew. So far as he was concerned, there was quite enough weirdness in this reality that there was no need to go out of your way to look for alternate ones. And, there was quite enough that was wonderful about this reality that there was no need to search further afield for happiness.

Blake and Professor McInerny were now inviting the public to call in on the air if they were interested in finding out more about alternate reality transfers. The phones started ringing, which Wilfred viewed as a good sign, at least in terms of evidence of a TV audience.

The first caller was a solid-looking man of about 35 who looked as if he might have put in a couple of seasons with the Green Bay Packers before starting his own trucking business.

"How much does this cost?" he demanded.

Professor McInerny and Blake looked a little taken aback.

"Uh ... you mean, how much is the program costing the taxpayers?" Professor McInerny said.

"No," the man answered. "I mean, I want to visit one of these here alternate realities. How much does it cost to do that?"

"Ah, I see," said Professor McInerny, clearly relieved at the direction the conversation had taken. "We'll have to call you back on that, once the rates have been approved."

"You mean we can't go now?" said the man. "How long do we have to wait?"

"That depends on the recreation commission."

"Look — money's no object," the man said. "I just want to make sure I'm one of the first. All over Zirconia, people are going to be getting in line. Can't I pay in advance?"

"You're dealing with the government," said Professor McInerny. "We can't take your money at this stage. We don't even have the right forms developed."

"We can put your name on a waiting list," Blake suggested. "We'll call you back in the order received as soon as we get approval."

"All right," the man said reluctantly. He gave his name. "You sure you couldn't just take a deposit, to guarantee my place in line?"

"Not until the rates have been set," Professor McInerny explained once more. "As part of the federal government, we're legally restricted from making a profit."

"Well, *that's* one less thing to worry about," said Bzzpt.

The second caller wanted the same information: how soon could she go, how much did it cost, and could they put her name on a waiting list? The third caller wanted the same; so did the fourth, and the fifth.

Selena turned to Wilfred.

"We'd better contact EDSEL," she said. "We're going to need some help in keeping everyone straight."

"Good idea," said Wilfred. Moments later, EDSEL's cheerful voice added to the general conversation, displaying a database on one of Blake's computers, and even volunteering to absorb the backlog of calls into its own communication banks.

"We can't use EDSEL for this purpose indefinitely," said Professor McInerny. "We'll need to hire our own receptionists."

"Too bad we can't use the Handymen," said Blake. "The few who haven't retired, that is."

"Why can't we?" said Wilfred.

"We hired them to do nothing, so that's their official job description," said Blake with a shrug. "It's automatic overtime if they do any actual work."

"At least we'll be able to pay for all that now," Professor McInerny said. "It's nice to have some financial security."

A rapping sounded at the door, barely audible over the noise level.

"Get that, somebody, would you?" Blake called out.

Wilfred went to the door and opened it. An imposing figure robed in dark blue stood on the threshold.

"Mother Ismeralda!" he exclaimed.

"Wilfred!" She swept inside, closing the door behind her. The imperious eyebrows went up as she turned in his direction. "Congratulations on your victories against the Centaurians."

"Well, it was really nothing ..."

"Now, about your propagation assignment." She raised her voice a little louder, compensating for the noise in the room. Wilfred looked around anxiously. Already, her mere presence was starting to attract reporters, even drawing them away from the food table. In particular, he noticed Jennifer edging her way closer. He drew Mother Ismeralda aside.

"Well, I'm afraid I haven't really ..."

"You mean, you haven't even started yet?" said Mother Ismeralda in ringing tones.

"I really have meant to get to it." Wilfred lowered his voice still further, hoping Mother Ismeralda would follow his example. "I've just been so busy."

"I'm relieved to hear it," Mother Ismeralda intoned.

Despite the clarity of her voice, Wilfred wasn't sure if he'd heard correctly. "What?" he said.

"This is wonderful news!" Mother Ismeralda could hardly

contain her rejoicing. "We've averted a national catastrophe."

"What do you mean?" cried Wilfred indignantly. It was one thing to have people express disappointment at his failure to perform as planned, but to see them deliriously overjoyed was another.

"As you pointed out, the purpose of your propagation assignment was to introduce a non-militaristic element into the gene pool," Mother Ismeralda explained. "It would hardly be appropriate to have our top military hero sponsored by the federal government as the official stud for the next century. Even the government has to show some level of responsibility."

"But wait ... I mean, I haven't even had a chance yet!"

"Just as well," said Mother Ismeralda.

"I mean, here I've been, defending the planet ..."

"My point exactly."

"And this is my reward!"

"I'm afraid so. Unfortunately, society tends to reward people in inverse proportion to their actual contribution."

"Look ..." Wilfred racked his brains for a new approach. "I didn't do anything in those victories. I was an innocent bystander. I—"

"Sorry." Mother Ismeralda patted his shoulder benignly. "And you showed such promise."

"But ..."

Wilfred glanced around at the reporters who were avidly getting down every nuance of the conversation before rushing to follow Mother Ismeralda to her next photo opportunity with Blake and Professor McInerny. Jennifer caught his eye long enough to give him a sympathetic shrug before going off to join the others.

Selena came over to him. She brought her face close to his, so that the tips of their noses touched.

"I don't think it's such a bad deal," she said. She pressed her nose gently against his.

"That's fine for you to say. You're not the one who's being paraded around on national TV as some type of genetic misfit!"

"I don't mind genetic misfits." She rested her forearms on his shoulders, linking her hands behind his neck. "I just kind of like having them all to myself."

Wilfred looked into Selena's eyes. In the background, he could hear Mother Ismeralda praising the Bureau of Alternate Reality for a technology which would not only provide recreation for millions but would also bring in revenue and help balance the budget, and Professor McInerny praising Mother Ismeralda's Council leadership and economic foresight which had made programs like this possible for the Zirconian public.

Mother Ismeralda asked if there was anything else she could do to help the Bureau, and Professor McInerny said that members of the public were anxious to start putting down money to guarantee places in line.

Mother Ismeralda said if that was what the people wanted she was all for it and she would provide a special dispensation, and Professor McInerny said the public would be appreciative of Mother Ismeralda's red-tape-cutting leadership style but there was still the matter of the recreation commission.

Mother Ismeralda said even though it was after five she would personally arrange the necessary paperwork, and Professor McInerny said this was truly an example of government at work.

Wilfred remembered back to a time when he had seen some visiting Japanese students perform a demonstration of Kabuki theater, in which all the roles were played out according to a centuries-old ritual. He opened his mouth to say something to Selena, when he heard a knock at the door.

He opened the door, and to his surprise found Santa Claus and his reindeer standing on the doorstep.

"Sorry to trouble you," said Santa Claus, "but is this the Bureau of Alternate Reality?"

"If it wasn't before," said Wilfred, "it certainly is now."

23

"Don't worry," Bzzpt called out from across the room. "They're with me." He went over to where Santa Claus stood blocking the door with his reindeer and sleigh. "How are you guys doing?"

"Fine," said Santa Claus. The reindeer grunted, as if "fine," as a description of how they were doing, was a definite exaggeration.

"I'd like to introduce my friends from Polaris," Bzzpt said. "Xrrpp—" he indicated Santa Claus, "—and Kppkt." He pointed to the reindeer and sleigh.

"Ho-ho-ho," said Xrrpp jovially. Kppkt pawed the threshold with his hooves.

"Come on in," Bzzpt invited. He ushered them in through the doorway — a tight squeeze that Wilfred would have thought impossible, but, on reflection, was probably an easier fit than the average chimney — and closed the door behind them. "We're just starting to have some fun."

"That's what I was afraid of," said Xrrpp. He moved closer to Bzzpt, trying to look official despite his red and white suit and fluffy white beard. "Did you succeed with the alternate reality shift?"

"I'm afraid not," said Bzzpt in a serious tone. He took off his blue mechanic's cap and swept back his hair. "We managed to find a way to visit other realities, but changing our existing reality proved impractical."

"The Great Speaker will be disappointed to hear that," Xrrpp said, fingering his whiskers.

"I can bet he will," said Bzzpt. "You'll just have to tell him that such a reality shift is not available. Still, look on the bright side — we staved off the Centaurian invasion for the time being." He leaned over to Wilfred, adding: "Maybe now our leader can even win his election without the aid of a reality shift!"

"Listen," said Kppkt. "I'm getting really hungry. Being a Death Ray for 36 hours without a break takes it out of you, and we've still got the journey back to Polaris. Can we go now?"

"Yes, we should get going." Xrrpp tried to tighten his jolly black belt, found it wouldn't tighten, and winced behind his beard. He climbed aboard the sleigh. "Ho-ho-ho, just five more shopping months to go!" he announced with a cheerful wave.

Bzzpt said his goodbyes to Wilfred, Selena, and Professor McInerny. He acknowledged the assembled reporters and Mother Ismeralda. Finally, as he walked towards Blake, his shape shifted ... imperceptibly at first, then more quickly, though still maintaining its human form. The color drained away into shades of gray, and he stood before Blake in the perfect black-and-white movie likeness of Humphrey Bogart.

"Here's looking at you, kid," he said.

Blake, speechless for once, merely nodded. Bzzpt touched the brim of his hat, then walked to the *Spade and Archer* window and opened it. He went back to the sleigh and climbed aboard beside Xrrpp, changing his form once more into a giant sack which Xrrpp hoisted over his shoulder.

With a jingling of sleigh bells and a final wave from Xrrpp, the craft sped through the open window and disappeared into the early evening sky.

No one else moved as Blake walked slowly to the window and closed it behind them.

"Pardon my asking," said Mother Ismeralda after a moment, "but is this a normal day in your department?"

"That depends on what you mean by 'normal,'" said Professor McInerny.

"I see." Mother Ismeralda smiled as she moved to the door. "Well, keep up the good work." She paused in the doorway. "If that's what it is you do around here."

"Talking of work," Professor McInerny said after Mother Ismeralda had left, "I believe we were getting ready to develop the federal regulations governing alternate reality transfer." She turned to the group of reporters, many of whom were still shaking their heads in wonder at the events they'd just experienced. "You're welcome to stay if you want," she said, "but I think setting up government regulations may be a slightly slower process than you're looking for in terms of live entertainment."

Several reporters sidled in evident agreement towards the door.

"I think we've got it covered," said Jennifer Jordan with a smile. As the other reporters slipped out, she walked over to Wilfred, shaking her head at him in friendly admonition. "See what happens when you keep a nation waiting on the hottest news story of the year?" she said. "On the other hand …" She appraised Wilfred from head to foot. "Sometimes forbidden fruit can make just as good a story. You'll be sure to contact me the minute you have any new developments, won't you?"

"Um …" said Wilfred.

"Count on it," said Selena, taking Wilfred's hand firmly and pulling him towards her.

"That's perfect!" said Jennifer. She pulled a matchbox-sized camera from her bag and held down the button, running off several seconds of footage. "'Sex Pariah Wilfred in Alternate Reality Love Nest.' Got it! Thanks, guys." She slipped the camera back into her bag, waving cheerfully as she left. "Let me know if there's anything I can do for you," she called through the doorway. "You know where to find me."

Selena put her arm around Wilfred's shoulders.

"Once a celebrity, always a celebrity," she said with a grin. She tilted her head towards the door. "Hungry?"

"M-hm." Wilfred watched Selena's face, allowing himself

to be towed along by her movement. He wasn't hungry, especially, but at that moment he would have said yes to acupuncture.

"Hey!" Blake called from his desk, where he and Professor McInerny had already seated themselves to begin the task of developing regulations. "Where are you two going? There's work to do here!"

"Since we're not officially members of your department ..." Selena began.

"We thought we'd head out for a bite to eat," said Wilfred.

"We'll be back in a couple of hours." Selena moved Wilfred further towards the door. "See you then. Oh, and ... keep up the good work."

They left.

"Almost done," Blake announced wearily when Wilfred and Selena returned from dinner a couple of hours later. He was slouched in his armchair, collar loosened, while Professor McInerny sat, immaculately tailored as ever, across the desk from him.

"One more quick review of the paperwork," said Professor McInerny, "and we should be ready to proceed."

Blake narrowed his eyes at her, and groped among the papers on his desk. Professor McInerny turned around to Selena and Wilfred.

"You're welcome to help, by the way," she said.

"We don't mind watching," said Wilfred.

"Always a pleasure to see the pros in action," said Selena.

"Thanks," said Blake. "Thanks a whole lot."

"All right," said Professor McInerny, getting back to business. "Let's review this application form AP-001-R you filled in for one round-trip alternate reality transfer." She glanced down at the paper in her hand, and looked back up at Blake. "You wrote here under 'criteria' that you want an alternate reality where Monica falls in love with you."

"That's right."

"You also indicate on the form that you want a 1940's Humphrey Bogart ambiance."

"I do," Blake said. "That too."

Professor McInerny leaned back in her chair.

"This is a government program," she said. "We're supposed to be establishing definite regulations. You don't just waltz around picking one from column A and one from column B. You pick one from column A. Period."

"All right," said Blake. He considered for a moment. "I'll take the Humphrey Bogart."

"Good choice," said Selena. "When I go visiting an alternate reality, I don't plan on spending my time hobnobbing with Monica van Patten."

"OK," said Professor McInerny. She made the adjustment on the form with her pen, then turned the page over for a final glance at the other side. "Next, I just run this form through the scanner, and it programs the alternate reality automatically, to order?"

"It should," said Blake. "Give it a try."

Professor McInerny got up and slipped the paper into the thin slot at the front of the scanner that sat on top of one of Blake's computers. For about 15 seconds, all four of them stared at the scanner, while nothing seemed to happen. Then a red light began flashing on the computer underneath.

"What's that light?" said Professor McInerny, a note of concern in her voice.

"That means it's ready," Blake said. He got up and walked over to the coat-rack. He slipped on his trenchcoat, and adjusted his hat brim to the appropriate level for his prospective Bogart milieu.

Professor McInerny took a quarter from her suit pocket and flipped it across the room to him.

"What's this?" said Blake, grinning as he caught it, and opening his hand. "My raise?"

"It's a lucky quarter," she said. "They always have that kind of stuff in those 1940's novels, don't they?"

Blake looked at the coin in his palm.

"Thanks," he said. He flipped the coin up into the air and caught it again, walking towards the circular doorway and the time machine beyond. "I'll see you around."

"Enjoy yourself," said Professor McInerny.

"Good luck," said Wilfred.

"Have a good time," said Selena. "Send us a message."

Blake patted the printer as he passed. "Don't sweat it, angel," he said, half-turning back towards them and tugging the brim of his hat down a shade lower. "I'll see that you folks know the score."

The portal materialized across the time machine entrance in response to the proximity of Blake's voice, and glittered with a faintly blue crackle of static. Blake turned and stepped through it, disappearing from view. At the same instant, the main door of the office flew open, and Monica van Patten stormed in.

The impact of Monica's entrance was diluted for a moment by her apparent confusion as to what she had just seen. She stopped three or four paces into the room, her attention drawn to the time machine beyond the circular doorway.

She approached it cautiously, peering first into the time machine itself, then venturing a little way around the edge into Professor McInerny's office before coming back to the machine's entrance where the alternate reality portal still glimmered. She reached a hand towards the portal, retracting it quickly as the electrostatic buzz and the play of light around her finger-ends startled her with its sudden display of contact.

"You can't hide from me, Blake!" she called, her voice echoing back at her from the dark interior of the time machine. "I know you're in here somewhere!" Then she turned, her expression set, and stalked back through the circular doorway into the main office.

Wilfred hadn't seen Monica since the second of his two encounters in the marble-staircased hall, the time when she had tried to have him arrested in front of the union president for not having the right union membership card. In spite of her breathtaking physical attractiveness, he nevertheless gave her a wide berth, stepping back instinctively when she first entered the room, and again now as she reentered from Professor McInerny's office through the circular doorway. Selena did the same. Only Professor McInerny, seated behind Blake's desk, held her ground, her chin raised, eyes gazing levelly at Monica's, arms folded confidently across the desktop.

Monica glanced at Wilfred and Selena, dismissing them as a lion might dismiss a couple of field mice when there was an antelope for the taking. She moved closer to Professor McInerny.

"I'm here to confiscate your equipment," she said with a smile. "All of it."

"Why?" Professor McInerny's smooth face was a picture of innocence. "It's all registered to our agency." She reached for the portable computer on Blake's desk, and made as if to call up a file. "I can provide you with the inventory, if you wish."

"Never mind that." Monica brushed the suggestion aside with growing irritation. "Your agency is behind on its retirement benefits to over 11,000 former employees. We both know you can't pay them."

"Yes, we can." Professor McInerny held up a printout of several hundred names, representing a list of prepaid orders for the alternate reality transfer. "Do you think we don't plan ahead for such contingencies? We intend to use the money generated from these orders."

Monica moved closer, a taut smile forming on her lips.

"You've collected money before your procedure has been approved?" she said wickedly. "That's illegal!"

"I'm afraid not. Not this time." Professor McInerny rummaged on Blake's desk, and held up another piece of paper. "Special dispensation."

Monica leaned in over the desk and peered closely at the paper, as if verifying that Mother Ismeralda's signature was genuine.

"This isn't enough," she said. "You also need a license from the recreation commission."

Professor McInerny located another piece of paper on the desk and held it up practically in Monica's face. "All taken care of," she said sweetly.

Monica pulled herself up with dignity to her full height, and looked down across the desk at Professor McInerny.

"So, where's Blake?" she asked, reinstating the musical charm into her voice as if remembering a technique she had momentarily let slip. She crossed the room to the time machine and the still-glimmering alternate reality portal. "I'm sure I saw him go in here."

"You can't go through there without completing the paperwork." Professor McInerny got up from the desk and followed Monica over to the circular doorway, where she handed her a blank application form AP-001-R. "There's also a charge." She held up the advance orders. "And a waiting list."

"Don't be ridiculous! I know Blake's in there. I saw him go through there with my own eyes. And this is what I think of your paperwork!" Monica tore up the blank form AP-001-R, retearing it three, four, five times with her strong, slim fingers and placing the pieces into Professor McInerny's hand. "The minute I get back to my office, the Bureau of Alternate Reality is finished — and your paperwork won't count for a thing!" She strode to the time machine and stepped through the portal, disappearing from view in a crackle of static.

24

Late that evening, Wilfred and Selena were waiting up in Blake's office for a message from Blake. They had agreed to stand guard in case of an emergency, while Professor McInerny went home for some needed rest — her first relaxation since her jury duty ordeal that morning.

Selena had fallen asleep on Wilfred's shoulder, which would have been extremely pleasant, except for the fact that his arm, underneath her, had fallen asleep as well. He had spent the last ten minutes trying to extricate his arm without waking her, and had met with zero success: that is to say, he had been a hundred percent successful in not waking her, but had met with zero success in terms of extricating his arm. Every time he had managed to gain a couple of inches through painstaking work, she had stirred slightly, made a "Mmmmph" sound, and snuggled back against his shoulder a little more securely than before. Each time, the sight of her coppery red hair drifting across her face, her lips gently parted in repose, had weakened his resolve, and each time the tingling in his arm had grown more unbearable, and strengthened it.

Finally, just as he was about to wake her, the printer dropped a piece of paper into the bin. She awoke with a start and sat upright, rubbing her eyes.

"What was that?" she said.

Wilfred massaged his upper arm and flexed his fingers, bringing the circulation back with a tingling rush.

"I think it's a message from Blake," he said.

"Oh-h-h." Selena yawned and stretched her arms, bonking

Wilfred on the nose with her wrist. "Be a sweetheart and go get it, will you?"

Wilfred went over to investigate.

"Did we get anything?" Selena said. "Is it a message from Blake?"

"Looks like it," said Wilfred. A second page dropped into the bin, followed by a third. He fished them out. "Kind of a long one."

"What does it say?" Selena's face clouded with concern, and she got up and came over to Wilfred, taking his hand. "I hope he's OK."

"I expect he is," said Wilfred. "If he had time to send us a three-page message, he can't have been in any immediate danger."

"Let's see what he says," Selena said. "Just think — our first real message back from an alternate reality!"

"Better call Professor Mac and get her down here," Wilfred said. He cleared some space on Blake's desk and spread out the pages, while Selena made the call. Then, together, they read the message:

> It was morning in Manhattan — a gray, empty morning — the kind of morning when the wind off the East River brushes the ghosts of yesterday's papers up against the hard curbstones of reality. I wrapped my coat tighter around me, and pulled the brim of my hat down low.

Wilfred started to wonder what this message had to do with an alternate reality shift. Then he remembered that Blake had requested an alternate reality based on a 1940's Bogart milieu. Blake was probably just setting the scene.

He read on:

> A black, early 1940's sedan pulled up to the curb, driven by two men in dark suits. More accurately, it was driven by one of them. The other leaned out of the rear window.
>
> "Hey, Studs," he called to me.

I took out my lucky quarter, then flipped it up and caught it. The guy was twice my size. He wore his suit the way an iceberg might wear the *Titanic*. I said nothing.

"You Studs Malone?" he asked.

I flipped the coin up once more.

"Depends on who wants him," I said.

The man's massive face relaxed into a grin.

"Cut the small talk, buddy," he said. "You wanna do business with the Boss, you better get in."

So that was how the ground lay. Malone was looking to unload the Black Bird. I needed to find out who was buying.

I got in.

My companion introduced himself as Harry, and the driver as Louie. "So, Studs, I guess this puts you in pretty good with the Boss," Harry said.

That was welcome news.

"Yeah," Louie put in, glancing around to the back seat as he drove. He had the facial topography of a man who has satisfied his curiosity as to how many rounds he can go with Jack Dempsey. "So long as you got the genuine article."

"Don't worry about that," I told them.

A few minutes later, the sedan pulled up outside a restaurant called Marconi's. We went inside, and on through to a back room.

"Make yourself comfortable, Mr. Malone," Harry said. "Whatever you want is on the house. I'll let the Boss know you're here."

Marconi's. So that was the Boss. Nicky 'The Rat' Marconi.

I watched Harry and Louie leave through the door. Hearing a noise behind me, I turned. A blonde had entered from a sliding panel in the wall. She wore long black gloves up past her elbows, and a similar amount of clothing over the rest of her. She was built like January on a garage mechanic's calendar. She came towards me, a martini in each hand. The way her hips swiveled when she walked, I was concerned that the martinis seemed in danger of spilling with each step.

She tasted one of the martinis and offered it to me, turning the imprint of her jungle red lipstick in my direction.

"You must be Studs Malone," she said.

"Must I?" At that moment, being Studs Malone didn't seem such a bad idea, but the prospect of an interview with Nicky 'The Rat' Marconi still hung like a dark cloud on the horizon.

"One of us must," she said, eyeing me closely from beneath her long lashes. "It can't very well be me, can it?"

"I guess that leaves me," I said. I finished my drink in a couple of gulps.

She sipped hers. "I'm glad we understand each other."

I hadn't understood a word, but I didn't want to rain on her parade.

"Known Marconi a long time?" I asked her.

"Long enough to know he's never met Studs Malone." She sipped her drink again, and ran her finger up over my shoulder. "If you play your cards right, he'll never need to."

The boys came back in. I walked over to meet them.

"Thanks, January," I said. "I'll see you around."

I followed Harry and Louie to Marconi's office. They showed me in, then left. Nicky the Rat was sitting behind a desk. He pointed to a chair. I picked a different one, and sat down.

"So," Nicky the Rat said. He smiled unpleasantly, and I had no trouble seeing the resemblance. "They call you Studs?"

If by 'they' he meant Harry, Louie and January, he was correct.

"So far they have," I said ...

Well, as you can see, guys, the alternate reality here couldn't be better. I ran into the van Patten dame — Monica, I mean. Seems she was holding the Black Bird for Studs Malone all along. At least, that's what I told the Feds when I turned her in.

As for January, this could be the beginning of a beautiful friendship ...

"What do you think it means?" Wilfred said, when they'd read to the end.

"I guess it's Blake's way of saying things are OK," said Selena.

Professor McInerny arrived, looking professional as ever in spite of the late hour and her evident haste in getting there as quickly as possible. Wilfred and Selena showed her Blake's message and summarized it for her.

"Well, clearly the alternate reality shift and the message transmitter are working fine," said Professor McInerny. "I suppose he'll send us another message as soon as he's ready to come home. I'd better get started on the paperwork." She sat down at Blake's desk and began checking the requisite forms.

Selena took Wilfred's hand and pulled him towards her. He looked into her eyes. In the 1940's lamplight of Blake's office, they looked deeper, more filled with mystery than he remembered. Their lips touched.

A short while later, they heard the hum of the printer starting up, and the sound of a page falling into the print bin.

"Could one of you get that?" Professor McInerny called. After a pause, she added: "If it's not too much trouble."

Wilfred went to the print bin and took out the message from Blake. It was shorter than the first, and read as follows:

Everything fine this end. Get ready to bring me back. Check the coordinates — oh, and of COURSE make sure the paperwork is in order!!

P.S.: I'm bringing January, so I assume we'll need some paperwork on her as well. We can count it as research. See you soon!

Professor McInerny looked up, shaking her head like an indulgent parent.

"Doesn't he know we need the paperwork in advance?" she said. "We just finished setting up that regulation."

"That was for people starting from here," Selena pointed out. "January — or whatever her name is — comes from a different reality. The same rules don't necessarily apply."

"You'll probably need a different form altogether," Wilfred put in helpfully.

Professor McInerny acknowledged his remark with a wry smile.

"I suppose you're right," she said. "Well, that's why we do these test runs — to iron out any new situations that may come up."

"Like Monica," said Wilfred after a moment.

"Monica?" said Professor McInerny. "What about her?"

"Well, she started from here," Wilfred said. "Without filling in an AP-001-R."

"Yes," said Selena. "How's she going to get approval to get back?"

Professor McInerny shook her head and sighed.

"In a case like this," she said, "there's only one thing to do. We'll simply have to appoint a committee to look into the matter."

"But that could take years!" cried Selena.

Professor McInerny allowed herself the most modest of smiles.

"Never underestimate the value of bureaucracy," she said.

COMING SOON:

THE FEDERAL BUREAU OF
Paperwork Reduction

sequel to
The Federal Bureau of Alternate Reality

by Douglas Watson

❦

AVAILABLE NOW:

DARKHAVEN
(BOOK 1)

GHOSTS OF DARKHAVEN
(BOOK 2)

THE EPIC FANTASY SERIES
BY DOUGLAS WATSON

www.twinstarbooks.com

About the Author

Douglas Watson was born in the U.S. and raised in England, and enjoys the nationalities of both countries. After earning his Bachelor's and Master's degees from Oxford University, he moved to Portland, Oregon, where he divides his time between teaching and writing. In addition to his novels, he is the author of several plays, which have been produced in Portland, Seattle, and elsewhere. He has one daughter, Kimberley, born in 1980.

About the Illustrator

Erica Ritter grew up in Oregon. She attended Hampshire College, in Massachusetts, where she studied physics and fine art. She works at the Oregon Museum of Science and Industry, and pursues her illustrating career as time allows.

☆ ☆
Twin
Star
Books